Cape Maybe

A Novel

Carol Fragale Brill

all the best,
Carol Fragale Brill

ISBN: 149097959X

ISBN 13:   9781490979595

Published in the United States of America by
Brilliant Beach Books 2013

Cover Photographs by Isabelle Cameron and Malorie Massaro

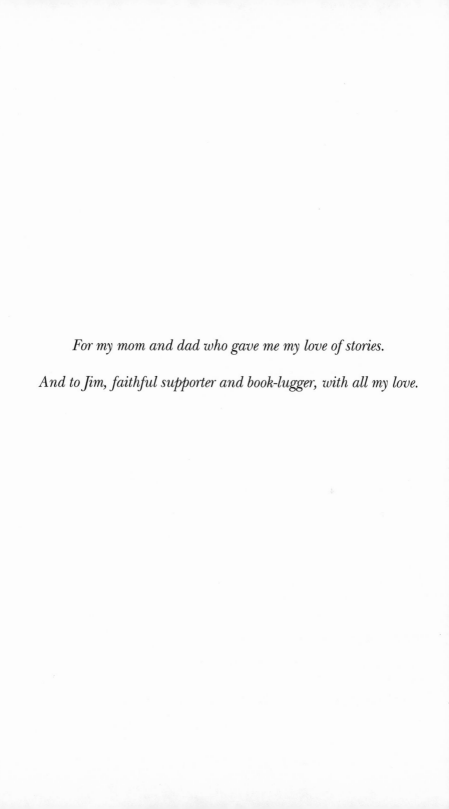

For my mom and dad who gave me my love of stories.

And to Jim, faithful supporter and book-lugger, with all my love.

Part 1

Chapter 1

R ay's truck parked half off the curb next to our VW is just the beginning of what isn't right today. When I pull open the door to go inside, a flap of torn screen scratches me under my sore eye. The kitchen stinks of beer and burned weeds. My cereal bowl is still on the counter from this morning, but now a cigarette butt floats with the soggy Corn Pops, like they forget I have to eat out of that bowl tomorrow. All you can hear is metal squeaking from my mother's room down the hall.

There's no way I want to be here with Ray, but it's drizzling and there's no place else to go. Nobody but next-door Lucy and us lives in this trailer court off season. Lucy's car isn't out front, and her shades are pulled way down like ours. It's no use calling my grandfather, Poppi. Even if him or Uncle Nack is there, they can't hear the phone when they're working out back.

I throw my hip against the door to slam it shut. When the squeaking doesn't stop, I drop my school bag so it thunks on the floor.

"Katie?"

It takes a few minutes for Mama to come out of her bedroom wearing her cut-offs and what looks like Ray's tank top slipping off her shoulder. She sways barefoot the couple of steps down the hall. "You're early," she says through a yawn.

I scowl and punch the light switch. The florescent light buzzes and flickers. It finally goes on, and both of us squint. Mama's mascara is all streaky under her eyes. Poppi calls our eyes sweet molasses-colored, but today hers are black stones. She sneaks the baggie and rolling papers off the table into her pocket, like I didn't already see them.

"Why is *he* here?"

Instead of answering, she sits and stares at herself in the toaster, moving the cross on her necklace back and forth with her thumb. She makes a big deal about that necklace, as if God forgives the rest of it as long as you wear your crucifix.

"Why are you early?" She says it like I'm the one who should apologize.

"We *always* get out early on Tuesday."

She pushes an open box of liquid chocolate cherries across the table as if she didn't hear me. "See what he brought us," she says, like she really wants to believe it, but we both know he brings the cherries for her, not for me, and she stupidly falls for them every time. I could tell the first time I met Ray you had to be careful around him. Some cheap drugstore chocolates don't change that fact.

"You promised Poppi," I hiss.

"You promised Poppi." She sounds like the wicked witch imitating me. Her eyes are closed so she doesn't see me stick out my tongue, but I know she hears me grab my schoolbag and stomp to my bedroom, which is about the same size as a closet.

My mother never calls where we live a trailer. She always says we live in a mobile estate outside of Cape May. Even at eleven, I get why she needs to believe that. The truth is we live in a dinky tin can in Rio Grande in the South Jersey sticks.

She goes back into her room. To drown out their voices, I put my transistor radio on the pillow near my head and listen to the only rock station you can get in these boonies. I start with my math homework. I'm good at arithmetic, probably because I have enough real problems to make the ones they give you in school easy as stepping on ants.

On my long list of problems, Ray is right at the top.

By the time my mother's bedroom door opens again, I've finished my math. I pray Ray is leaving, but his footsteps stop in the kitchen. The refrigerator door opens and closes. "I'll start dinner," he hollers.

Although I'm hungry, this is not good news.

The last time the three of us had dinner together, my elbow hit my mother's highball when I reached for the bread. Gold-brown liquid splashed across the table and sprinkled the mashed potatoes in Ray's TV dinner tray. He kept right on shoveling in food and growled at me to clean it up. After wiping the table, I tossed the dishrag at the sink. It missed and landed on Ray's snakeskin boot. Mama thinks those boots make him some fashion plate, but to me, they make him look like a pointy-toed devil. A wet stain the size of Texas on the map at school spread across his boot. Ray acted like I did it on purpose. He yanked off his boot and threw it at me. The purple mark under my eye faded a few weeks ago, but it still hurts when I press on it. All hell broke loose when I told

Poppi. He made Mama promise to keep Ray away from me. Said he would take me to live with him if not.

She kept her promise for almost two months. For her, that's not half bad.

Ray rattles pans in the kitchen. It's a good thing my door is locked. Mama's in the hall, jiggling the doorknob.

"Baby, open the door," she purrs.

"I'm doing my homework," I snap, rolling on my back on my half of the trundle bed. Poppi fixed this bed so my mother can use the other half in her room. I force myself not to blink while the water stain on the ceiling changes from an Indian papoose to a horse's head. Too bad that horse can't gallop me out of here.

"It's time for dinner." It sounds like she's scratching my bedroom door.

The smell of fried onions is making me starve, but I'm not about to admit it. "I'm not hungry."

"Come on, Katie,"

"I'm doing somethin'."

"Open this door." The purr is gone from her voice.

Rain leaks off the plastic window curtain. To keep my socks dry, I walk around the drops on the floor and wedge my foot behind the door to open it a crack. "I don't want to see him," I grumble.

She reaches through the slit and brushes my bangs out of my eyes, touching the scratch from the screen with her fingertips. "Honey, can't you be nice to him for me?" Her shoulder slumps against the wall. You can smell the booze when she breathes out. Her eyes are glassy, but you can still see the worry in them. Even when Ray isn't around, my mother is full of worry, like she's always dreading something. It makes her seem breakable and is why I usually end up giving in and doing what she wants.

When I get to the kitchen, Ray pivots in those pointy boots I hate. Right away, I sit and stare at my over-cooked hotdog instead of looking at him, even though I know he's gawking at me. I spoon myself some macaroni and cheese, pushing it around so the elbows make a line on either side of the crack on this Melmac plate. You can tell Ray set the table. Mama knows my food touching that stain skeeves me.

"Say hi to Ray," Mama says too cheerfully, but I don't.

The slogan on his shirt says IF THEY CALL IT TOURIST SEASON, WHY CAN'T WE SHOOT 'EM. If that was on Poppi's or Uncle Nack's shirt I would laugh, but Ray could mean it. On his shirt, it's not so funny. His stringy brown hair falls across his eyes when he leans forward.

"Did you hear your mother?" He drums his fingers on the table.

Out of the corner of my eye I see Mama press on her temples. She looks sorry she said anything, which means in spite of her thing for Ray, she probably loves me some, too. I reach for the mustard and squeeze some on my hotdog.

"Just let her eat." Mama's voice is so quiet, you just about hear her.

"She should learn some manners," he barks.

I thump down the mustard on the table. "Look who's talking."

"What'd you say?" His hand covers mine. The creases on his fingers are pitch-black from fixing boats at the marina. Mustard squirts on his thumb when I try to jerk my hand away.

Mama picks up her beer with both hands and drinks half of it down. "Can we just eat?"

Deep in his throat, Ray makes a laugh that is not one bit funny. "We'll eat when she says she's sorry." He won't let go of my hand.

"I didn't do anything." My throat aches with the effort not to let him see me cry. I fake letting my hand go slack, so Ray thinks I don't care. My heart pounds so loud, I don't hear the screen door open. Poppi is halfway across the kitchen before I see him.

"What the hell?" Poppi usually talks real soft, but now his voice booms. His scalp looks bright pink through his wavy hair. He almost throws the bag of groceries on the counter. He usually grocery shops for us on the weekend, but last weekend was his Sons of Italy meeting. A can rolls out the top of the bag and crashes to the floor. Ray lets go in surprise. I bolt from the table to Poppi. He gathers me under his arm and I bury my nose near his elbow. His flannel shirt smells like pipe smoke and wood chips.

"Are you Ray?" Poppi's voice sounds husky.

"That's him, Poppi," I say, feeling brave.

"Who the hell are you?" Ray growls.

I wiggle around to see Poppi's face. He glares at my mother, but she won't look up at him. "I thought we agreed to keep him away from her."

Mama puts both hands flat on the table to get to her feet. Her hair hides her eyes when she shakes her head.

Ray pulls out a cigarette, crumbles the empty pack, and tosses it on his plate. "I don't need this shit. I'm goin' out for smokes."

Poppi watches Ray's back until he's out the door. "What the hell were you thinking?"

"She wasn't supposed to be here," she says lamely.

"He's not supposed to be here." I stamp my foot for emphasis.

Poppi shushes me. My mother's eyes seem to free float when she tries to stare him down.

"Pack your school things, Katie. You're coming home with me."

"No. You want to stay here, right?" The way her eyes plead makes it hard to look at her face.

Poppi leans over the sink to look out the window. "He left his truck. I don't want her here when he comes back."

I hug my schoolbag to my chest and go back to stand with Poppi.

She keeps shaking her head no, but she empties the groceries onto the counter and takes the brown paper bag down the hall, bracing herself with her hand on the wall.

Poppi stoops to my level, resting his hand protectively on my head. "Did he hurt you, Scungilli?"

I show him my hand and say yes, even though there's no mark. He takes off his jacket and wraps it over my shoulders. "Let's get you into my truck so I can talk to your mother," he says.

"I'll wait here," I say, dying to hear what he says to her. He ignores me and scoots me out the door.

My socks get soggy walking beside him over the broken clamshells out front. My mother thinks this shell path Ray put in makes our outside look fancy, but really, it just adds the stink of old clams.

Poppi opens the car door, moving his Daily Racing Form so I can sit down. He rolls down the window about an inch and pushes the button to lock the door. "Keep it closed until I get back," he says.

I pull off my wet socks. "Don't forget my shoes."

My mother meets him at the door with a bag of clothes. When he reaches for it, she steps back and stumbles. He has to grab her elbow to steady her. Her voice is a high-pitched whine, but I can't make out the words. She sounds like a lost baby lamb. Just as I'm feeling guilty and thinking I better stay with her after all, a stray cat slinks across the clamshells to hide under Ray's truck. One look at that truck makes me stay put.

My mother pulls away when Poppi tries to take the bag. My shoes fly out the top. He bends over to pick them up. The way he holds one in each hand, arms down at his sides, makes him seem weighted down. I open the window wider to listen, but close it again when that screech in her voice sends a chill down my spine. She shoves my bag into Poppi's chest. I bite my lip so hard there's salty blood on my tongue. She pounds the sides of her head with her fists.

Poppi reaches up to make her stop, but she slaps his hand away and slams the door.

Chapter 2

*T*here's so much to ask Poppi, but no way to start. Each time we pass under a street lamp, he clenches and unclenches his jaw. It makes his false teeth rattle and sound loose.

"Why do you do that?" I ask.

"Do what?"

"Click your teeth like that."

He rubs his hand over his chin, considering my question. "Guess it's the way I chew on my thoughts."

He keeps one hand on the wheel and rests the other one on my head, making circles in my hair with his thumb. In my shadow on the dashboard, my hair sticks out and my head look gigantic.

"You got lasagna noodle curls," Poppi teases.

"I hate when the rain frizzes up my hair," I sulk.

At the bottom of the bridge, he turns to go my favorite way along the canal. "Are you sure he didn't hurt you?"

"I hate him. How can she like him? She must hate me."

His fingers nuzzle my hair. "Nah, your Mama loves you. She just doesn't show it so good when she's nervous."

"I want a different mother." I fold my arms tightly across my chest.

Poppi blows out a lungful of air.

If I can't have a different mother, I want her to go back to being how she was before she was nervous all the time. On good days back in first grade, she held my hand at the bus stop and cut my sandwich into stars with a cookie cutter. One time I'll never forget, she wrote I love you on a shell we'd found on the beach and tied it to my thermos with a string. Poppi always makes excuses for her and says she would be different if my father didn't die in Vietnam. I don't remember my father, but I miss him as if I do.

If I can't have a different mother, I want to be someone else, but only if I can still keep Poppi.

Poppi is quiet except for rattling his teeth again, so I know he wants me to change the subject. He turns on the high beams. The thick fog turns smoky in the brighter lights. The cedars on the side of the road seem more twisted than usual, creepy like the trees in the Wizard of Oz that might grab a kid and eat her. I move closer to Poppi and catch a whiff of Clubman's Talc.

"Get your ears lowered?" I ask.

"Yup, got a haircut."

"Looks like you got 'em all cut."

We both chuckle at our old joke. I roll his racing form between my fingers.

"Did Cheatin' Arthur win?" I ask.

"Yup, he's a good mudder."

Poppi always says that when his favorite horse, Cheatin' Arthur, wins on days the track is muddy.

He lowers the headlights when a car approaches. We drive like that in the semi-dark until he turns at Green Turtle Creek Road. The aged wooden sign Poppi and his brother, Uncle Nack, made when they were teenagers that says THIRTEEN ACRES swings on its chain when we pull into the driveway.

This is the house where Poppi and Uncle Nack grew up. Except for the screened-in porch with the towering blue spruce in front, the white-shuttered farmhouse looks pretty much the same in the old family pictures Poppi keeps in an album in a dresser drawer in his work shed.

Poppi parks beside the huge blue spruce. My mother keeps a worn picture in her wallet from the day they planted that tree. In the picture, my grandmother, who died before I was born, has her arm around my mother's waist. Both of them have smiles so wide, you can hear them laughing just gazing at it. Mama is younger in the picture than I am now, but standing on her tiptoes on the porch, she looks taller than the brand new tree. I wish I could have known her when she was happy like that.

We go inside and Poppi drops my bag on the bench in the mudroom. He plops down to take off his boots. I go right into the kitchen. Poppi's brother, Uncle Nack, turns from the sink and grins. He has the same ruddy complexion and wavy white hair as Poppi, but his is thicker on top.

"Hey, Number Two." Uncle Nack calls me that because he says he's the prettiest person in Cape May County, but I'm a close second. His real name is Nicholas Nacaro. His nickname used to be Nick-Nack, but it got shortened.

"Hi, Uncle Nack."

He turns back to finish filling the spaghetti pot with water and puts it on the stove. "Didn't know you were coming to dinner." He pinches my cheek and kisses the top of my head.

"Me neither."

He sets another place at the table, sits down, and rests his hand on top of mine. I put my other hand on top of his. His hands are rough and red because he's always outside planting and picking. He lays his other hand on top of mine to make a hand sandwich. I slide out my bottom hand and place it on top. He slides out his bottom hand, like he might upset a house of cards if he goes too fast, and puts *it* on top. I do the same thing, then he does, then I do, quicker every time, until our hands move so fast, we whack the air. You can't talk to Uncle Nack about serious stuff, but he's fun to fool around with. I follow him to the butcher block. He rips a hunk of crusty bread, dips it in the gravy pot, and hands it to me.

"Blow on it," he says.

I blow and lick a drip of tomato sauce before it burns my thumb. "Um, good."

Uncle Nack bounces his hand in the air near my face. "Good? Good? Who calls Number One's tomato gravy just good?"

I giggle. "It's great. It's delicious. The best I ever tasted."

This time, he pinches both of my cheeks. "Thatsa better," he says.

After dinner, I wash the dishes and Uncle Nack dries while Poppi spreads my homework pages on the table.

"Spell spaghetti, macaroni, ricotta, manicotti," he says.

"Hey, they aren't on the list."

"They're on mine," he says, tweaking my nose.

I spell them all, because I'm even better at spelling than I am at arithmetic. Besides, after he says each word, Poppi looks right into my eyes with this look that says this is what I look like when I know you are going to get it right. His confidence makes me feel like one of the Websters.

"Take your bath, Scungilli," Poppi says when spelling is done.

After my bath, I stand in the upstairs hallway and listen to them talking. I can't make out the words, but I know from the way Uncle Nack hugs me careful like I might break when I go back downstairs that Poppi told him about Ray. Only the television picture lights the room.

"Can I put on Happy Days?"

"We're watching this," Uncle Nack says. It's that boring underwater show with that Jack Cousteau guy.

"Come on," I bellyache.

Uncle Nack throws Poppi a look, but Poppi is rummaging for something in the drawer and isn't paying attention. Uncle Nack thumps back in his recliner and crosses his hands behind his head. "Go ahead." The way he snorts when he says it makes it sound like ahead has three syllables.

I switch to my show and curl up on the end of the couch. At the other end, Poppi taps his pipe on an ashtray and fills it. He holds the pipe lighter to the bowl until it glows red. Swirls of sweet cherry fill the air.

"I thought the doctor said no smoking," I scold. Even though Poppi says playing the ponies is his only vice, I know smoking is one, too, and I want him to stop.

"Mind your business." He bites down on the pipe stem.

I turn up the TV volume when Uncle Nack starts to snore. As soon as the show ends, Poppi points to the grandfather clock and says it's time for bed.

Upstairs, in my mother's old bedroom, the bed bounces when Poppi sits on it to say goodnight. I push and pull at a thread on the bedspread until it comes loose. Being in this bed instead of my own makes it sink in how everything is unraveling. "How am I getting to school tomorrow?"

"I'll drive you."

I let out a deep breath. "Do I live here now, Poppi?" I ask in a raspy whisper.

He rubs my arms. "We'll see." The room gets quiet except for the clock ticking.

"Is that why you and Mama were fighting?"

He gives my arms a reassuring squeeze, kisses my brow, and turns off the bedside lamp without answering. He looks like a shadow walking across the room.

"Will Mama be okay?"

Except for a sigh, there's still no answer, which isn't that unusual in our family. He stops at the door to whisper our goodnight song. "I love you truly," he sings.

"Truly I do," I sing back.

His footsteps are already on the stairs, and I'm humming alone in the dark.

Chapter 3

*O*n Friday night, my worst fear is that this pinochle game with Poppi and Uncle Nack could go on all night, even though playing cards might be better than going to bed. It's impossible not to miss Mama when I'm tossing in my bed. It's like every day that ends without seeing her makes it harder to hope tomorrow could be different.

There are little purple spots on the table from the light shining through the grapes in the ceiling fixture. I fan my cards and twist them so the dots line up with the clubs on my ten. "What's trump again?" I ask.

"Spades," Uncle Nack says.

Poppi snaps down the Jack of Hearts. "You need to pay attention." Usually his voice only gets strict like that when he quarrels with Mama.

It seemed like a good idea when he said he would teach me to play, but he acts so serious, it isn't any fun. Like, how could not knowing trump make him as mad as he gets at Mama? This must be why she never plays cards with him. I wonder what she'll say when I tell her I'm learning.

I stretch my arms up over my head and yawn.

Poppi folds his cards and slaps them on the table. "All right, go on to bed. We'll play again tomorrow."

On my knees beside my bed before Poppi comes up to tuck me in, I say a special prayer for God to make Poppi too busy tomorrow for pinochle.

Sometime later, I'm halfway out of bed before I realize the phone woke me up. In the half-dark from the nightlight in the hallway, it's hard to tell if the hands of the cuckoo clock point to two or ten-after-twelve. Poppi's gruff voice climbs the stairs. I cup my palm over the mouthpiece and lift extra slow so there isn't a click. The receiver is chilly against my ear.

"Jesus, June, it's the middle of the night," Poppi grumbles.

"Let me talk to her." My mother's words have that thick, sloppy sound that always makes the hair on the back of my neck stand up.

"Damn it, she's sleeping. So was I."

"Drop dead."

"I'm hanging up."

"No. Please. Just let me talk to her." Now Mama's voice sounds whiny and sorry.

My mother rambles, repeating, "You can't just keep her," and "She belongs with me." There's rustling like Poppi is moving the phone to his other ear so he might not

hear her when she says, "I want to die. I should kill myself."
But I hear it, and my heart slams against my rib cage. My
thoughts race, counting all the things she could use—pills
or bug poison or anything sharp.

Now my mother sobs. "I don't want to be like this. Oh,
God. Why did Kenny die?"

Poppi talks quietly like he always does when she cries
about my father. He doesn't sound mad anymore. He just
sounds tired. After a while, she's quiet except for sniffling
and says she needs to lie down.

"Do you want me to come over?"

"I need to sleep."

"Good. Go to sleep. I'll come tomorrow."

She blows her nose. "Bring Katie," she says.

I wait to hear two clicks before I hang up and creep back
to bed, burrow under the spread, thinking about what she
said about killing herself, praying God has a rule that after
one of your parents dies, the other one isn't allowed to.

All night, the same dream keeps waking me when I try
to get back to sleep. I dial my mother's phone number on
Poppi's clunky, antique phone. The dial is too heavy and
makes a dent in my finger when I push it around. Every
time I get to the last number, my finger slips off and I have
to start all over.

In the morning, dust floats in the stripes of sunlight
coming through my bedroom blinds. So much light makes
it hard to open my eyes all the way. I squint to see the clock.
Ten after eleven. I jump up so fast, it feels like the ocean is
rushing through my ears.

There's no answer when I yell for Poppi. I hop around
my room, one leg in my overalls, tucking in my nightshirt,
flying down the stairs, shoes in my hand. His truck isn't in
the driveway. The note on the table says the foil-wrapped
plate on the pilot light is a stack of pancakes, nothing about
where he is. The screen door slams behind me. Uncle Nack

is out back in the middle of his grapevines, hammering a bent section of barbed wire tight to a wooden post.

"Where's Poppi?" I ask anxiously.

He moves his nails to the corner of his lip with his tongue before he answers.

"Grocery shopping. Want to give me a hand?"

"Is he going anywhere else?"

"Didn't say."

Back on the porch, I put on my sneakers and pace, worrying he went to Mama's without me, until his truck finally rumbles up the dirt drive. He lowers the gate on the flatbed and hands me a bag filled with paper towels and tissues.

"I didn't know where you were," I say accusingly. He frowns and nudges me to traipse along inside and help empty the bags. I'm thinking any minute now, he'll tell me when we're going to visit Mama. Instead, he asks if Uncle Nack is still out back, mentions the price of milk is up, and the kind of orange juice we use is buy one get one, and isn't that a good deal? There's no way I can ask him when we're going since I'm not supposed to know. After a while, I stop listening and go back outside. In a few minutes, he comes out, jiggling his car keys in his palm.

"Wanna' come to drop off your mother's groceries?"

"Let me comb my hair."

"Be quick so the frozen stuff doesn't melt."

I take the steps upstairs two at a time, rip off my nightshirt, and pull on my favorite pink tee with the little ribbon roses on the neckline. When my part looks straight, I clip in a silver starfish barrette. From a dusty old bottle on the bureau, I splash Jean Naté on my wrists and behind my ears.

"You stink pretty," Poppi says when I climb into the front seat of the truck.

The first thing you see when we turn the corner is the empty spot where her car should be. "She's not even here." I bunch my fists and jab at the dashboard.

Poppi gets out anyway. His key sticks at first and he rattles it around and pushes the door with his shoulder to open it. Even though I know she's not here, I follow him inside and check every room for empty medicine or poison bottles, pulling so hard on the string in the hood of my sweatshirt that it breaks off in my hand. Butts overflow in the ashtrays. They stink like they've been there since I left last week. In front of the open refrigerator, Poppi loosens the lids on containers and sniffs, throwing out the old stuff before he puts anything in. He holds up the empty brown grocery bag. "Anything you want to take along?"

My magic eight ball, pickup sticks, jacks, and all my Nancy Drew books go into the bag. I leave the stuffed animals and dolls. At first, I leave the wagging-dog-tail music box Mama gave me when I was six, but go back for it. While Poppi locks up, it plays "How Much is That Doggie in the Window."

Next-door-Lucy rakes leaves into a pile near her curb. Her thick glasses slip down her nose. She stops raking to push them back up, blinks her turtle eyes, and waves. I wave back quick before I hop into the truck so she won't see me cry.

The next morning, even though Poppi isn't much of a churchgoer, he puts a dollar into my yellow envelope, and drops me off just in time for the ten o'clock Sunday mass. I'm halfway out of the car when he says we're making homemade macaroni when we get home. He usually watches football on Sunday, but homemades are my favorite. I know he's trying to cheer me up.

At Sunday mass, we have to sit with our grade in church. My best friend, Cam, sits beside me, looking for split ends in her straight red hair. Her real name is Campbell, and I'm the only one besides her parents who is allowed to call her Cam. All the other girls are jealous she picked me for a best friend because she's the only redhead in sixth grade. She has navy blue eyes to go with her perfect red hair. Dottie Gerhard, who was my best friend before Cam, says the only reason Cam picked me is to boss me around, but what does she know?

Mass is so boring, I slip my foot out of my shoe and wiggle my toes on the kneeler. Cam elbows me in the ribs and points across the aisle where one of the boys nods off. We snicker out loud when spit dribbles out of his mouth. Two pews up, Sister Patrice turns around, glares over her wire rims, and shushes us. I sit up straight and jam my foot into my shoe.

As soon as mass ends, Cam and I run through the parking lot to find her mother and beg until she says Cam can come home with Poppi and me to make the homemades.

We squish together in the front seat of Poppi's truck. We're almost home by the time I find the radio station that always plays Beatles on Sunday morning. Even after Poppi parks and turns off the car, we keep singing "Maybe I'm Amazed."

All you can smell when you open the kitchen door is roasting pork and garlic. A flour sack sits on the table beside a dozen eggs.

Poppi grabs three long, white aprons off the peg in the utility closet. Uncle Nack gets the aprons from his lady-friend, Ursula, who owns a restaurant.

"Put these on," Poppi says. He makes a big hill of flour in the middle of the table, letting us take turns cracking the eggs into the nest in the center of the flour. After working the dough until it feels just right against his hands, he gets the macaroni cutter that was his mother's out of the sideboard. We call the macaroni cutter a guitar because it has wire strings that slice through the sheets of dough to make strands. Cam and I take turns with the rolling pin, flattening the dough into sheets that are thick as a penny. Uncle Nack drapes the dining room table and chairs with tablecloths and helps us separate the macaroni strand by strand to lay it out to dry.

When we finish, Cam and I go upstairs to wash up, so we don't hear my mother's car pull up the driveway. Halfway back down the stairs, the click of high heels on the kitchen floor and her voice freeze me in my tracks. I stop so abruptly, Cam bumps into me, and I have to grab the banister to catch my balance.

I turn with my finger on my lips. Cam rubs her forehead as I drag her back upstairs into my bedroom and close the door.

"Don't you want to see her?" Cam asks.

I punch the lock on the doorknob with my thumb. I want to see her more than anything, but I am not about to admit it to Cam. "No."

"You have to." Her eyes make that Campbell-know-it-all look I hate.

"Do not."

"I'll go with you." She says it as if that helps.

She tugs on my arm. I pull away and press my back against the door, squeezing the knob behind me with both hands. The only sound is the lock button clicking in and out.

"What if she comes up here?"

The thought of her up here with us makes every breath feel like a broken shell poking me in my ribs. I open the door a crack. A shiver passes through me. "You stay right there." I try to sound as bossy as she is, and it must work because Cam makes a face and plops down on the bed.

Downstairs, I watch from the shadow of the china closet in the dining room. My mother wears a low-cut, dark sweater tucked into black jeans. She smokes up a storm. It's chilly, but her toes are bare in her high-heeled sandals. Her hair is frizzed like she walked through a downpour.

In between puffs, she keeps tapping her cigarette against the edge of the ashtray. Uncle Nack comes in to get a cigar from the can in the refrigerator. You can barely hear Mama utter hello. He mumbles hello and goes back outside. She waits for the door to close before she talks again.

"I'm taking her home." She tries to sound tough, but the hand holding her cigarette shakes.

"She's better off here," Poppi fires back.

A mouthful of smoke curls up to the ceiling. "I swear I won't let Ray come over," she says defensively.

To keep quiet, I take little sips of air. Poppi coughs and runs his hand through his hair. "She's staying here."

"You can't just keep her," she snaps.

Poppi pushes the ashtray closer to catch her ashes. His face looks like his throat hurts. "I want you to give me custody." His voice is a raspy whisper.

The way her head whips around, you'd think she just got punched. It feels like I did, too. She whacks the table and her cigarette pack falls to the floor. "Do not start that again." Her words are like sharp little knives in the air.

Poppi's chair scrapes the floor. He opens the freezer, and ice clunks into his glass. "You never keep your promises," he says sadly.

Outside, Uncle Nack's rocker creaks back and forth.

Mama bends to pick up her cigarettes. She lights one even though there's a half-smoked one in the ashtray.

"I will this time. I'm going to quit."

Poppi grabs his car keys off the hook near the door. "Show me. Let's go to detox right now."

Show me, too, is all I can think. In a few steps, Poppi is back across the room, dangling the keys in front of her.

My mother lets out a mouthful of smoke. "I can't just up and go."

"Why not?" He rattles the keys in her face.

She slaps his hand away. "I need to think about it."

"You either want to stop or you don't." You can tell by the way he tosses the keys on the table that he's disgusted.

"I can stop on my own."

Poppi gives her a look like he has heard this all before.

Her voice is a whisper, but it echoes in my head. "I can," she says.

I have heard it all before, too, yet for no good reason this time, I start to believe her. She brushes both hands under her eyes and wipes them on her jeans when she sees me come out from beside the china closet. She holds out her arms. "Give me a hug," she says like it is part question and part prayer.

Poppi always says if you want to know what a person really means, look straight into their eyes. When I do, it scares me how I almost see myself in her dark pupils.

Her arms feel limp and clammy pulling me into her. Her breath smells like sour mints when I bury my face into her neck to make myself not cry.

"I miss you," she says, tearing up when I pull away.

I miss her, too, but there is no way to say it.

She taps her Zippo on the table. "Do you want to go out to dinner?"

"Cam's here." I back up a few steps to lean against Poppi, pointing at the macaroni draped on the dining room chairs. "We made homemades."

She tries to smile. Her shoulders go up and down. She holds her cigarettes over her heart and glances up at Poppi. "I can't compete with macaroni Sunday."

The wind rattles the blinds and gives me goose bumps. A gush of cigar smoke comes in through the open window. Poppi gets up to close it. I plant myself in his warmed-up chair.

The creaking from Uncle Nack's rocker stops. "Starting to drizzle," he says when he comes in. He goes right to the dining room. Everyone is quiet except for him whistling "Moon River."

"I should probably go," Mama says awkwardly.

My fingers make a steeple in the air. "You just got here."

"Stay for dinner," Poppi says.

"I can't," she says quietly.

"Why not?" I stamp my foot.

She forces a fake-looking smile. "I'll come back tomorrow." She stuffs her cigarettes into her pocket and backs herself toward the door. "Tomorrow, I promise," she says too happily.

"Right." Like I haven't heard that bull before. I'm halfway upstairs by the time the screen door thuds behind her.

It takes a few minutes standing outside the bedroom door for my heartbeat to go back to normal. When I open the door, Cam sits cross-legged on the rug in a triangle of shade, an open book in her hands.

"Your mom was prom queen?"

"Give me that."

I try to yank the yearbook from her hands, and she swings it to the side. She reads the caption. DREAMS FULFILLED IN THE SPLENDOR AND GLITZ OF PROM NIGHT. Cam holds the book out of my reach and flips to another page. I plunk down on the bed, pretending not to care.

"And a cheerleader?" She scrambles off the floor to sit next to me, draping the book across our laps. In the black-and-white picture, my mom and a bunch of girls with face-wide smiles kick and hold up pom-poms.

Even though I have seen the picture a hundred times, I study it before I turn to the section in the back of the book titled TODAY'S SENIORS, TOMORROW'S FUTURE. In his cap and gown, my father's head leans a little to the right. His wide-spaced eyes and his lips smirk in a way that make you wish you knew him. Next to his picture it reads <u>Kenneth Drennen, Intramurals 1, 2; Community Service Corps 1, 2, 3, 4; Football 2, 3, 4; Student Council 2, 3, 4.</u> His sloppy handwriting fills the margin.

J, I love you more today than yesterday, but not as much as tomorrow. The future is ours. Love, K.

"What do the numbers mean?" Cam asks.

"The years he did that stuff."

A few pages later, my mother's picture shows off her dreamy eyes. Her hair falls to her shoulders in a soft flip.

Her life story says <u>Cheerleading 1, 2, 3, 4; Decorations committee 3, 4; School Show 2, 3, 4; Film Study Club 2, 3.</u>

I close the book and shove it back under the bed. "It's time to eat."

It's after seven when Cam's mother picks her up, almost nine when Poppi tucks me in and sings "I Love You Truly." He turns out my light, and his footsteps fade down the staircase.

When I'm sure he's downstairs, I take out the yearbook and my flashlight.

What was it like to be her back then, and to turn into who she is now? No matter how many times I plump up the pillow, it's impossible to sleep with that question boomeranging in my head.

There must be a way for me to make her happy like that again.

Chapter 4

The frost seems like lace on the dirt where Uncle Nack and me dig up tulip bulbs. The grass looks sprinkled with sugar.

Uncle Nack straightens up real slowly and presses both hands into the small of his back. He pulled something taking down the Halloween decorations at the farm stand last week and it still hurts. He keeps taking stretch breaks. "I'm taking these bulbs back to the carriage house to wrap them in brown paper."

As soon as he goes, I sneak into the side garden with the tulip bulbs I hid in my pocket and replant them in the shape of an M for Mama. If they grow, I'll be able to keep an eye on them from my bedroom window. I wish it could be that easy to keep an eye on Mama. Too bad those tulips can't bloom in time for her to see them when she's here for Thanksgiving dinner. Something like that might make her feel at home enough to stay.

Uncle Nack is taking a long time in the carriage house. Years ago, he lived back there with his wife, Aunt Nettie. After she died, he moved back into the big house, and now the carriage house is just storage. If you ask about Aunt Nettie, everyone in this family clams up and looks down, so even though I want to know more, the only thing I know for sure is she died too young and her real name was Annette.

I'm blowing on my fingertips to warm them up when Uncle Nack finally comes back, lugging the concrete horn of plenty he only puts out for Thanksgiving. He probably shouldn't be carrying it with his bad back. Most people would be satisfied with a birdbath, but Uncle Nack is really hot on lawn ornaments, so besides the special holiday ones, we have a concrete donkey pulling a cart, an elf sitting on a flower, and a guy in an orange raincoat holding a lantern. My favorites are the baby ducks with yellow beaks, trailing their mother across the grass.

It has to all look perfect for Mama on Thanksgiving. I am rearranging the horn of plenty near the bird feeders when a clacking sound makes me look up. It's a boy riding a blue bicycle with a baseball card in the spokes. He goes slow, balancing a pitchfork on the handlebars. The sleeves of his red sweatshirt stretch over his hands.

"My mom said to return this, Mr. Nacaro." He holds up the pitchfork.

It might be rude, but I can't stop looking at his eyes. They're the best color of blue, like a robin's egg or my prize glass marble.

Uncle Nack pushes his floppy hat back off his forehead. "How many times have I told you to call me Nack?"

The boy chews a big wad of gum with his mouth open. "My mom says to call you Mr. Nacaro."

Uncle Nack unbends an inch at a time and takes the pitchfork. He grins. "Guess I know better than to disagree with your mother." He takes off his hat and wipes his brow with the back of his hand. "Number Two, this is Dennis, my lady-friend Ursula's son."

Last weekend, when Uncle Nack and Poppi took me to meet Ursula at her restaurant, she talked non-stop about her son. The way she called him *my son the pitcher*, made me think he was a lot older.

He's taller than me and so skinny, his Adam's apple sticks out a mile when he repeats *Number Two*, like it's a question. The way he grins at me right before he looks down fills my stomach with lightning bugs. "I'm Katie," I say shyly. Cam and me would kill for his curly eyelashes.

He licks his lips, watching Uncle Nack spread mulch around the hollies. "How come he called you Number Two?"

He might laugh if I tell him Uncle Nack calls me the second prettiest person in Cape May. I wish I could think of something to say to impress him. There are no other kids in this neighborhood, and I want him to be my friend. "I'm visiting my grandfather," I say stupidly.

"My mom says you live here."

For a second I want to punch him for knowing. What else did Ursula tell him about me? The night we met, she talked a mile a minute about him. She said he wants to be a baseball player, or a pilot, or a fireman like his father. He's an honor student, and pitches a un-hit-able fastball that she called his ticket to college. The way she talks so much makes me worry she probably told him all about Mama.

Dennis wheels his bike toward where Uncle Nack pitches mulch from the big pile on the lawn into the wheelbarrow.

"My mom says I should help 'cause your back hurts," he says.

Uncle Nack looks grateful. "Can you push the wheelbarrow?"

Dennis nods and leans his bike against the trunk of the weeping willow. Uncle Nack's gloves swim on my hands as I help spread the mulch Dennis dumps. When neither of them is looking, I sneak sideways glances at Dennis. I want him to notice me and smile again, but he keeps his head down while he works. Neither of us talks until he blows the biggest, most amazing bubble I have ever seen.

"Nice one," I say enviously.

He sucks it back into his mouth without breaking it. Uncle Nack leans on his pitchfork. "I can finish from here. You two go play."

Dennis gets up and brushes dirt from the knees of his jeans. All I can think is *please don't leave*, but he goes for his bike like he can't get out of here fast enough. He probably doesn't want anything to do with me, probably thinks I'm weird because I don't even live with my own mother. I try to look nonchalant, pulling off these gloves. They're stiff with dirt. I clap them together and dust floats in the air and makes me sneeze.

"Bless you." Dennis picks up his bike and swings his leg over the bar. "Want to ride bikes?"

I screw up my lips and tuck my hands inside the sleeves of my jacket. "I don't have a bike."

"Hop on. I'll lend you one." Dennis flips the top up on a rusted rack on the rear fender.

It doesn't look like much of a seat, but I'm so excited he wants to be friends with me, I get on anyway. No matter how I squirm around, the rack pinches my butt. Uncle Nack takes the towel draped around his neck and folds it square. "Try sitting on this," he says.

I scooch up and pretend the towel under me helps. We wobble down the driveway, me balancing with my toes.

Dennis waddles us onto Green Turtle Creek Road and peeks at me over his shoulder. "Ready?" His breath smells of grape bubblegum.

"Ready," I say eagerly, in spite of the metal grid jabbing into my back.

We follow Green Turtle Creek Road to Shun Pike. My legs are out straight, but after a few blocks my thighs burn so much, I bend my legs back. The toes of my sneakers drag in the street.

"Stop dragging your feet."

"My legs hurt."

"You're slowing us down," he complains, standing on the pedals and pumping harder.

As soon as we get to his driveway, I jump off, trying to rub my butt before he turns around and catches me. He points to a barn-shaped shed. "Get a bike in there. I'll be right out."

The spring on the screen snaps and the door bangs when Dennis runs inside to go upstairs. The place looks more rundown from back here than when you go in the restaurant's front door on Broadway.

I hold my nose inside the shed because it smells like skunk, but at least in here, no one sees me knead my sore backside. There are a few bikes with flat tires and a twenty-inch with no fenders, but the tires look okay, so I wheel it outside and take a deep breath. Out here, you can smell the garbage from the dumpster, but it beats smelling skunk.

Ursula is on the back porch, wiping her hands on her apron. There are mustard stains on her short-sleeved white tunic. She looks happy to see me. "I got that bike at a yard sale for three bucks."

In the light, the bike looks like crap, but for three bucks, I tell her it was a good deal.

This time of year, she only serves dinner, so the parking lot is empty except for a sign truck. She tells me she's getting a new sign. "Look in back," she says like she's about to share a secret.

Up on my tippy-toes, my chin just makes it over the side of the truck. The sign is pinker than a flamingo and says, Mae's West Cape Café.

"Why is it called Mae's instead of Ursula's?"

"It's a play on words. You know the actress, Mae West, and being in West Cape May."

I don't really get it, but I don't tell her. "I thought maybe it was your middle name."

"Like you," she says.

"Kate Mae's a stupid name. My mother named me that on purpose to sound like Cape May."

"I like it."

I can't tell whether she's being serious or just being nice and if maybe she's wondering like I do why a mother would do that to her kid.

Unlike my mother, she has this way of looking right at you when she talks to you. That, and the way her gray-streaked hair is cut straight across like a knight's makes her seem solid. Dependable.

I decide she probably means it about my name.

The door bangs. Dennis flies past her down the steps.

"Hey bud, not so fast. No kiss?"

His cheeks turn red as his sweatshirt. I make myself look busy rechecking the air in my tires. He jumps on his bike and heads to the street. Ursula smoothes down her apron. "Where're you going?"

"Around," he says.

"Be back for lunch. You too, Katie."

After we ride a few blocks, my bike chain keeps jamming. Every time it happens, my foot pops off the pedal and I lose my balance. Dennis is way in front of me. I'm breathing hard when I follow him onto Sea Grove Avenue. It's quiet except for our tires crunching knee-deep leaves. One side of the street is all trees; the other side has some closed-up cottages and a few big new houses. Seagulls circle overhead. Dennis stops near the end of the street, and I finally catch up beside him.

"Wouldn't it be cool to live here?" The dimple on his chin gets big as a thumbprint when he smiles, making my insides tingly.

Up ahead is Cape May Point. On the map in Poppi's glove box, it really is sort of a point, with the ocean on one side and the Delaware Bay on the other. We pedal past the red and white lighthouse to the parking lot beside the souvenir shop at Sunset Beach, riding in big circles and slamming our brakes so our tires make ridges in the gravel.

"Want to look for Cape May diamonds?" Dennis asks.

I follow him down to the water's edge. It's a funny beach, more pebbles than sand. These diamond things are supposed to be all over. A few times, Mama brought me here to look for them. Even though we didn't find any, it was worth it just to be here with her. When I catch up to Dennis, he proudly holds out his fist to show off his palm full of pebbles. I say how nice they are even though to me, they look like plain old milky white stones.

When we get back to the restaurant, Ursula arranges two stools at the counter in the kitchen. It's the first time I've been in a restaurant kitchen. Thick steam rises from a huge pot on the stove. Everything is silver and shiny; thick-bottomed pots hang from the ceiling on hooks. At my school, they joke about restaurants that use cats to make hamburgers, but you can tell there's never been a cat in here.

Ursula slices stubby hotdogs in half and puts them on thick rye bread with a handful of chips and a pickle on the plate just like when you eat in her restaurant.

"I called your grandfather to tell him you're staying for lunch." She slides a plate in front of me.

"Those hotdogs are really fat," I say.

Dennis shoots me a you-are-too-weird look. "It's kielbasa."

"Kill *whatta?*"

"Just try it," he says, rolling his eyes and taking a big bite of his.

It smells like garlic and smoke. I nibble the edge. "Yum." I take a bigger bite.

"I told you you'd like it."

After lunch, when I say I'll put the bike back in the shed, Ursula says to keep it. Dennis rides with me all the way home. When we get there, he chews his lip before he circles, lifts the front wheel of his bike in the air, and does a perfect wheelie. "Want to ride to the canal tomorrow?"

It's only a bike ride, but all night, I pretend it's our first date.

The next morning, Cam and I only have a few minutes before we go into mass, so I talk fast, telling her about Dennis, and the Point, and how he gave me the bike. Her eyes flash when I get to the part about riding bikes again today. She flips her hair over her shoulder, kicking a pebble so hard it bounces off the sidewalk into the grass.

"It's your turn to come over my house," she says all bossy.

I wish I could take back telling her.

Her lips are pursed, arms folded across in front. "I came over your house last Sunday."

"I'll come next Sunday."

"I'll be at my grandmother's for Thanksgiving weekend."

I am not sure how I forgot Thanksgiving because until yesterday, Mama coming was all I could think about. "Come with us."

"Don't do me any favors." She flips her hair again and makes the snorting sound that goes with her bossy-beg-me look.

"Please." I tug on her folded-up arms. "Pretty please with jimmies on top."

Now she looks bored, but she unfolds her arms. "I guess."

The last thing I want is to share my new friend with her, but it beats her being mad at me.

Later, from the second I introduce them, you can tell Dennis is pretending not to stare, but he can't take his eyes off her in the turquoise sweater that turns her hair copper, the one that makes the boys' eyes pop out when she wears it to school. Not like yesterday, when he met me and kept his head buried in the mulch. We squat in the beach grass on the bank of the canal near the railroad bridge. The dark mud near the water's edge smells ripe with fish. Every time Cam glances at Dennis, he looks away quick and pulls at his shoelace. Cam chatters one minute and acts stuck up or pouty the next. It makes me sick, but I don't think Dennis notices. It's like even though he's supposed to be my friend, all he can see is her turquoise sweater and red hair. On the way back, they ride side by side in front of me. No matter how hard I pump the rusty pedals on this clunker, I can't keep up with them.

He was my friend first so it's not fair, but all he asks when we get back is if Cam will be here tomorrow. She shrugs her shoulders, rippling her hair down her back.

He does a killer wheelie on his bike and takes off. I pick the petals off dried mums in the window box, saying in my head *he loves me he loves me not*, hoping there are enough petals to make it come out right. "Did you see that wheel-ie?" I ask, awed.

"What a showoff," she says, as if she has room to talk.

"He's not a showoff."

"He's skinny, and he has Brillo hair."

"Does not." His hair does look like steel wool, but there is no way I'll agree with her.

She straddles her bike. "Skinny, Frizzy Dennis. Skinny Frizzy Dennis." She chants her spiteful sing-song until she is halfway up the block.

On Thursday, the sky looks too blue for Thanksgiving, the clouds too fluffy and white. Ever since noon, I have circled from the kitchen to the dining room window, then to the living room to peek through the drapes before I head back to the kitchen. The whole time I pray *God, get her here no matter what.* The sun is going down when I decide to wait on the porch. On the lawn, a squirrel stops near the weeping willow to gnaw something it picked out of the mulch. Maybe, like me, it senses danger because it darts up the trunk to a high branch. It's colder out here than it looks from inside. My fingertips are numb from holding my sweater closed in front. Shivering, I go back inside.

We planned to start dinner at four, but it's after five and Mama's not here. When you dial her number, the phone just rings. About a half hour ago, Uncle Nack soaked a new white hand towel in hot water and laid it over the turkey to keep it from drying out. Now he's sharpening the knife. "It's time to carve the bird," he says, clearly annoyed.

"Can't we wait a little longer?" I plead.

He nudges my hand on the table like he wants to play sandwich hands, but I pull my hand away. "We better go on and eat," he says, sounding more apologetic than mad.

All during dinner, I can feel Poppi watching me, but I don't look up, just push turkey and stuffing around on my plate.

After dinner, at first I say I don't want to play when Poppi gets out Monopoly. He sets it up anyway, and after a few rounds, it cheers me up some. I take it as a good sign when I get to buy St. James, New York, and Tennessee. I pass Go and reach for my $200 from Poppi when headlights flash across the kitchen. A crash like thunder shakes the table. A car horn blares.

"Holy cripes!" Poppi's chair goes one way and my two hundred bucks goes the other.

I race after him to the door. Uncle Nack touches my shoulders to get around me. "Stay inside, honey," he says.

Mama's VW is lodged on top of the bottom porch step, the motor racing. Vines from the weeping willow trail over the headlights, throwing snake shadows on the porch. This is not my idea of get her here no matter what. You'd think just once, God could hear one of my prayers and get it right.

Uncle Nack flips on the porch lights. Poppi runs down the steps, reaches inside to turn off the car, and moves Mama's head off of the steering wheel. The horn stops blowing. Uncle Nack runs back inside for a towel. He passes me on the bottom step and nudges me. "Honey, go back inside."

As if I don't have more reason than anybody to be out here.

Poppi taps Mama's cheeks, rubbing her hands. "Can you hear me, June?"

Her eyelids flutter and she moans. A thin line of blood runs down the side of her face into a tadpole-shaped puddle on her collar. Poppi wipes at the blood and presses the towel from Uncle Nack near her temple.

Every few minutes, Poppi moves the towel, but puts it back when a thread of blood drips down her face.

Suddenly, her eyes open wide. She pushes at Poppi's hand. "Get off," she whimpers.

"You're bleeding. We need to go to the hospital."

"No."

"You might need stitches."

"Shit, shit, shit."

Her body looks limp when they half-carry her to the truck. "Katie, grab my keys," Poppi hollers.

"I'm coming."

"No, you stay with Uncle Nack," he says.

Poppi stands near the open truck. I turn to go inside. "Just let me get my shoes."

"I said you're staying here," he says in the stern tone he usually saves for my mother.

I clam up, reach inside the door to snatch his keys off the hook, and toss them over the railing. He grabs them mid-air and climbs into the truck.

Uncle Nack drapes his arm protectively over my shoulders. "Come on inside now. We'll have apple pie and hot chocolate before bed."

Three hours pass before Poppi calls to say she's all right, but she needs five stitches over her eyebrow. More hours pass as I toss in bed with my eyes squeezed closed, but no matter what I do, it's impossible to sleep.

Chapter 5

ince her accident, my mother is in a special hospital. The rules say you have to be twelve to visit.

To look old enough, I wear my best blue sweater and plaid wool skirt with tights instead of socks. My hair is parted at the side with no barrettes, the way Cam always wears hers. I sit up tall as I can in this chair, legs crossed, my chin so high, the back of my neck hurts. Except for one teenage boy with a ponytail, it's all grownups in this waiting room. I worry somebody will notice me, but everyone stares straight ahead at the movie you have to watch before you visit anybody. It's called the *Bottomless Bottle* and it's hard to hear because Poppi keeps shifting around and picking at a strip of silver tape on the seat of his chair. The whole room smells like burnt coffee.

After the movie ends, Mama stands in the doorway, twisting her hands together, looking around for us. All I want to do is run to her. I grip the seat of my chair with both hands to make myself stay put. Her fingers are cool on my face when she kisses me on the lips. She pecks Poppi on the cheek before she pulls her chair up so close in front of me, her knee bumps mine every time she jiggles her leg. She wears a yellow sweater that makes the whites of her eyes look whiter. Her pupils have little gold specks I never noticed before. The corner of her right eye keeps twitching, making the stitches over her eyebrow where her head slammed the steering wheel look like grinning pumpkin teeth.

Her knee bumps mine again, and she shoots up out of her chair. "Let's go out on the enclosed porch," she says nervously.

The porch is like a tent, all screens with plastic rolled down that doesn't do much to keep out the cool. It's foggy because most of the people wearing plastic bracelets like the one my mother picks at with her thumbnail smoke like there's no tomorrow. To fill up the quiet after we sit down again, Poppi gives Mama the carton of cigarettes we bought at the Save-way on the way here. The whole time she tugs at the cellophane to open them, she keeps twitching her nose like a rabbit. She looks relieved and shy when she finally gets them open, but not as happy as when I give her my homemade card decorated with lace from Nonna's old sewing chest in the attic.

"I made a card for you in arts and crafts, but it's back in my room," she says.

I want Poppi to ask why a grown-up has arts and crafts, but when he doesn't, I don't either. "What else do you do here?"

Her hand shakes when she strikes a match to light a cigarette. "We see counselors and have an hour in the afternoon before dinner for exercise. Mostly we have group."

"Group?" Poppi says like it's a curse word.

"Like in the movie?" I ask timidly.

"Yeah." She stands up and shakes her leg. Sits back down and looks right at Poppi for the first time. "Thanks for watching it."

"They said we had to if we wanted to see you." Poppi rattles the change in his pocket. "How's the food?"

"We help cook some days." She makes some smoke rings and smiles at me, stubs out her cigarette, and turns to Poppi. She keeps slipping her foot in and out of her shoe. "You know about the family meeting with my counselor at three, right?"

Poppi shakes his head yes, but this is news to me.

A woman with a ridge of white fat between her tank top and her stretch pants taps my mother on the back. "Your family showed. I wish mine would," she says sadly.

"Dee's my roommate." Mama points with her cigarette. "This is my father, Louis, and my daughter, Kate Mae."

I have to act twelve, so I let it slide when she uses my whole silly name.

Dee makes a half smile that shows the gap where her front teeth should be. "My old man's probably out catching a load. Not that I miss him, but I'd like to see my kid."

Poppi stands up and offers Dee his chair. She shakes her head. "No thanks, I'm gonna grab a coffee."

We are all quiet while she shuffles back inside in her flip-flops.

"Do you want a tour? My room is off-limits, but I'll show you the cafeteria and library." She touches my hair. "You can wait there while we're at our meeting."

"I want to come to the meeting."

"It's just for your mother and me."

"She said it's a *family* meeting."

"Adult family."

"That's not fair." I cross my arms over my chest. "I'm *family*."

Poppi purses his lips and shakes his head no, so it surprises me when Mama chirps up. "She can come."

An hour later, we are all in the family meeting. From where I sit in the corner, I can see Poppi's whole face and the counselor's, but only the side of Mama's. Poppi' been studying a water spot on the side of the desk, but he looks up when the counselor says there's a problem with the insurance. She says Mama might not be able to stay for the whole twenty-eight days like she's supposed to.

"How much is it if I pay cash?" Poppi asks.

"You can't do that." Mama shakes her head and wrings her hands in her lap.

Poppi ignores her. "How much?" He sounds impatient.

"In group, they keep saying AA is our insurance. I'll go to AA if I can't stay here." Mama laughs like what she said is a joke, but Poppi doesn't laugh back. I ask what's AA, but nobody is listening to me.

"What the hell does that mean?" Poppi asks.

"I'm just saying. People get sober in AA without rehab."

Poppi looks at Mama like she just talked in Russian. He dabs at his forehead with his handkerchief before he leans his elbow up on the desk. "Could that work for June?"

"Ask June," the counselor says, and Poppi frowns at her.

I try to stare right into my mother's eyes, but I can't get the right angle from where I sit.

"I can go to a meeting every day," Mama murmurs.

The counselor raises her eyebrows. You can tell she's waiting for something more.

Mama reaches up to rub her eyes, bows her head so you just about hear her. "And if I stay away from Ray."

"You'll move in with us. That S.O.B. won't come anywhere near you." Poppi growls.

Mama's eyes twitch. She stares so hard at the carpet, I look down to see if there's something there.

Her voice is a shaky whisper. "Maybe Katie and me could move into the carriage house."

"No. We'll all live in the big house." Poppi sits back in his chair and folds his arms like it's a done deal.

In the quiet, the second hand on the wall clock tick, tick, ticks around the face. The counselor squares up the papers on her desk. "Is that what you want, June?"

Mama finally takes her eyes off the rug and, for a split second, glances over at me. Her knuckles are white from clutching the arms of her chair. "I think . . ." She takes a deep breath, bites her lip, and lets out her breath in a loud whoosh. "I think we should be on our own in the carriage house."

Another week goes by before the counselor calls to say the insurance company approved a total of 21 days and no more. Since dinner, Poppi and Uncle Nack have been in the kitchen whispering. I know they're talking about where Mama and me will live even though they stop talking every time I go into the kitchen. So far, I have gone in there to sharpen my pencil, get a glass of water, put whipped cream on my Jell-O, and refill my glass with ice. I'm out of reasons to go in there. Luckily, Uncle Nack's voice is loud enough to hear some of what he says. From Poppi, all you hear besides his teeth clicking is his pipe drumming on the ashtray.

Hard as I try to snoop, I get nothing.

The next afternoon, Poppi is supposed to be restoring the woodwork at an inn in Cape May, so I'm surprised his truck is in the driveway when I get home from school. I drop my school bag on a kitchen chair and wander through every room downstairs before I find Poppi and Uncle Nack out back, moving stuff from the carriage house to the shed.

They're in what Uncle Nack calls the everything room, because it's the kitchen and living room combined. While I was at school, they got the plumbing working and cleaned up and placed the wrought iron table and chairs from the patio in the middle of the room. There's a rocker and over-stuffed loveseat against the wall. The nook that will be my bedroom is full of odds and ends furniture. Poppi stops grinding his teeth long enough to say if I get my homework done, we can polish up nightstands and dressers and a few extra chairs after dinner.

"We'll stop at Sears tomorrow to get new beds," he says.

"Can't we move the beds from the trailer?"

"They're crap," is all he says and goes back to clicking his teeth.

On Saturday I like to sleep late, but today, Poppi woke me up early. Uncle Nack and me are in Handy Man Haven picking paint colors because in the daylight, the cleaned-up carriage house walls still look dingy. There are so many colors, but I finally pick blue sky for the bedrooms and laser lemon for the rest.

"You don't think that yellow is too bright?" Uncle Nack scrunches his face into a squinty frown.

The yellow is bright, but both are happy colors, like beach balls and bathing suits and sun and sky. Happy colors could make a difference.

After we got home this morning, Uncle Nack got to work using the paint roller. It looked like fun when he was rolling on paint, but now that he's inside making lunch, it's my turn to paint. My arms feel heavy, like I've been roll-ing on paint for a month. Across the room, Poppi is on his hands and knees, carefully lining the woodwork with masking tape. Hearing Dennis's bike clack-clacking outside is just the excuse I need to stop rolling. I peek through the window. "Can I go out?"

Poppi says no without looking up.

If I don't go, Dennis might ride to Cam's without me. There should be a rule that they can only do things when I'm there since I'm the reason they even know each other in the first place, but I'm not taking any chances.

I drop the roller in the paint tray, stick my head out the door, and tell Dennis to wait up. "We won't go for long," I tell Poppi.

"I said no."

"That's not fair."

Poppi rocks back on his knees and gets up slow.

"Please," I whine.

He scowls at me, but he doesn't really look mad, and I can tell he's about to give in. "I'll finish when I get back," I promise.

He shakes his head, checking his watch. "Eat your lunch first."

"I'll take it with me," I squeal over my shoulder because I'm halfway out the door.

"Let's stop for Cam," Dennis says when I catch up to him.

It irks me that the first words out of his mouth are about Cam, like he's even allowed to call her that. My fingers are crossed behind my back so the fib doesn't count when I say she isn't home.

Chapter 6

On Sunday morning after church, Poppi took me to the trailer to get some of Mama's things because I want to make it look like home in here when she gets out tomorrow. Now, I keep rearranging stuff, unsure if the silver comb and brush look better on the mirrored tray with her lotion and cold cream, or in front of it shaped in a V. Finally, I decide to go with the V but now the pictures I lined up at the edge of the mirror don't look right. There's a picture of Mama and my father holding me in my christening outfit, and my favorite picture of Mama sitting at a picnic table in a yellow bathing suit. Next to that is a picture of my father shoveling snow and one of me in my communion veil staring down at my praying hands. Mama always says I look like an angel in that picture.

I don't remember anything about the pictures of my father. Like the few stories I have heard about him, the pictures seem incomplete. Just once, I would like to hear a grown-up tell a story or look at a picture of him and say this is what he did that day, how he smelled, what he sounded like when he laughed. His parents and his sister probably know that stuff, but they didn't approve when my father quit college to get married. After he died, they moved to Arizona and never kept in touch.

I rearrange the picture of my father and pick up the one of Mama. I will always remember the day Mama wore that yellow bathing suit to the water park in Wildwood. Every time I went up and down the water slide in the kiddie pool, she caught me at the bottom in her wide-open arms, hugging me until I stopped shivering. The way she smiled up at me when she held her arms out, I knew she would catch me every time.

Uncle Nack thinks the yellow paint I picked for the bathroom and kitchen is too bright, that you need sunglasses when you turn the light on, but I'm glad I picked it, because it reminds me of that bathing suit.

It's almost bedtime, so I check out the vanity one more time before I close the door and skip across the yard.

Last night, no matter how much I begged, Poppi would not let me skip school today. Now, I run all the way from the school bus. I'm out of breath when I reach for the carriage house doorknob. You can hear Poppi's voice through the closed door, but as soon as it opens, he stops talking. Mama turns quickly from the window. Smoke curls out of the side of her mouth, twirls up to the ceiling. She squints like the smoke stings her eyes, and she makes a shaky little wave. Ashes flutter to the floor.

Poppi motions for me to come in and close the door. Mama puffs away, tugging her black sweater down at her waist. Her foot jiggles like she's keeping time to music only she hears. She looks at the kerosene heater in the corner, stares at her hand holding her cigarette, tugs some more at the edge of her sweater. Her eye twitches like in the hospital. Her nose twitches, too, like a rabbit when you surprise it in the flowerbed. I'm not sure what to do next. We should all be happy, but it feels wrong. Maybe it would be better if I had made a sign, big black letters that said WELCOME HOME.

She stubs out her cigarette in the clamshell ashtray, looking down at my shoes. "Can I have a hug?"

I'm not sure who moves first, but we meet somewhere in the middle. Her arms are like claws pulling me in, pressing my arms at my sides. My forehead bumps her shoulder. Even though the carriage house is warm, her whole body shivers. I wiggle an arm free and wrap it loosely around her. We hug until it feels like too long. I pat her back a few times and let go.

Poppi rolls his lips together and pulls up a chair. His arms are crossed over his chest. I back up closer to him.

"It's nuts for you two to be cramped in this carriage house when we have that whole big house," Poppi says.

Mama silently bites her thumbnail.

"At least stay in the big house until you get used to being home."

For once, Mama stares Poppi right in the eyes. "I can't talk about this again."

Four days later, like every day now when I get home from school, Mama sits at the wrought iron table, drinking coffee, reading her blue book in the glare of the bare bulb hanging from the ceiling on an extension cord. She calls that book her *big book* and reads it night and day, lips moving with the words, legs jerking up and down. The ashtray is full.

She closes the book and stretches her face up for me to kiss her. I breathe in deep when my lips touch hers to get a good whiff of her breath. The knot in my stomach unties some when she only smells like cigarettes and Chiclets.

"I made us hot chocolate," she says bashfully.

She moves past me like the floor is covered with egg-shells and she's trying not to break one. It's been that way all week, both of us walking around here on tiptoes. I sit at the table to be out of her way. She locks the door when she goes by it, then checks the lock on the window over the sink while she reheats the milk. She hardly ever locked up the trailer, but now it's like she's afraid there's something out there that might get inside. Her hands shake so much, some cocoa spills out when she sets my cup on the table. She lights another cigarette, watching me closely while I drop in a marshmallow, poking at it with my fingertip. Besides twitching and shaking her legs, she has taken up humming since she's been home, and now she hums "Oh Holy Night" with the portable radio.

"I went to my meeting with Dee," she says.

The only time she goes outside is when Dee, her hospital friend, picks her up for one of those meetings. She doesn't know I secretly read the pamphlets she gave Poppi and know when she says that about going to her meeting I'm supposed to encourage her. The way I nod my head and grin, I probably look like a goofy, bobble-head doll. "That's good."

Later, while I do my homework, she paces near the window, staring at nothing outside. It's the same thing every night. The way she sucks her cigarette sounds like she's in a tug of war.

Later, I'm not sure how long I slept when I wake up to go to the bathroom. I must have dozed off doing my home-work. Mama paces back and forth, clutching the phone. She must be talking to Dee, because she's whispering and there's nobody else she calls. The way she stalks reminds me of a tiger in a cage at the zoo.

By the time I finish in the bathroom, she's off the phone, standing still in front of the window. She doesn't turn around when I say goodnight. Her finger traces the mark her breath leaves on the glass. Her dark reflection stares back at me.

When I woke up this morning, Mama was whispering on the phone again. She waved me away and blew a kiss good-bye when it was time for me to leave for school.

Now, like every Tuesday, I'm home from school early. From out here on the porch, I hear the Beatles blaring "I Feel Fine" on the kitchen radio. When I open the door, Mama turns around at the sink. She looks like a different mother than the one who couldn't sleep last night, the one I left this morning. She wears black jeans and a red sweater. Her hair is tied back in a red gingham bandana. Instead of cigarettes, the room smells like bayberry candles. The song stops and "Eight Days a Week" comes on.

She sings the words, waves her arms, and shimmies up to me. Her breath smells like candy canes when she kisses me and takes my schoolbag. She tugs at my arms and we're dancing, arms swinging, hips swaying all over the place.

I want to sing the words about loving every day with her, but the change in her has me all jumbled up inside. She keeps pulling me along in her dance. At first, my body is stiff and my voice is hushed, then suddenly, I'm singing "Eight Days a Week" with her at the top of my lungs.

We make big loops around the table before I knock into a chair. We're moving too fast to stop, and I step on her instep. We fall into a laughing heap of arms and legs twisted together on the floor. I wish we could never untangle.

When we finally stop laughing, Mama stands up and dangles the car keys. "We're going to buy a Christmas tree."

"A real tree?" Poppi always has a real tree, but in the trailer, we only ever had a scrawny artificial tree, or straggly evergreen branches in a bucket of water.

Her hair falls over her forehead as she shakes her head up and down, her wide-open eyes mirroring the surprise I feel. She scoots me back out the door. Across the yard, Uncle Nack dumps out the trash. I skip past him to the car.

"Where you going?" he asks.

"To get a real tree," I yell.

"Pick a good one, Number Two."

My chuckling bubbles over and fills up the whole VW.

Chapter 7

*A*ll night I dream about sleeping in the forest, so I'm not surprised when I wake up and the whole place smells like pine from the Christmas tree propped in a bucket against the wall.

"Can I stay home from school to trim the tree?"

Mama's eyes look bleary, like she didn't sleep again. "I don't know."

"It's only a half-day."

She shrugs and gets out two bowls.

"Come on, please."

Her head jerks. Something flashes in her eyes. She slams the bowls down on the table so hard, I duck.

"I said I don't know." Her voice is a robot voice. My heart pounds in my ears. The way she flipped so fast creeps me out, reminding me of Ray.

She grips the back of the chair with her eyes closed. Her lips move but no words come out. You can hear her raspy breathing when she sits down. Her hand trembles lighting her cigarette and opening her big book. Her leg jiggles so much, the whole table vibrates. After her second cigarette, her quiet voice is back. "You don't have to go," she says.

I don't take my eyes off of her when I reach into my school bag for my Nancy Drew book.

After she settles down, there's something nice about sitting here together reading even though the table still shakes in time with her wiggly leg. While she reads, she hums along with the radio, first "Piano Man" with Billy Joel, then something disco by Donna Summer. Cam and me don't know if we like disco, but her mother promised to take us to see *Saturday Night Fever* over Christmas vacation, because we know for sure we love John Travolta.

As soon as the news comes on, Mama stops humming and gets up. She stares into the fridge like she forgot why she opened it. "Damn. Damn. Damn. There's no milk."

I grab my jacket off the back of my chair. "I'll get some from Poppi."

The cold in the yard goes right up my nightgown. Zipping my jacket doesn't help. My whole body is one big goose bump by the time I get into Poppi's kitchen. He sits at the table, blowing on his oatmeal.

"We need some milk," I say.

He points at the open half-gallon on the table. "Take this. We have another one." His eyes get squinty. "Why aren't you ready for school?"

"I'm not going."

"You sick?"

"It's just a half-day."

Poppi wipes his mouth with a napkin. "You can't skip school."

My feet are planted, hands on my hips. "Mama says I can."

He harrumphs and pushes the milk across the table. "Go finish breakfast and put on your uniform. I'll drop you off on my way to the lumberyard."

I stamp my foot. "Mama said."

He takes his time arranging his spoon on a saucer, puts both hands flat on the table. The way he pushes out of his chair real slow, a warning on his face, you can tell he means business. "Be ready in ten minutes."

I'm out the door in no time flat.

Back at our kitchen table, I bang the milk carton down hard enough for drops to fly out the top. Mama marks her spot in her book with her finger and looks up.

"Hey," she says, absently.

"Poppi says I have to go to school." I kick the table leg.

She just sits there chewing her lip.

"Go tell him I don't have too."

She slaps her book closed and shuts her eyes, but even closed, her lids twitch. Her lips move and I'm not sure, but I think she's counting to ten. When she opens her eyes, she starts reading again.

I ball up my fists on my hips. "Are you gonna go tell him?"

"Don't get me in the middle," is all she says.

After school, I can't wait to tell Poppi what a waste going to school was—spending the entire morning helping the first graders make holiday cards. To top it off, the bus was late and now I'm starving, walking the three blocks from the bus stop. The sky is gray; the air smells like it could snow. I'm about to march up the driveway and give it to Poppi when I hear him cursing under his breath before I see him. He must have just knocked over his can of nails.

He kneels in the dirt, grumbling to himself, plucking the nails out of the dead leaves one at a time. I ditch the idea of giving him crap and make a beeline for the carriage house.

Mama sits at the table just like I left her this morning, except instead of her bathrobe, she wears a sweatshirt and jeans. "Do you want to trim the tree?" Her cheeks flush like she can't wait to get started. Before I can say let's eat first, she walks to the loveseat. There are boxes stacked on the floor with June written on them in big, black letters. Right away, Mama opens a box, starts unwrapping ornaments, and spreads them out on the loveseat. I've never seen most of these ornaments. There's a purple rocking horse, red glass taffies on silver strings, a cheerleader waving pink pom-poms.

I pick up a woven crystal bonnet that looks like sugar candy. "Where did you get these?"

"The attic; my mother used to give me a new one every year. It was always the first thing we put on the tree."

She reaches behind a pillow and pulls out a little green box. The box looks old, with yellowed tape marks on it, but the peppermint-striped ribbon tied in a bow makes it seem new.

"What's that?"

"Open it," she says eagerly.

Inside is a ceramic angel wrapped in thick layers of wrinkly tissue. While I hold it with both hands, Mama threads a hook onto the gold ribbon behind the angel's wings. It takes a while for me to find the special place near the center of the tree where the angel twirls in the gap between the branches.

"Perfect." Mama looks so happy. "Now we untangle the lights."

After the lights are strung on the tree, Mama hands me the decorations one at a time, letting me decide where to hang them. We drink hot chocolate and stuff ourselves with popcorn and biscotti instead of the casserole Uncle Nack cooked up for dinner, listening to Johnny Mathis and Nat King Cole sing Christmas songs.

I stir my hot chocolate with a candy cane, sucking on the melted candy. Out of the blue, Mama says, "Your father used to drink his hot chocolate like that. And if we didn't have candy canes, he'd stir it with a red licorice Twizzler. He'd bite the ends off and use it like a straw. I never tried it, but it looked disgusting."

I stop stirring and stare at my cup. It feels like I am breathing in slow motion. My mother almost never talks about my father. There are a million more things I want to hear about him, but I learned a long time ago asking about him is one of the things that makes her nervous.

I'm afraid if I make a sound, she'll realize what she's doing and stop. There's a minute or two of total silence, and then I know I missed my chance because when I look up, she's opening the last decoration box. She hands me an egg-shaped ornament covered in sequins with an olive-sized hole in the front and a miniature reindeer inside.

"Nonna and me made these," she says.

"No way." It looks like a real egg.

She cradles it in both hands. "We made dozens, but there are only a few left."

I sit next to her on the loveseat. "How did you make the holes without breaking the egg?"

"We broke plenty." She smiles a faraway smile. "Poppi ate omelets every day for a month."

I carefully take it from her and let it dangle from the ribbon to check it out.

"Can we make more?"

"We'll see," she says, touching my fingertip gently.

Last night, I must have fallen asleep on the love seat after we decorated the tree. I'm huddled under the quilt from Mama's bed. Sunlight pours through the window. I jump up to look outside. There's a light dusting of snow on the grass and trees. Mama's car is gone.

Where can she be? Except for her meetings with Dee, she never goes out. I pace back and forth between the window and the door, pretty sure nine o'clock is too early for her AA meeting. Uncle Nack's uneaten casserole is still wrapped in foil on the counter, reminding me how hungry I am. I grab the cereal box and eat handfuls while I try to decide if I should get Poppi.

I'm seriously thinking about getting on my bike to go look for her when I hear the unmistakable sound of the VW chugging into the driveway. The clock says I have only been waiting for nineteen minutes. It seems like much longer.

I open the door and stick my head out. "I didn't know where you went."

"Shush, you'll wake up the neighborhood." She holds up a 7-eleven coffee cup and a plastic bag, squeezing by me to come inside.

"You have to tell me when you're going out."

"You were sleeping."

"You should've woke me up."

"I just went to get eggs so we can make ornaments."

"You can't just *leave* like that."

"Stop shouting at me!"

She's the one shouting. She yanks out an egg carton, bunches up the plastic bag, and tosses it at the trashcan. It totally misses, floating in the air, and falling near her feet.

"You *left* without telling me." I am so close to tears.

She runs her fingers up through her hair, holds onto the top of her head like she is afraid it might pop off. "Jesus frigging Christ, I'm trying to do something nice here." She stamps off into the bathroom and slams the door.

I stomp to the bathroom door. "You have to leave me a note or somethin'." I want to yell more but I'm hiccupping so hard, my whole body shudders.

The pipes squeak when she turns on the shower. I cross my arms over my chest and plop down on the loveseat. She's in there so long, her skin is probably shriveling. When the door finally opens, she pads barefoot into her bedroom, wearing a towel. For a few minutes, neither of us says anything when she comes back out dressed in sweats. Out of the corner of my eye, I see she carries the small scissors from the manicure set she never uses. She places a bowl next to the eggs on the table. The kitchen chairs scrape the floor when she moves them closer together and sits down. "Do you want to do this or not?" she grumbles.

I take my good old time getting up to sit next to her. Her hands tremble when she takes out an egg and taps the front of it with the point of the scissors. Our chairs are so close, I can smell her vanilla shampoo, feel her breath on my arm. She bites her lip and wedges the tip of the scissors into the eggshell to cut a hole the size of a quarter. The egg drips into the bowl under her hands. She holds the empty shell at arm's length to inspect it. The opening is lopsided with rough edges, round on one side and oval on the other. "I guess I'm out of practice," she says apologetically.

She hands me an egg and moves the bowl over under my hands. "Your turn."

I tap the way she did with the scissors and nothing happens. I hit it harder. The egg cracks in every direction, my thumb crushing the shell.

She almost knocks her chair over, grabbing for the paper towels, and laughing playfully at the egg leaking down my arms. By the time we get through the whole dozen, we have four good shells and a bowl full of broken eggs.

"Let's take a break and eat," she says.

She beats the eggs my favorite way, with milk and grated Locatelli cheese. They sizzle when she pours them into the buttered-up pan. I make the toast in our second-hand toaster that never pops up fast enough, always burning the toast on the edges, but not too dark to eat.

When we finish breakfast, she rinses the dishes in the sink. I run over to Poppi's attic to hunt for a tin of sequins and beads she saw up there when she brought down the Christmas decorations.

Uncle Nack is on the porch breaking up stale bread for the sparrows when I come out carrying the tin. "What are you up to, Number Two?"

"Making decorations from eggshells like the ones Mama made with Nonna."

He rolls his eyes. "Hope you like scrambled eggs," he says and grins.

An hour later, my fingers are tacky with glue from trying to stick on the sequins, concentrating so hard, I jump when there's a knock on the door. Mama gets up and uses her knuckle to push up a slate in the blind and look out. "It's a boy." She opens the door.

"Is Katie here?"

I can't get up fast enough, wiping my sticky fingers on my overalls.

"You must be Dennis. Do you want to come in?"

Uncle Nack or Poppi must have told her about Dennis because I know I didn't. Before he can come in, I scoot around her, opening the screen door just enough to slip outside. "We'll talk out here," I say quickly, pulling the door closed behind me.

Dennis's earlobes are pink where they peek out from under his navy ski cap. A piece of fuzz clings to the tip of his eyelash. "Why are you back here?"

I shrug my shoulders. The snow from this morning is melted, but it's cold out here without a jacket. I squeeze the metal doorknob behind me so tightly, my fingers are turning numb.

"Can you come out?"

"I don't know." From inside, water runs in the sink.

"Is Campbell here?"

"No."

"Is she coming over?"

"No."

"Why are you whispering?"

I rub my hands together and blow on them. "I'm not whispering," I say too stubbornly, even though I was.

Dennis makes a snorty sound. "I'm going to the shell shop at the Point to get my mom's present."

"You didn't buy it yet?"

His cheeks turn pinker than his ears. "I like to shop on Christmas Eve," he says impatiently.

"What if they aren't open?"

He lets out a puff of air you can see in the cold. "Do you want to go or not?"

"Wait for me," I huff back at him, slipping inside, making sure the door is shut tight behind me.

Back inside, Mama sits at the table, puffing away on her cigarette. "Why didn't you invite him in?"

I sweep my arm out over the table. "Can we finish later?"

"I thought you wanted to do this."

I screw up my face and shrug. I do, but I want to go with Dennis more. "Can't we do it later?"

All of a sudden, she starts shoveling the sequins into the tin, twisting the cap on the glue, tossing the tube in with the sequins. I shift from one foot to the other. She seems so angry, I'm about to give up, go back out and tell Dennis I can't go. Just as suddenly she stops throwing stuff around and lights another cigarette.

For a minute, she has a routine going with her cigarette, three taps on the ashtray, a big drag, and two more taps. She keeps doing it that exact same way, puffing so fast there's a smoke cloud all around her.

"I'll stay here and finish the eggs if you want."

She sighs. "I skipped my meeting this morning. I'll call Dee and see if she wants to go this afternoon."

"Why do you have to keep going to meetings?"

She pushes her arms out in front, like she wants to push the question away, so I'm surprised when she answers. "To get better."

"Didn't you get better at the hospital?"

Her face is turned away from me. She lights another cigarette, doing the tapping and puffing thing again. I'm sorry now I brought this up. She tap, tap, taps her cigarette. "The rehab was surface stuff. The meetings dig deeper."

I think that over. "Sounds like dandelions."

She scrunches her eyes. "Dandelions?"

"Uncle Nack says you can't just cut the part you see. You have to get the root or it comes back."

She grunts. Smoke comes out her nose. I can't tell if she's laughing or getting ready to cry.

By the time I get back from the shell shop, Uncle Nack is almost finished cooking Christmas Eve dinner. Just like he does every Christmas Eve, he cooks seven different fishes. It's some kind of tradition and makes the whole house smell like seawater. Uncle Nack and Poppi eat some of everything, picking bones out of smelts and flounder, making a big fuss over the smelly baccala. Like Mama, I stick with the lobster, crabmeat, scallops, and shrimp he simmered in tomato gravy.

Poppi and Uncle Nack always have the biggest Christmas tree in front of the parlor window. The star on top touches the ceiling. Every Christmas Eve after dinner, we are only allowed to open one gift. We save the rest for Christmas morning. Uncle Nack and Poppi just pick the gift on the top of their stack, but I can't decide which one to pick from my pile. Uncle Nack raves about the cigar in the glass tube Poppi helped me pick out for him. Poppi holds up knitted potholders from great Aunt Lena, who we never see because she lives in an old people's home in Reading, PA. Instead of just picking the top box, Mama digs into her pile and picks a box from me. It's the seashell key chain I bought this afternoon when I went to the Shell Shop with Dennis, just something extra, not her real gift, but she fusses over it like it is. Since she picked my gift, I pick one from her—a tie-dyed tee shirt she made in arts and crafts at the hospital. I slip it on over my skirt and blouse. It swims on me, hanging below my knees. Mama's lip and eyes crumple into a sorry-looking pout.

"It's so comfy, I can't wait to sleep in," I say, pretending I love it, relieved when a smile replaces the worry on her face.

By the time we clean up the wrapping paper, it's time to leave to hear Christmas Carols before midnight mass. We pile into Uncle Nack's caddy. Parking takes forever, and by the time we make our way through the crowd to the church, the choir is singing "Silent Night" on the side lawn near the life-size manger. You can't see them, but droplets of ice sting our noses and cheeks while we listen. The bells chime and three priests and the altar boys come out the side door. We line up behind them to file into church.

The church smells like radiator steam and damp coats. Ursula waves like crazy from a pew in the middle. She slipped inside early to save us a good spot. We all stand in the aisle while Uncle Nack whispers to introduce Mama to Ursula. All day, I have dreaded Mama talking to Ursula and Dennis, afraid she might say something stupid like how cute he is or about how sweet she thinks it is that we are boy-girl friends, like she did when I got back from the shell shop this afternoon, but she just shakes Ursula's hand and darts her nervous smile at both of them. Ursula slides into the pew first, and Uncle Nack sits next to her. I'm between Dennis and Mama, with Poppi on the end. It's boiling hot in here. I take off my coat and bunch it up to sit on it. The hair on my arms sticks up with electricity. Mama can't sit still; she keeps squirming and jabbing my ribs with her elbow. Every time she kicks the kneeler, Poppi makes a tsk sound with his tongue. I'll die if Dennis notices and thinks she's weird, but the whole, entire mass, he thumbs through the hymnal, oblivious.

On Christmas morning, after being out late for mass last night, Poppi thought we would sleep in, but it's not even eight o'clock, and I already opened all my gifts. There are two sweaters—a navy blue button-down for over my school uniform, and a pink pullover—blue jeans, roller skates, a Mickey Mouse watch, the newest Nancy Drew books, Bee Gees and Michael Jackson albums, Clue and the Game of Life. My favorite present is the silver cross on a chain from Mama. She helps me with the clasp and steers me into the hall with her hands on my shoulders so we can check it out together in the mirror.

Poppi follows us into the hall, holding out a trash bag filled with wrapping paper he just scooped up off the parlor floor. "Mind putting this out on the porch?" he asks me.

I slip Uncle Nack's moccasins onto my bare feet and slide ski-like across the porch to drop the trash bag near the rail. As soon as I turn around, I see it, a shiny new bike, silvery blue with streamers on the handles and a bell on the handlebars. A white wicker basket sits over the front fender. Uncle Nack clicks away on the camera.

"Merry Christmas, Scungilli." Poppi bends down to show me the license plate. "I had to get Kate, they didn't have Katie."

I throw my arms around his neck. "You're the best, Poppi." I bury my lips near his ear. "I love it better than anything."

Over Poppi's shoulder, my mother takes a deep drag on her cigarette. She flicks the butt onto the porch, grinding it into the wood with her foot. The screen door thuds softly behind her when she goes back inside.

Chapter 8

*T*omorrow is New Year's Eve. All day today, dark clouds hung low in the sky, but the rain held off until bedtime. Now it beats the roof and leaks through a seam in the gutter, going plunk-doom on the trashcan below my window. It keeps waking me up from the same dream where I try to zip up a suitcase. When I can't get it closed, I gather the open suitcase in my arms and start running. My stuff drops out behind me, leaving a trail. I wake up before I know what I'm running from.

I roll over, bunching a pillow over my head when a car horn blares. There's a long angry blast, then a bunch of short ones. I bolt up and peek through the blinds. Grayish light fills the yard. Ray hangs from the open door of his pickup, punching the horn with his elbow.

By the time my feet find my slippers, Mama is in the kitchen fumbling with the key in the door.

"Don't open it," I warn, trying to wrestle the key from her hand.

Her eyes look like she isn't in there when she pushes me away. Her hair sticks out at odd angles from her face. She twists the key into the lock and goes outside in her bare feet, covering her ears with her hands. Behind her, I shiver in my flannel nightie.

Ray wears an orange hunting vest over a denim shirt. His hair falls over his face, hiding his eyes. "I'm taking you home, Babe," he yells.

Poppi's back porch light flicks on. He comes through the door hitching his overalls over his pajama tops. Uncle Nack follows in long underwear tops and bottoms.

"What the hell?" Poppi's face is flushed red in the glow of the porch light.

Ray jumps from the truck and moves toward Mama. She stands still with her hands over her mouth. Ray reaches his hand out to her.

"Get in the truck, June."

"Stay away from her," Poppi hollers.

Ray acts like he didn't hear him. "Get in, June."

Uncle Nack gets between Mama and Ray with Poppi on Ray's other side. Ray plants his feet wide apart, watching all of us.

"She's coming with me."

"She's staying right here." Poppi's voice is gruff.

"Shut up, old man." Ray spits in the dirt near Poppi's feet.

Uncle Nack raises his open hands, patting the air. "We don't want any trouble," he says evenly.

"You already got trouble." Ray runs his fingers through the hair on his forehead. His eyes look black in the dawn-colored air.

"Just get in your truck and go," Poppi says.

"She's coming with me."

"She doesn't want to.

"Ask her what she wants."

"Leave her alone," I say in a squeaky voice.

Ray sneers at me. I back up until my butt hits the door.

"June and Katie, go inside," Poppi says firmly.

I tug my mother's arm. "Come on."

She shakes me off, standing there, pulling on the belt on her terrycloth robe. Ray picks up a branch with both hands and swings it at Uncle Nack.

Uncle Nack jumps out of the way and steps hard on something. He hops and swears, rubbing his foot, keeping his eyes on the branch. Ray swings it full circle when Poppi tries to sneak up behind him. The limb hits our VW, shattering the headlight and spraying glass all over. The sound echoes in the icy air.

"Get in the fucking truck, June."

Poppi grabs for the branch, and it hits him in the palm. "Katie, call 911."

"No. Don't, Katie. Please," Mama begs.

Torn, I look from her to Poppi. Ray swings the branch again, just missing Poppi's arm, and that decides me. I reach behind me for the knob to open the door. Mama's whole body sags as if her spirit is seeping out of her.

Ray yells the whole time I'm on the phone. When I get back outside, he's sweeping the branch back and forth, backing Poppi and Uncle Nack against a tree. He tips his head at Mama. "Get. In. The. Truck."

Mama sits on a cinder block, humming, her arms wrapped around her knees. The closer the sirens get, the louder she hums. Two police cars race up the driveway and pen Ray in near his truck. Mama rocks back and forth. The policemen circle Ray, pointing their nightsticks out in front. One is the son of Poppi's barber, and the older one is an usher at church. Ray lunges at him and his partner grabs Ray's arm and twists it behind his back until Ray drops the branch. He bends Ray over the hood of the police car.

"Get off my arm, shithead."

"Calm down."

"You fucking, fuck, fuck. Get off my arm."

"Watch your mouth." The older cop jabs Ray behind the knees with his stick. Ray falls forward and smacks his face on the hood. He seems dazed while they snap the handcuffs and put him in the back of the police car.

Uncle Nack lifts Mama under her arm to pull her inside. It's like she's sleepwalking until we get inside, then she starts to come to. She yanks so hard to open the drawer where she keeps her cigarettes, everything dumps on the floor. She leaves the stuff there, fidgets with the cellophane, trying to open the pack. When she can't get them open, she curses and throws the pack on the floor with everything else. I pick them up, rip the cellophane, and hand her one. Her lips move a mile a minute, but she isn't saying anything. Poppi comes in and slams the door. Mama starts blinking, like she's trying to make something register. "You can't press charges," she says.

"The hell we won't."

We are all so quiet, you can hear the spigot drip. Her cigarette hisses when she tosses it into the sink. "Why does it always have to be your way?"

Poppi's eyes bulge. "My way?" He jerks the door open so fast, it bangs the wall as he storms out.

Chapter 9

ince the morning Ray showed up, everything about Mama is different. Some days, she's still in bed when I get home from school. I try playing the Beatles, but nothing seems to bring her back. When she does get up, her voice is flat and hollow-like, and she rocks near the window, cradling the phone in her lap.

"Don't dare call him." My voice is part pity and the rest defiance.

She gazes blankly at me like she doesn't recognize me.

All night, she paces and chain-smokes. Her shoulders droop, shrinking her body. She looks like half of herself. When Dee calls about going to a meeting, she says she can't talk right now and hangs up. She wears her robe all of the time. The front is stained with coffee, and there are cigarette burns on the sleeve. She hasn't been outside in a week.

Poppi hovers, making us breakfast, packing my lunch, and bringing us dinner every night. Tonight it's baked chicken and rice. Mama hardly eats. She sits at the kitchen table, tightening the belt on her robe after each puff of her cigarette, while he tries to convince her we should move into the house with him and Uncle Nack. He keeps his voice low, even though he keeps having this same argument every night.

"Did you take your medicine?"

She nods, looking like one of the feral cats that roam the woods behind Uncle Nack's grapevines.

"Maybe you need to go back to the rehab," he says.

Her eyes and voice are empty when she says, "I didn't drink."

Later, when I wake up in the middle of the night to go the bathroom, she's not at the window. She sits crossed legged on the kitchen floor, the phone pressed to her ear. Her fist is jammed against her teeth, and she makes little choking sounds. I try to pry the phone from her hand.

"Go back to bed," she hisses.

"Who is it?"

Her eyes don't focus. "Go to bed."

I try again to jerk the phone from her hands. "It's him. I know it's him."

"I said go to bed." Her voice is so shrill, I don't recognize it; it makes me jump and bang my hip on the table. "Go. To. Bed. Now."

"I hate you." I run to my nook, throw the quilt on the floor, and stomp it with both feet. I punch my mattress until my arms ache.

I don't know when I fell asleep. The sound of the kitchen door opening is just a whoosh of air, but it wakes me.

From the window, she looks like a shadow running across the lawn, disappearing around the front of the house. In the distance, there's a thud and a gunning motor, and then a flash of blurry, dim red taillights, as if I'm dreaming underwater.

I pull a chair up to the window to wait, leaning my head on the cold glass. One-thirty. Two-twenty. Ten to four. The fog my breath makes drips down the windowpane.

When I can't pretend any longer that she's coming back, I put on my robe and bunch the quilt over my shoulders. The black air outside pinches my cheeks and nose. It takes a minute for my eyes to adjust. Holly leaves and pine needles pinch right through my slipper socks. My feet feel numb, but with each step closer to the house, the frozen ground feels more solid. I pat around under the clay flowerpot for the back door key. My eyes adjust again to the filmy dark in the kitchen. The stairs creak when I get near the top. The quilt swishes on the hard wood floor. I throw it on the bed, and roll myself up in it.

In a minute, Poppi is in the doorway. "What are you doing, Scungilli?"

"Mama left."

"Left, where?" He comes in and sits on the edge of my bed. His flannel pajamas feel soft on my face when he scoops me into a bear hug. I breathe in his smell of woodchips and pipe-smoke. His voice is husky and quiet and sad. "I love you truly," he sings.

I snuggle against his chest, pressing my ear to his heartbeat, feeling warm and safe. "Truly, I do."

Chapter 10

E very night back in Mama's old bedroom in Poppi's house, I make private deals with God and the Blessed Mother. I'll go to mass every day, give my recess money to the pagan babies, study hard for every test. I'll eat broccoli rabe *every* time Uncle Nack makes it. Some nights, I promise to become a nun.

Every day, I wait for my prayers to be answered. Mama will call to say she went back to the special hospital. She would have let us know sooner, but the new rules don't allow phone calls. No matter, she's out now and completely cured. She comes for dinner wearing an A-line skirt and a white eyelet blouse with a ruffled high-necked collar, sensible shoes, a stack heel or loafer. We sell the trailer so we can live with Poppi forever.

It's hard to stay awake at school when I don't sleep all night. As soon as Sister Patrice turns her back to pull down the map of the Western Hemisphere, my eyes close. They pop right open when Cam pokes me in the ribs with the eraser end of her pencil. The map sticks and Sister Patrice yanks on the cord. Cam jabs me again and points out the window with her pencil. The map makes loud flap-snapping sounds as it rolls back up so I don't think anyone but Cam hears me gasp.

Mama paces in the shadow of a leafless oak near the line of orange school buses parked at the curb. She stops for a second to light a cigarette from the butt in her other hand. She wears heels, black stockings that might be fishnets, and a too-short dark skirt. If Sister Patrice looks out this window, she will say she looks cheap.

I wait for Sister to secure the map's cord to the hook below the blackboard before I raise my hand. It doesn't matter that it's never a good idea to ask to go to the bathroom in the middle of class. Sister Patrice lets my hand go numb in the air while she gives me the why-didn't-you-go-at-recess look.

"Make it quick," she says, with annoyance.

I go straight past the girl's lavatory to the old classroom at the end of the hall that we use as a library. We don't have a librarian, so it's easy to sneak in here to use the phone. There's no way I will walk out front to get my school bus, so I tell Uncle Nack I have to stay an extra half hour after school to try out for cheerleading. He agrees to pick me up at the back door near the gym.

My mother is still there when the dismissal bell rings. Cam leaves to catch the bus without me after I tell her Uncle Nack is picking me up for a dentist appointment. To kill time, I help Sister Patrice clean the blackboards. I throw my jacket over my shoulders to stand in the open-air fire escape and watch the school buses pull away while I clap the erasers. Hiding in the dusty chalk clouds, I watch Mama, but she can't see me.

The bomber jacket Ray gave her last year is open at her neck. You might have thought that jacket was the most special present when she opened it, but it's not even leather, just leather-look. She shivers, trying to hold the collar closed with her hand. She watches the main door for another minute after the last bus pulls away. A gust of wind blows chalk dust into my face. She's gone by the time my eyes stop watering enough to go back inside.

For the next eight days, the February wind-chill is below zero, too cold for Mama to show up at school.

Instead, the late night phone calls start up again. Whenever the phone rings at night, I bury my head under my pillow, but there's no way to shut out Poppi's worn out voice coming up through the floorboards. This week, he started taking the phone off the hook every night when I go to bed. Just like that, Mama vanishes again into the quiet in the middle of the night.

On Saint Patrick's Day, we get out of school early and Poppi and Uncle Nack are in the woodshed when I get home. After I change out of my uniform, I go down the cellar to look for clothespins for a school project. Now, Poppi doesn't know I'm hunched on the cellar steps in the dark, listening to him talk on the kitchen phone. From my perch on the third step from the top, I hear him say, "Tony the Barber says you're a good lawyer." I don't know why Poppi needs a lawyer, but I don't think needing a lawyer is good. Poppi says something about papers he wants Mama to sign. He's quiet for a long time except for saying, *right* and *uh-huh* until he hangs up. The back door scrapes the floor, and I hear his footsteps on the porch. I wait until I'm sure Poppi is out back before I come out of the stairwell.

The next day, Uncle Nack drives me to school so I won't get soaked at the bus stop because a nor'easter blew in overnight. In front of school, he runs around the car to open my door. Sheets of rain blow sideways, dripping big, navy splotches on my purple jacket. The wind turns Uncle Nack's umbrella inside out.

Inside our classroom, Sister Patrice claps her hands for quiet, but it's no use. Everyone buzzes about the storm. She gives up and says it's time to change seats since we haven't changed for a few months. We pack up our desks and stand around the room, waiting for her to call our names. I stand near the window. The raindrops turn to slush and crawl down the glass like slow-moving spiders. The grass and trees are covered with snow. Sister calls Cam's name to sit in the first seat in the second row. I pray to be called next, but I'm not, pray again when Sister gets to the first seat in the third row, but she doesn't call my name until there are only four seats left. I'm in the last row again, one seat from my old one, nowhere near Cam. Annoyed, I let my schoolbag thunk on the desk. Sister Patrice peeps over her glasses at me. Her mouth is a straight-line reprimand, but she doesn't say anything. I slump into the seat and start to unpack my books. The intercom cracks with static. The principle announces school will close at noon, but there won't be any buses because of the snow. We line up outside the library to call home. Cam can't reach her mother, so I call Uncle Nack to come and get us.

The whole way home, big, mushy flakes chase each other out of the sky, clinging to the car windows. The wipers swish the icy clumps into hard-packed triangles at the edges of the windshield. Uncle Nack hunches over the steering wheel, swiping at the windshield with his hankie to clear a half-moon spot in the fogged-up glass. At the top of the canal bridge, we catch up to a snowplow and follow it down Broadway. The plow is a converted trash truck. I wonder if Ray is driving it because his second job is working for the county, picking up trash. That's how Mama met him. He used to pick up the trash in our neighborhood. The first time we saw him, he impressed Mama when he put the cans back at the curb instead of letting them roll around in the street. He took off his big glove and made a fake salute when Mama thanked him. His hand looked huge. That night, Mama oozed all over the kitchen about how handsome he was when he smiled, but the way he winked at her made me wonder what he was thinking behind that smile.

The next morning, I wake after ten-thirty to find that it snowed all last night. School is closed today, and Poppi let me sleep in.

Sun glares off the snow outside of my bedroom window. Poppi already has the plow hitched to the front of his truck and is finished plowing the driveway. From my bedroom window, I watch him hand his keys over to Uncle Nack, who is probably going to Ursula's to plow her out. By the time I get dressed and go downstairs, Poppi is stomping his feet on the porch to knock the snow off his boots. He shakes out his cap. I walk barefoot into the mudroom to watch him change from his boots to his moccasins. He opens the dryer and takes out a pair of his wool knit socks for me to put on. They're still warm from the dryer, reach up to my knees, and make my whole leg toasty.

"How much did it snow?"

"About a foot."

"Goodie. No school tomorrow, either."

He smiles and tweaks my cheek. "After I wash up, we'll make waffles."

Back in the kitchen, we use a soup ladle to dribble the batter onto the waffle iron, making a dozen waffles by the time Uncle Nack gets back.

"Look what the storm blew in," he calls from the mudroom.

Icy snow clings to the tips of Dennis's hair around his ears.

"Pull up a chair," Poppi says cheerfully, and Dennis can't wait to plop down and fork a waffle.

After breakfast, Uncle Nack and Poppi go to the wood-shed to varnish the custom kitchen cabinets Poppi has to deliver this week. Dennis and me try building a snowman, but the snow is so heavy, it's hard to roll it into a ball. We give up, go back inside, and peel off our wet jackets, throwing our hats and gloves into the dryer.

We set up the checker board and play a zillion games by the time Uncle Nack comes in to make us grilled provolone cheese sandwiches and hot chocolate. We are both starving and we eat so fast, the cheese burns our tongues. When we finish, Dennis calls his mother to beg her to take us sledding. She agrees to come and get us on her way to the grocery store.

There are two sleds in the back of the van. I know the shorter, rusty one will end up being mine. Ursula pulls over to unload near the foot of the canal bridge. When everything is out of the van, she stands between us and lifts both our chins so we have to look her in the eyes. "Only this hill, not the one near the water."

Dennis glances at the steeper hill. "It's not that close to the water." He stoops to pick up the cord of his sled.

As soon as he stands up straight again, she swivels his chin back around. Her head is angled to the side. "Promise," she says.

"Geez, Mom."

"Dennis. Don't even think about it."

He shields his eyes to study the bigger hill. "I'll roll off my sled if I get close."

"Be careful, you two," she says less sternly and gets back into the van.

An hour later, we have been up and down the smaller hill enough times for my fingers to be cold and soggy inside my gloves. My toes are numb.

"Let's go down the big hill," Dennis says.

"You mom said . . ."

"Just one time, I swear." He slogs away so fast, I have to run to catch up to him. We are almost up top when he says, "Lay on my back and we'll go down together."

I push my sled out of the way under a tree. Overhead, in the bare branches, a sparrow chirps its heart out. I feel wobbly stretched out on Dennis's back. To keep from sliding off, I grip the sleeves of his jacket.

"Hold on near my neck so I can steer," he says.

I squeeze a fistful of jacket near his collar.

"Ready?"

I bend my legs back at the knees. "Ready."

He wiggles his feet to push off. I slide all over the place, trying to shimmy my hips back over his butt. His head smells like wet hat and hair sweat. About halfway down the hill, the sled pops in the air when we hit something solid. We bounce hard on the ground. I bite my tongue and taste salty blood in my mouth. When I look up, we're heading right for a tree stump.

"Ditch," Dennis yells.

I tumble off on my back in the snow. Something stabs my forehead, and it feels like there are ice cubes seeping down my neck.

"Are you okay?" He pries my fingers away from my face. "Let me see."

He braces my arm to help me sit up. My eyebrow stings like crazy. Blood drips down my cheek and makes three little dots in the snow. I close my eyes tight to keep from crying.

"Do you have a tissue?" he asks.

The palm of my glove is bloody. I bite the fingertips to pull it off, feel around in my pocket, and pull out a crumpled tissue. He takes it and presses it over my eyebrow.

"Ouch."

"Stay still."

"Don't push so hard."

I snatch the tissue from him and dab at the cut. His sled is upside down in the snow. He flips it and swipes at the wet on it with his glove. "Sit on this," he says.

"Stop bossing me."

"Don't be such a baby."

My butt is cold but to spite him, I don't get up. The way he stands over me, the sun is a bright flash over his shoulder, making me squint when I glare up at him. The skin over my eye pinches. Really slowly, I move the tissue. "Is it still bleeding?"

He nods and takes the tissue from me. He presses hard again. It hurts, but instead of telling him, I count to fifty in my head. He lifts the tissue and stares for a few seconds. "It's almost stopped."

We're both quiet as we trudge in the slush to the side of the hill to get my sled.

"Do you think I'll need stitches?"

"If you do, you'll be just like your mother," he says.

I hate that he noticed the jagged scar on her forehead from her car accident, but not as much as I hate him saying I might be like her. "I will not." I kick snow at him and stomp away.

He is so wrong. Just living with Poppi, where she never wants to be, proves I am *nothing* like her. I stamp my feet through the snow until I'm at the side of the road. I sit on my sled with my elbows on my knees, chin on my fists. Dennis pulls up his sled beside me.

"Don't even think about sitting here." I shimmy around on the sled so my back faces him.

"What's wrong with you?"

"It's your fault for making me get on your sled." I jam my hands into my pockets.

"Crybaby."

"Just shut up."

"Geez-oh-man." He huffs and tramps away.

I wait for the noise of his sled slogging through the snow to fade before I sneak a peek over my shoulder. He's back on top of the big hill, talking to three boys I don't recognize. Who cares? I have other friends, too. He flops on his sled and whirls down the hill. I lose him in the sun's glare before he gets to the bottom. I'm still looking for him a few minutes later when he shows up out of nowhere and plops on his sled beside me.

"You dropped this." It's my bloodstained glove. I don't say a thing when I snatch it and stuff it into my pocket. He picks up a pinecone and sits, snapping pieces off of it. I pull my glove from my pocket and pull it over my icy fist.

"Your mom isn't so bad."

I lift the empty glove fingers one at a time and let them fall against my closed fist. "Who asked you?"

"I'm just saying."

He throws his pinecone against a tree. It bounces and sinks deep into the snow. "My mom says when my dad drinks, he can't help it."

I sneak a sideways glance. He picks up another pinecone. "She says it's because he's sick."

I spread my fingers one at a time to put the glove on right. With my boots, I dig slushy grooves in the snow. "Do you believe her?"

Instead of answering, he shrugs and dropkicks the pinecone into a bank of snow.

Chapter 11

*A*fter a soggy spring, today is the first day of
summer vacation. Last week, Sister Patrice let me
bring in Uncle Nack's camera to take pictures of
my classmates because now that I live with Poppi in Our
Lady Star of the Sea Parish, I'm not going back to Saint
Raymond's next year. Neither is Cam, since her family
bought a bed and breakfast Inn and moved to Cape May.
That means next year, we get to go to the same school as
Dennis.

Poppi is refinishing a dining room set in the woodshed
when I take my pictures out there to put them in one of
the albums he keeps in an old bureau. He sings along with
Frank Sinatra on the radio while he works.

"When I finish, want to take a walk through the Bird Sanctuary?" He opens a tin can. The smell of turpentine fills my nose. Between that and the dust that floats up when I open the picture drawer, I sneeze four times in a row.

He offers me his hankie. After I blow my nose, I lift a box of old pictures out of the drawer.

"Let's stay here and look at old pictures."

"Wouldn't you sooner get some fresh air?"

"I'd rather look at pictures."

He shrugs his shoulders and tightens the lid on the turpentine.

After lunch, Poppi lugs the picture box into the kitchen. We have to open one envelope at a time so we don't mix up the negatives. I hunt through a few before I find the black and white prints from a football game. I've seen them a hundred times before. Five teenaged boys dressed in football jerseys huddle in a semicircle. Their shoulders and legs bulge with padding. In the center, my grinning father clutches his helmet in one arm. The next picture is almost the same, except he's sticking out his tongue.

"He was a good ballplayer, your father," Poppi says and sighs.

He always says that when we look at these pictures. Usually he adds, "Could have turned pro," but today, he's busy looking at the next picture, which is one of the ones I was rooting for. In it, my father's arm is draped over my mother's shoulders, his fingers twined in the ends of her hair. She gazes at him like there's nothing else in the whole, wide world to see, the way I probably gawk at Dennis.

"Did my mother have other boyfriends?" I know the answer, but want to hear him say it again.

"Just him. From the first year of high school, they were crazy for each other."

Even though they were so young, Poppi and Nonna let them go steady because they loved my father like a son. Not like my other grandparents, who tried to break them up. "Can I keep this picture in my room?"

He says sure, and I steal another look at it before tucking it into the bib of my overalls. It doesn't make sense that she can like Ray after being in love like that with my father. I could never love another boyfriend the way I love Dennis.

In the next packet, my mother wears a cap and gown, standing between Nonna and a younger, thinner-faced Poppi.

"How old were you?"

He squints to read the date on the bottom of the picture. "In '58? Thirty-nine, I guess."

"When did your hair get white?"

"Few years after that."

"Do you think Mama's and mine will do that?" "Nah. You and your mama got Nonna's hair."

In this picture, Nonna's hair is still dark and thick. I've seen every picture in this box. The only ones from when she was sick were taken two years after this one, at my parent's wedding. In them, her hair is so thin, you see right through it to her scalp.

I pick up my father's graduation picture: full open face, wide-spaced eyes, pug nose. "Did I get anything from my father?" I ask anxiously. I want him to say the part that makes you not drink.

He points to my father's head. "You got his little ears."

True. The Nacaro ears are on the big side. "What else?"

He picks up my hand and stretches out my fingers. "You got his long fingers. People used to say he should play piano." I run my finger over a callous on Poppi's palm. I wouldn't have minded getting Poppi's hard work hands, but I like having my father's fingers.

"What else?"

He raises his eyebrows like he doesn't know.

"There must be something."

He rubs his hand over his chin. "He liked to ride his bike, and he loved to read. He used to complain his stomach hurt when he drank coffee—or maybe it was orange juice, just like you do."

Good, an inside thing.

"You'd be in your playpen and he'd come in the back door and put his arm straight up in the air and sing out, "Who's my best girl?" You'd put your arm up just like him and giggle and baby talk. He swore you repeated who's my best girl back to him. Some days it did sound like that."

"How old was I?"

"Maybe eight or nine months."

"I think I remember."

"Nah. You were just a baby."

"Still, I think maybe I remember."

After we put away the picture box, I cannot get Mama out of my head. Cam is visiting her cousins in Lancaster and Dennis is at baseball camp until three, so I decide to ride my bike to the trailer. There are no cars around when I get there. The windows are grimy and one of the panes in the door is boarded up. Everything is locked up tight. There's nothing to see when I try to peek through the blind on the kitchen window. I turn around quick when I hear a door squeak. It's next-door Lucy coming down her front step.

"She isn't there, honey. I haven't seen her since Memorial Day."

I want to ask if she saw her leave, what she took with her, where she went. How can she want to be with Ray more than she wants to be with me? Instead, I pick up my bike out of the nasty clamshells and straddle it.

"Want to come in for a cracker?" Lucy asks.

"I have to get home."

I pedal hard, making my legs ache and my whole rib-cage burn. The hot, humid air makes it hard to breathe. I have to stop to catch my breath when I get to the bottom of the canal bridge. I sit in the gravel at the side of the road, picking pieces of broken clamshells from the hateful driveway out of my tires. I'm not getting up until I pick out every piece.

Chapter 12

My summer job is helping Uncle Nack in the early morning before he opens the farm stand. It rained last night, so today, we slog through the mud in the grapevines. He's a fanatic about these grapes. Every time it rains we have to check every leaf and stem and reattach any loose vines to the wire lattice. Heaven help us if a grape gets bruised.

The sun is so hot this morning, you can almost see steam coming out of the dirt. All that wet makes the mosquitoes wicked; there must a hundred bites on my ankles. They don't bug Uncle Nack, but every time I turn around, I swat another one.

We have one more row of vines to check, which is good. I can tell by where the sun is in the sky that it's almost time to go to the beach.

As soon as we finish with the grapes, I skip back to the house to put on my bathing suit and lather on my suntan lotion. From my bedroom window, I see Dennis and his friends the Raymond brothers ride up on their bikes. Joe and John Raymond look so much alike, they could be twins if John wasn't three inches taller. They both have hair the color of iced tea and a ridge of freckles on their nose. Their towels are rolled up in their belts and slung over their handlebars. Dennis wears a backpack. I run down the steps, my beachbag bouncing against my hip. I shove the salami sandwich Uncle Nack made earlier into it and head outside. As soon as I stow my bag in my bike basket, we pedal back out the driveway to pick up Cam.

Like every day when we get to the beach, Cam getting set up is a production. She arranges her body on her beach towel so she is perfectly lined up with the sun. I spread my towel out next to her, but before I can sit down, John Raymond asks if one of us can put Coppertone on his back. It's no big surprise when Cam doesn't get up to do it. The hair on John's back tickles my fingers, making it hard to rub in the lotion without leaving a bunch of white streaks.

Dennis is next. Touching the silky blond hairs on his back, mixed up with the sunshine smell of Coppertone, makes me dreamy when I close my eyes.

I am almost finished when he says, "Scratch my back." My hand glides over his back. An electric current moves through my fingertips and up my arms. It's like my nails are fireworks shooting out sparks. He doesn't seem to notice, rapping my arm with his knuckles before sprinting to the volleyball net.

I try to copy the way Cam lounges, one leg bent up at the knee, the other one straight with painted toes pointed and palms flat behind her hips. In my one-piece with a skirt, it's hard to look as glamorous as she does in her pink-check bikini.

I sift sand through my fingers, watching the volleyball game. Dennis makes an unbelievable diving save. His arms are stretched like a big V, his belly hits the sand. I jump to my feet, clapping wildly.

"Hey, watch the sand." Cam flicks a few grains off her leg.

"Sorry."

"He's kind of cute when he plays sports," she says.

I dig grooves in the sand with my heels, burrowing my toes. "Do you like him now?"

Her hair ripples down her back when she shakes her head. "He's okay."

I deepen the ridges in the sand with my feet. "But, do you, you know, like him?"

Before she can answer, Dennis appears out of nowhere, digs into his backpack, and pulls out a half-gallon of iced tea. He chugs it down right from the bottle.

As if he's not there, Cam looks me up and down with squinty, disapproving eyes. "You need a real bathing suit, instead of one that looks like a mom's."

Dennis chokes and tea sprays through his teeth onto the sand.

I'm seriously thinking about crawling under my sandy towel. Instead, I stand up. "I'm going in the water."

Dennis screws the lid back on his tea as I sprint away. "I'll go with you." He has to run to catch up.

We're quiet while the chilly foam laps at our toes. I go in further. My calves are so cold, I have to shift from one foot to the other.

"She's mean sometimes," he says.

"It's just how she is."

"She's supposed to be your best friend."

"*You're* my best friend." I turn my back to him, but the yellow sun makes me blink, so I turn around again. "Besides, she's right."

His hand cups the water, like he might splash me. The way he stops to pay attention makes me keep talking.

"I don't have anyone but Cam to tell me girl things. Like, how's Poppi or Uncle Nack supposed to know about makeup or two-piece bathing suits . . ." I slap the water so hard drops spray his face. "Or a bra."

Dennis' mouth drops open. The sun looks like little high beams in his pupils. I dive head first into a wave. Salt water burns up my nose and around my eyes. A watery echo fills my ears. It feels like my head might burst. I shake the water out of my ears.

"You could ask my mom about stuff."

I slap the water. "Right."

Before he can say anything else, Joe Raymond swims up on a blow-up raft. "Get on," he says.

I hang on, ready to be carried wherever the wave decides to take me.

The next Saturday morning, Poppi takes me to Ursula's for breakfast—a real treat because on Saturday morning, he is usually busy running errands. We just finished eating and I'm out on the sidewalk, watching through the lace curtains as he pays the bill. It's taking a long time. You can tell by the way their heads are bent close that they're talking about something serious. He comes out chewing on a toothpick.

"Let's take a ride to the Point," he says.

When we get to Cape May Point, he parks across the street from the huge St. Joseph's Convent. All the rocking chairs on the red and white wrap-around porch are empty. The nuns must be inside praying.

"Ursula offered to take you shopping."

"What kind of shopping?"

"New school clothes." He clears his throat, staring straight ahead. His ears turn pink. "And girly things." He shifts into park and lets the truck idle.

I swear, Dennis tells her *everything*. I'm not sure if that makes me thankful or mad. I play with the radio dial, change it from Poppi's AM Frank Sinatra station to FM rock. Usually, the rule is he gets to pick, but he doesn't say anything when Elton John starts singing "Someone Saved My Life Tonight." I raise the volume a few notches too loud. He lets that go, too.

He guns the motor a little, even though we're parked. "I know it's hard for you without your mom around."

I put my window all the way down. Beach grass leans on the breeze along the path leading to the sand. The exhaust fumes from the revving motor are so thick, you can almost taste them. "Do you know where she is?"

He lowers the volume on the radio, turning sideways in his seat. "Somewhere in the Villas with Ray."

My old school, St. Raymond's, is in Wildwood Villas. Is that why she showed up those times out front? "How do you know?"

"The bartender at the Villas Fishing Club sees them. He's a friend from Sons of Italy."

My eyes water a little in the glare from the windshield. I wipe them with the back of my hand. He rests his hand on my shoulder. I run my finger along the grooved edge of the glove compartment, like it is a road that could take me somewhere. "Do you think she misses us?" I ask uncertainly.

He nods his head. His hand is still on my shoulder and I can hear his watch tick in my ear. I change the radio dial back to Sinatra and stare straight out the windshield. "Do you think she's the one who calls and hangs up?"

He moves both hands and squeezes the steering wheel. "Don't know," he says.

I want him to say "yes, for sure," even if it isn't true, but that's the thing about Poppi. I know there are things he doesn't tell me, but I don't think he ever lies.

"I guess I'll go shopping with Ursula," I say.

On Monday when her restaurant is closed, Ursula drives to the bigger Dellas General Store in North Cape May instead of the crowded tourist one in town. I'm in the dressing room by myself, trying on the four bathing suits she helped me pick. Each time I change into another one, I open the door and model it for her. The one I have on now is hot pink gingham.

"I like that one best," she says.

"Cam might be mad that it looks too much like hers."

Ursula purses her lips. "Give me a minute." She comes back with the same bathing suit in royal blue. "It's even prettier in blue," she says wholeheartedly.

I change into it and check myself out from all sides in the three-way mirror. She convinces me when she adds that the blue is perfect for my complexion. She tells me to pick one more because Poppi said I can get two.

I settle on the aqua one with crocheted daisy trim after Ursula says it's dainty and very grown up.

I'm heading up to the register when she stops me. "Try on a few of these." She picks several bras out of a bin. My heart thumps. I keep my head down, staring at the bras— I'm too mortified to look Ursula in the face.

She touches my shoulder. "Don't worry. You don't have to show me, just pick what fits the best."

I exhale and head back into the dressing room. With the door shut tight and my foot jammed against it, my arm feels like it's stretching out of the socket trying to hook this bra behind my back. I give up and try the one that fastens in front. The lace trim itches, but at least I can get this one hooked. I get dressed without trying on the last one. "This one, I guess." I study Ursula's shoes when I hand it to her.

"Let's see if they have a few more in your size."

"Do they come without lace?"

She smiles and smooths the hair at the side of my face. "I hate lace, too." She says it with a wink like we're schemers and makes me feel like we're part of a special club.

After Dellas, we go to the bookstore. In the health section, she pulls out a thick book about puberty and hands it to me. My cheeks blush all the way to my toes.

"Let's go pay," she says. I trudge behind her up to the register. After she pays, we go back outside into the muggy air. I hug my bags to my chest, head down, being careful where I walk, putting each foot in the center of the concrete. Don't step on a crack; don't break your mother's back. At the car, I toss my bags into the backseat and Ursula sets the book under her purse. "The book is yours, but I'll give it to Poppi to read first."

The only thing Poppi reads is the Racing Form and the newspaper. I can't believe Ursula thinks he will read this book with nothing but girls my age on the front.

Ursula must be reading my mind, because she adds, "I know. Weird, right?" The way she rolls her eyes and smirks makes me chuckle. And then we both laugh so hard, tears leak out of our eyes.

For the first time all day, I don't feel embarrassed.

When she drops me off at the house and I thank her for taking me shopping, I really mean it.

Chapter 13

*I*t has hardly rained all summer and the grass is so dry, it pricks my bare feet as I run across it to get inside before the phone stops ringing.

"Kate Mae." Mama's voice sounds thick from crying.

I know it has been exactly one hundred and sixty-two days since the last time I heard her voice because before I go to bed, I write it in red on the calendar hidden in my vanity drawer.

"He left me."

My heart beats so loud in my ears, it makes me dizzy.

"Everyone leaves me." She sobs too hard to make out what she says next. The back of my throat feels all slimy. Is she talking about me?

"I want to die."

"Don't say that, Mama."

Just then, the back door opens. Poppi's face looks flushed from the heat. He rushes in and pries the phone from my hand. Her voice gets smaller in the air between us. Poppi motions for me to leave the room, but I'm staying right here.

"June, it's Pop."

He clasps his hand on my shoulder and steers me out the door. I make sure the door slams behind me. I can hear his voice through the holes in the screen. Part of me wants to listen and the other part wants to cover my ears and scream.

"Did that son of a bitch hit you?" Poppi says.

There is a huge spider web between the porch rails with a ladybug stuck in the center, hanging by a see-through wing. I pick up a stick to poke it free.

Poppi coughs. It sounds like something is stuck in his throat. "I'll stop by in the morning to fix the door." A few minutes later, he says goodbye and comes out to stand next to me on the porch.

"I'm going with you tomorrow."

"We'll see."

I swipe at the spider web. The filmy threads cling to the stick. I throw it down and kick it off the porch. "I'm going and you can't stop me." I run off the porch and grab my bike from where it leans against the weeping willow tree.

"Wait." He starts down the steps, but I keep pedaling. "Where are you going?"

I pedal hard. "Nowhere," I scream. I'm going nowhere. Just like her.

Chapter 14

*I*n the morning when we get to the trailer, Poppi walks around, peeking in windows, while I sit in the truck kicking the dashboard.

She's not even here. Why did I bother to come?

When he gets back out front, he looks up and down at the screen door that hangs at an odd angle, nails sticking out of the broken top hinge. The wood panel at the bottom is splintered where Ray kicked that creepy snake boot of his right through it. Poppi shakes his head and tramps to the flatbed to get his tools. Ray's pickup rumbles to a stop at the curb. Poppi strides over to stand guard against my door. He sucks air in and out real slow, watching Ray.

Through the open window, I tug on Poppi's sleeve. "Let's go."

He doesn't move.

Ray swings his door open and jumps out. "What do you want?"

"I came to fix the door," Poppi says sharply.

"I can fix my own damn door."

He says it like he thinks it's really *his* door.

Poppi's neck turns blotchy, the way it does when his pressure is up. "June asked *me* to fix it," he says.

Ray's hair looks shorter, but it still falls across his eyes when he cocks his head. "Well, she ain't here."

Poppi shifts the toolbox. "Yeah? Where is she?"

Ray glares at Poppi and then glares at me. A vein in his temple pulses as he struts by us. He digs a key out of the pocket of his jeans and unlocks the door.

"When she gets home, tell her we were here," Poppi says.

Ray's lip curls up and shows his teeth. "Yeah, I'll be sure to do that."

Poppi chucks his toolbox back into the flatbed, climbs into the truck, and twists the key in the ignition. Neither of us says anything until we reach the first red light. My arms are crossed over my chest. I am trying so hard not to cry, I start to hiccup. "It's not fair," I say.

Poppi reaches over and pats me on the knee. "Tell me about it." His eyes look like he might cry with me.

I cannot believe I gave her another chance. From now on, I'm sticking on Poppi's side.

When we get home, Dennis' bike is propped next to mine in the driveway. He sits on the porch steps, tossing a pimple ball from one hand to the other. At this time of day, he's usually playing ball.

"Where are Joe and John?"

"At the dentist." His red Phillie's cap is turned backward on his head.

Poppi goes right to the shed with his tools.

"I'll be right out." I don't look at Dennis when I run up the steps in case my eyes are red. Inside, I splash cold water on my face and take a bunch of grapes from the colander in the fridge. I go back outside and hand him half of the grapes.

He pops one in his mouth and makes a this-is-sour-face. "Where were you?"

Instead of answering, I fill my mouth with grapes. They are so cold and tart, they shock my teeth, but I swallow like it doesn't matter.

We ride our bikes to our favorite spot on Sea Grove Avenue in Cape May Point, setting our bikes down in the tall grass on an empty lot. Honeysuckle and sweet clematis look like lacy snowflakes on the bushes and trees. The air smells syrupy. Every time we come here, Dennis pretends he's building a house. He drags the point of a stick, making a line in the dirt to show where he would put the in-ground pool. I follow his shadow. The birds chirp so loud, it feels like the air vibrates. I imagine this make-believe house is our house, Dennis' and mine, the wrap-around porch, the swings in the yard, the study with the telescope to watch purple martins fly in circles against the sky. Scratching the dirt with his stick, Dennis unearths two milky stones with tangerine streaks. He dusts them off on his shirt and hands them to me. The pearly streaks look like sunrays. He says keep them when I go to hand them back. I'm not sure why he gave me the stones, but after my crappy morning, this feels like winning a prize.

When we get back, Dennis does a wheelie in front of our driveway and says he will be back after dinner. I ditch my bike on the lawn and am on the back porch when I hear Poppi's voice through the screen door.

"It's the goddamndist thing if it's true."

I know he will stop talking as soon as I walk in. I stand out here listening instead. "She says she went to one of them AA meetings. Claims at 7-eleven last night, she ran into this gal she knew from going to meetings. They sat up talking all night at this gal's house. Then this morning, they go to this meeting."

"You believe her?"

A chair scrapes the floor and squeaks when one of them sits down.

"Who knows with her?"

As expected, Poppi and Uncle Nack clam up when I walk inside. Neither of them utters another syllable about Mama during dinner. Before I can work up the nerve to ask them about it, Cam knocks on the door.

"I have to do the dishes," I say, idiotically hoping she will offer to help.

She fans her fingers through her hair. "I'll wait out back."

When I get back there, she's sprawled right in the middle of the hammock. I try to nudge her over with my hip when I sit next to her, but she won't budge from the middle.

I know what she's doing.

Dennis shows up and has to sit on her other side. Three don't fit in the hammock as good as two. As soon as we lean back to watch the stars, you can't help sliding into Cam, rubbing up against her with your whole body. I shift around a little trying to get more room, and she lets out a yelp.

She puts her finger in her mouth and sucks on it. "You crushed my finger."

"Let me see." Dennis holds her hand so close to his face, if you didn't know better, you might think he needs glasses. I swat a low-hanging cluster of wisteria.

When she finally stops whining about her finger, we talk about nothing, last night's "Gilligan's Island" rerun, our favorite thing to eat at McDonald's, whether we will get a nun or a teacher when we go back to school.

We start telling riddles. The only ones I can think of are the ones I read on cereal boxes. Dennis tells us one about two elephants taking a bath and one of them says "no soap radio." He almost falls out of the hammock laughing so hard, but we don't get it. He keeps saying, no soap radio over and over, like he's saying how dumb can you be? He finally comes clean and admits he made it up—after all that, it doesn't mean anything.

Cam punches him in the arm. "No fair."

If I punched him like that, he would punch me back, but with her, he acts like it's hilarious.

In the middle of Dennis telling us about an old Dracula movie he watched the other night, Cam jumps up and says she wants to go home.

"It's not even 8:30," I say.

Dennis scrambles out of the hammock. "I'll walk you."

I'm stuck in the hammock's webbing. Nobody offers to help me up. I wiggle myself free. "You never leave at 8:30."

Dennis shoves his hands so deep into his pockets, he hunches over, scuffing the dirt with the toe of his sneaker. "She can't walk home alone."

"Poppi will drive her."

"I want to walk," Cam says.

"Why are you leaving?"

We must look pathetic, the way he can't take his eyes off her and I can't take mine off him.

"Don't be mad. I just want to go," she sulks.

I watch the parade of two; her in front, arms loose, her chin stuck out, leading the way. Dennis follows at her heels, his head slightly bent. Near the end of the driveway, he catches up and walks beside her. A big eggplant-shaped cloud blocks the moonlight. In the semi-dark, I can't tell if my eyes are playing tricks or if Dennis is holding Cam's hand. The whole way back to the house, I stamp my feet on dirt bombs until they turn to nothing but dust.

Poppi is on the couch, hands folded over his stomach, head back, making short, double-spaced snores. I tiptoe into the dining room, where dim light shows around the edges of the cellar door. Halfway down the steps, I plop down and breathe in the tart, musty smells of old wood and pressed grapes. Uncle Nack looks up from the corner where he works a cork out of the hole in one of his wine barrels.

"Number Two, what's with the pouty face?"

"Cam made Dennis walk her home."

He slips a thin rubber tube inside the barrel, puffs on it until wine drips out and half-fills a juice glass. He plugs the cork back in before he takes a sip, rolls it around his mouth, and swallows, licking his lips.

"Can I taste?"

"You know Poppi says no."

Uncle Nack started growing grapes to make wine a few years ago. He and Poppi don't fight about much, but they fight about that. Poppi says it's asking for trouble having barrels of goddamn alcohol in the basement.

"Just a taste," I say.

"You won't like it."

I slink down the steps on my butt, stand up, and jiggle his arm. "Please?"

He holds the glass to my lips and tilts up my chin. I know he wants me to just sip, but I take a big gulp. It makes a hot path down my throat and tastes putrid, but I like the way it makes my face tingle. I wipe my tongue on the sleeve of my shirt.

"Told you you wouldn't like it."

I watch for a while as he works on the cork on the second barrel. After he gets it out and starts to refill the glass, I work up the nerve to ask. "Is Mama better again?"

He clears his throat. "Better?"

"If she goes to those meetings, isn't she better?"

He wipes his cork with a terry cloth towel, plugs it back into the hole. "Why are you asking about that?"

I crack my knuckles. "I heard Poppi tell you."

"You shouldn't eavesdrop."

"I didn't. I just heard him."

He narrows his eyes and tastes the wine from the second barrel. The way he takes his time swishing it in his mouth, I can tell he's done with talking. I reach for the glass for another taste.

He puts his hand up in a stop sign. "You had enough."

After almost a week, I decide the whole thing about the AA meeting is a made-up story because nobody mentions it again. Wednesday night comes and goes, and so does Thursday—days 231 and 232 on the calendar where I keep track. How can she not want to see me for that many days?

Tonight, Cam went roller skating with the rest of the cheerleaders, so it's just Dennis and me in the hammock, staring up at the moon that looks like a crescent-shaped cookie. Dennis takes a bite of an apple, and juice sprays my cheek. He chews really loud, crunching right in my ear.

"What are you getting for your birthday?" he asks.

"I asked for a birthstone ring."

"What else?"

What I want more than anything is to see my mother— and for Dennis to like me better than Cam. I'm still trying to think of what else to tell him I want when a car horn shatters the stillness. We bolt from the hammock and dash to the front yard.

In the middle of the driveway, Poppi slumps against the steering wheel inside his truck. The truck's motor races, coughing exhaust into the chalky air. I shake the cobwebs from my head, trying to make it make sense. Poppi's limp arm hangs out the open window, just dangling there, not moving.

Dennis stands still like a big lump. I dart closer and grab Poppi's arm. Uncle Nack runs down the porch steps two at a time. He grabs Poppi's shoulders and shakes him. The horn stops. A creepy quiet completely fills the yard. Poppi isn't talking. His eyes blink every time I say his name, as if they are trying to tell me it's okay, but it feels like it might never be okay again. A thick, gurgling sound comes from the back of his throat. I squeeze his hand, praying with all my might for him to squeeze back.

"What's wrong?"

Uncle Nack shouts, "Dennis, call an ambulance; there's a sticker with the number on the phone."

Dennis finally moves, sprinting up the porch steps.

"Poppi, please . . ." I pump his arm.

"And call your mother," Uncle Nack yells just as the screen door slams.

It's been two awful hours since the ambulance raced Poppi to the hospital. Ursula keeps saying it will be all right, that Uncle Nack will call as soon as he can. This must be the fiftieth time I dialed Mama's number from Ursula's kitchen phone. I only let it ring five times, so I don't tie up the line. Dennis is half-laying across the table, arm stretched out, his cheek resting near his elbow. My face must have the same dumbfounded expression as his.

I grab for the phone when it rings, but Ursula gets it first. I hit the table with my open palm, splashing tea all over her new placemat. Serves her right for not letting me answer it. Ursula nods into the phone, murmuring about an operation, repeating words I never heard before. She hangs up without letting me get on.

"I wanted to talk to him."

"He was on a pay phone."

"How's Poppi?"

"Uncle Nack says he looks better." She dabs at the soggy placemat with a sponge. "He had a stroke."

"What's a stroke?"

"A weak spot, like when your bike tube gets a bubble."

"Will he be okay?"

In the split second she takes to reply the knot in my stomach knows he might not be. It sucks up all the space in my chest.

Every day, they keep telling me Poppi is a little better, but it all feels like lies because they won't let me go see him. Finally, after four days, I'm allowed to visit. I don't know how Uncle Nack got in touch with Mama, but he must have said something to make her feel guilty because she said she would meet us at the hospital. We've been on this bench in front of the hospital waiting for half an hour, but so far, she is a no-show. Uncle Nack stubs out his cigar and slips it into his tee shirt pocket. We go inside and get on the elevator without her.

Uncle Nack steers me out to the right when the elevator opens. The glare off the plate glass window makes me squint. At the end of the hall, there's a ghost with a shaved head sitting in a wheelchair.

That cannot be my Poppi!

What did Uncle Nack say about how Poppi looks on our way over in the car? Whatever he said, it wasn't enough.

My legs get so heavy Uncle Nack has to push me to make me keep walking. The closer we get, the more the deep purple bruise at the edge of the bandage looks like dried blood. As soon as he sees us, Poppi lifts his right arm and starts to wave. He looks so happy to see me, the right side of his face smiles, but the other side and his lower lip droop. His rasping sounds make me want to cry, but I know I'm not supposed to. I keep swallowing and trying to breathe. He must hate the flimsy blue gown he wears. I lean in to kiss his cheek and his good arm pulls me close. My head burrows into his chest, trying to find that safe place where I can hear his heartbeat.

We stayed at the hospital until dinner time, and got back hours ago. Uncle Nack has been in bed since before ten. I can't go to sleep. I sneak downstairs and pace back and forth in the kitchen, trying to work up the courage to pick up the phone, dial Mama's number, and make her tell me why she wants to drink and be with Ray more than she wants to see Poppi or be here with me.

After a few minutes, I open the cellar door, switch on the light, and sit on the bottom step, hugging my knees to my chest until the dampness seeps through my cotton nightgown. My arms are covered in goose bumps.

The siphon tube is where Uncle Nack always leaves it. In the semi-dark, I work at the wax cork with my fingers. When I get it off and put the tube in, the wine drips over my hand, making a bruise-like stain down my sleeve. Drops soak into the dirt floor.

The first few sips don't quench my thirst. I keep drinking. After half a glass, the pain in my chest starts to get dull. I sit back down on the bottom step and rock before I chug the rest, closing my eyes. My head spins off into a place where I start to forget.

The tolling of the grandfather clock upstairs reaches inside the purple-blue haze in my head. The twelve gloomy chimes remind me. Tomorrow is my twelfth birthday.

Chapter 15

*P*oppi should have come home from the hospital yesterday, but at the last minute, the doctor didn't let him. Uncle Nack told me it's just a fever, but I overheard him tell Ursula there's a complication with some kind of drain. Uncle Nack stayed at the hospital so late last night, I slept over Dennis's. Ursula made him give up his room for me, and he slept on the living room sofa. Since five a.m., I have stared out the window at the blurry rain coating the glass. The sky is one big steel wool cloud. No matter how many times Ursula reassured me last night that the fever is nothing, I keep worrying.

I forgot my robe, so Ursula lent me one of her flannel shirts to wear over my nightgown. I put it on and creep into the hallway. The sleeves hang almost to my knees. Ursula's bedroom door is open, and her bed is made. I tiptoe down the hall to the living room.

Dennis' ear and his fuzzy hair poke out the top of his sleeping bag. I sit on the couch and pull my legs up inside the flannel shirt, watching his sleeping bag rise and fall with each breath, thinking how dreamy it would be to run my fingers through his hair.

The smell of coffee floats in from the kitchen. It sounds like Ursula is putting away silverware. I lean down to sniff a vase of dried roses on the coffee table. The inside of my nose itches and I can't hold back a sneeze.

Dennis blinks and opens both eyes, but the lids are droopy. "What time is it?"

"After nine."

"It's still dark."

"It's raining."

He bunches the sleeping bag over his shoulders and hunkers down into it. "Go back to bed."

I work my hand out of my sleeve to bite the cuticle on my thumb. "I can't sleep."

He opens one eye and squints at me sideways. "You're a pain." I guess he can tell I'm not going anywhere because he sits up, yawns, and stretches his arms up to the ceiling. After he crawls out of the sleeping bag, he unzips it, fanning it out to cover us like a big blanket, with him huddled under it at one end of the couch and me at the other end.

We just settle in when Ursula comes in from the kitchen. "Morning."

"Did you talk to Uncle Nack?"

"Not yet, honey."

The sleeping bag smells like mothballs where it's tucked up under my chin. "Can I call him?"

"He got home late and might still be asleep."

I go back to gnawing on my cuticle.

She sits beside me on the arm of the couch, brushes my bangs from my eyes, and rests her hand on my shoulder. "I'm sure Poppi's fine. Uncle Nack would have called."

Her hand feels warm and solid. Just her being there makes me feel a little better.

"Let's have some breakfast," she says.

Twenty minutes later at the kitchen table, Dennis is on his third waffle and I still move little syrup-drenched squares from my first one around my plate.

"Don't you like your waffle?" Ursula asks.

"I'm not hungry."

She stares so hard at my plate, she might be counting the squares to see if they can still make a whole waffle. "Do you want oatmeal or eggs instead?"

I shrug, watching the second hand inch around the teakettle-shaped clock over the doorway. Ursula wipes her hands on the dishtowel and untangles the long cord on the wall phone. She holds the receiver out to me. "Here. I'll dial your house."

Uncle Nack says Poppi had a better night, but he has to stay in intensive care until his temperature comes all the way down. The rules say you have to be sixteen to visit intensive care, so I can't even think about going. I'm not sure I want to, anyway. His purple head, floppy arm, and lopsided smile make me want to cry.

Dennis swipes his fingers across the syrup on his plate. "Get dressed so we can go to Cam's when it stops raining."

The downpour sounds like bongos pounding the awning. "What makes you think the rain will stop?"

He licks his fingers one at a time. "It always has before."

A couple of hours later, walking over to Cam's, the wind stings my face; puddles and branches litter the pavement. When we get to Cam's house, a broken tree limb blocks part of the bottom step. On the porch, Mrs. McKee has on duck shoes and a yellow slicker over a long brown skirt. She picks twigs out of the mums in the window boxes. "Hi guys," she says. She calls through the screen door, "Cam, Katie and Dennis are here."

Cam comes out, letting the door slam behind her. I hop over the branch, but instead of following my lead, Dennis grips the broken limb in both of his hands. He puffs up his chest. "I'll just drag this off the steps."

"You'll hurt yourself. It's too heavy," Mrs. McKee says.

You can tell Dennis is trying to impress Cam, because he peeks at her before he plants his feet and tugs. It must be as heavy as Mrs. McKee says because his neck turns purple from the effort. When he gets it moved like eighteen inches, he gawks at Cam again. Serves him right—she's too busy touching up her lip gloss to notice him.

Walking to the beach, the three of us skip around puddles while Cam gloats about the cheerleading competition her squad won last night. There's no sense mentioning I didn't brag all over the place when I won the Halloween costume contest last week.

At the beach, the guy we call Twinkle Toes Tommy is up on his toes, doing his zany routine, gliding in slow-motion loops near the water's edge. While his feet dance in perfect circles, his arms jab the air, three quick thrusts in little sets, like he's boxing. Some days, he spins for hours. People around here say he was a heavyweight fighter who took one too many hits to the head. They call him crazy and homeless, but he smiles a lot and never looks dirty, so I don't know. I like watching him, especially when he turns to make the same moves in reverse as if he is unraveling what he just did.

This morning's storm churned up the waves, scattering dregs and seaweed all over the beach and wedging conch shells between the jetty rocks. Dennis reaches into the sludge and pulls out a perfect one, but before I can ask him if I can have it, he goes, "Here, Campbell."

He should give it to me. I'm the one all worried about Poppi. My hands are cold and my toes feel damp and numb. Cold mist sprays my face when a wave breaks against the jetty. I pull my hood tighter to march ahead of them back to the street.

After three more days, Poppi is finally out of intensive care. He might come home the day after tomorrow. Right now, it's just him and me in the patient lounge because Uncle Nack went to get coffee. His dingy gray vinyl chair with a tray reminds me of a high chair, except it has wheels. He must hate being trapped in by that tray, so I unhook it and push the chair close enough to the window for the sunshine trickling through the streaky glass to settle on his lap. Now that they took the tube out of his head and his hair has started to grow back in little spikes, he looks more like himself and less scary. I twist my new birthstone ring on my finger, trying to figure out what he is trying to say—a lot of his words get stuck in his throat. He ordered the ring for my birthday before he got sick. Uncle Nack wrapped it and brought it to the hospital today so Poppi could give it to me himself.

He mumbles something I don't understand.

"What, Poppi?"

"Ya, go . . . haaw . . . ." He points at me with his good right index finger.

"Me?"

He nods his head. "Gaa-go . . .?"

"Do you want me to go with Uncle Nack?"

He shakes his head no.

I pull so hard on the ring, it pinches my skin and makes my knuckle burn. "Do you want to know where Uncle Nack went?"

His lips are pursed; his arm flails the air. For a few seconds, his head drops to his chest. He points, taps my collarbone with his finger.

"Something about me?"

He nods.

"About school?"

"Nah, nah. Haa . . ."

"Is it something about Dennis or Ursula?" I'm so panicky and close to crying, I have to keep blinking and swallowing. I wish Uncle Nack would get back.

My face probably looks as puzzled as Poppi's. He squeezes his eyes closed so tight, it's like he's trying to look for something inside his head. A tear leaks from the corner of his eye. He breathes in really deep. He breathes out and pushes out the word.

"Hal-a–wee."

Halloween!

Every year, Poppi makes me a homemade Halloween costume for the West Cape May Firehouse party. Twice before, I came in first place—the year I was the Tin Man when I was seven, and last year as a tube of toothpaste. He made the tube from a canvas potato sack and cut eye and nose holes in a small trashcan and turned it upside down on my head as the cap. He makes such good costumes, Cam always wheedles him into making hers, too.

His idea this year was for me to be a bowl of raisin bran cereal and for Cam to be a spoon. Before he got sick, he painted a plastic tub to look like a china bowl and cut a hole in the center so it would slip over my head and sit on my hips. He bought me a purple sweat suit and stenciled "raisin" on the shirt. He had planned to fill the bowl with crumpled brown paper to look like flakes. It was his best idea ever.

"Halloween, Poppi?" I breathe out, so relieved, I almost jump up and down.

He nods so hard, the pillow behind his neck slides out. Half of his face tries to smile, but the other half sags down.

I pick up the pillow and squash it against my chest to stop the ache.

"Uncle Nack finished painting the rose on the bowl. We didn't have time to make Cam's spoon, so I used his wooden mixing spoon."

Disappointment flashes in his eyes until I pat his arm and tell him Cam's mom helped her dress up like a hippie, and the mixing spoon worked fine. I'm so thankful I figured out what he was asking me, it's almost harder not to cry now than it was before. A relieved quiet fills up between us.

"Wi-in?"

I wedge myself into the sunshine on his lap and drag his limp arm across my shoulder. "I always win with you, Poppi."

Yesterday, Uncle Nack and Ursula moved the dining room furniture out to the carriage house. It's turning into storage again, like living there with Mama never really happened. Two men dressed in blue coveralls set up the rented hospital bed in the dining room.

I don't know how he knew where to call Mama, but yesterday I overheard Uncle Nack ask her to move in with us to help take care of Poppi. She must have said it's too hard for her because his voice got huffy when he asked her if she ever thought about how hard it is on me and him. I would have liked to hear her answer.

Since Mama is no help, a few days a week, a nurse named Ronni with an "I" comes to check on Poppi. That's how she introduces herself, "My name is Ronni with an 'I'." She has shaggy brown hair that doesn't hide her big ears or bushy eyebrows. Everything she says comes out all singsong and nasal and high-pitched like a thirteen-year-old boy's voice that started to change and never finished. Poppi frowns at her the whole time she's here.

A few days ago while I was at school, Tony the Barber came to cut Poppi's hair. Now it doesn't look so spiky, but it still looks wrong, because *Ronni with an I* parts it in the middle and uses greasy gel to comb it straight down at the sides. The grease turns Poppi's soft waves into bumpy, comb-streaked ridges.

He growls at the hand mirror. "Nah, nah," he says when Ronni holds the mirror up to show him how he looks.

"I don't think he likes the greasy stuff," I say.

"It's styling gel."

"He doesn't like it," I say more firmly.

"His hair sticks up without it."

"And that's not how he combs his hair."

"Harrumph," Ronni says. She puts her big-boned hands on her hips in an exaggerated arc, the same showy way she does everything.

"I'll do it." I rub a washcloth on his hair to get the gunk out, before I comb it straight back from his face and forehead. His waves make soft little folds. I hold up the mirror.

"Good." He says it plain as day.

After that, I get up early every morning to help Poppi comb his own hair before Ronni gets here. It can still be hard to understand when he talks, but Poppi calls me his good little nurse. Yesterday and today, he splashed on Old Spice by himself too; all I did was help him open the bottle. The way he winks at me when he dabs it on his neck makes him look like his old self.

"I sti-ink. . . p-p-pretty," he says and winks.

When his hair is perfect, I clean Poppi's glasses with a tissue and put them on his face. He didn't used to wear glasses all the time, but since his stroke, it seems like he needs them. Every time I do things for him, Poppi says I'm the best nurse, much better than Ronni. After a few weeks, when Poppi can shuffle to the bathroom and the kitchen on his own with a walker, we say good riddance to Ronni.

I miss the old Poppi most at bedtime, when he can't climb the stairs to tuck me in. The nights like tonight when he's already in his hospital bed when I say goodnight, I put my lips near his ear and whisper our goodnight song. "I love you truly; truly I do."

He still can't sing all the words with me, but lately, he can hum.

Chapter 16

When I got home from school the last day before Christmas break, there were presents from Mama in a pile on the back porch. She must have dropped them off while Uncle Nack took Poppi to physical therapy. Instead of opening them right away, I made a deal with God to wait—God's part of the deal is to get Mama's act together enough for her to spend Christmas Day with us.

On Christmas Day, the morning and afternoon drag on without a sign of Mama. I know it's God's birthday and all, but it looks like he dropped the ball. After dinner, I finally give up and open the presents without her—a pair of jeans from J.C. Penney, a purple sweater, socks, and a Nancy Drew book—*The Clue of the Broken Locket*. When we lived in the trailer, if she had ever looked at my books on my bureau she would know I already have that one, but at least she got the Nancy Drew part right.

While I help Uncle Nack with the dinner dishes, Poppi sits at the kitchen table, filling his pipe with tobacco. There's no use reminding him again he's not supposed to smoke. Nothing about this seems like Christmas. Even the tree isn't real because with his bad back, Uncle Nack couldn't lug a big tree by himself.

My head hurts from wondering if Mama is sitting somewhere wondering what I'm doing the way I'm wondering about her.

"When we finish, let's take a drive through Cape May," Uncle Nack says.

"Do we have to?"

"Don't you want to see the lights?"

I rub the sponge so hard on an imaginary spot, it leaves little green specks on the tabletop. "I like to stay home on Christmas."

"We've been home all day."

I dig my fingernails into the sponge. "What if someone calls?"

Anger flashes in Uncle Nack's brown eyes. He swipes the sponge and tosses it into the sink. "She can call back," he snaps.

Ever since Mama didn't help out with Poppi, she's been on Uncle Nack's last nerve. He keeps reminding us she visited Poppi in the hospital exactly one time. I wasn't at the hospital that day, so this morning when I marked my calendar, it was 299 days since the last time I saw her.

Poppi pats my hand on the table. "I. Miss. Her. Too." He still talks slow and sometimes he stutters, but he can say whole sentences again.

In the car, Poppi sits with me in the back seat. Our legs are cozy under a stadium blanket. Uncle Nack drives up and down every street. Poppi points up at the lights—pink and lavender, green and white—they turn the Gingerbread houses into star-dusted castles against the blue-black sky. Even the ocean sparkles in the moon's yellow beam.

I can't help but hope, wherever she is, Mama gets to see this, too.

Chapter 17

*P*oppi got so much better over the winter, he can walk on his own with a cane—the kind with four prongs at the bottom. Every day, he walks a little further with it. Today, when I get home from school, he waits for me at the mailbox. I'm so excited about him being there, I almost knock the cane out of his hand, hugging him hello. He wobbles, and I grip the sleeve of his flannel shirt to steady him.

We take our time walking back to the house. About half-way, he sits on a tree stump to rest. Spring's first purple crocuses poke through frosty dirt. When Poppi is ready to stand up, I wrap both my hands over his on the cane. He's slower than he was the first half of the walk, taking smaller steps, leaning a minute on his truck when we get to it. On the porch, he sits heavily in a wicker rocker, a pile of saw-dust near his feet.

"What'd you whittle?"

He pulls a small bird and fish out from behind the pil-low. My fingers brush the callus on his thumb when I take them from him. There are a lot of rough edges, but they don't look half bad.

"I'll sand them for you."

"They're junk," he scowls, holding them up on his open palm.

I take them from him and hold them near my heart. "I love them," I say with such gusto that his wince softens into a smile.

A few weeks later, Poppi gives up the whittling and starts building birdhouses. At first, they were basic square blue-bird houses with slanted roofs and plain shellac, but now he gets fancy, putting on shutters and gingerbread trim. I help paint them, blending two or three colors like the inns in Cape May.

So far, we've made fourteen. Fourteen pieces in almost two months might not sound like much when he used to be able to make a kitchen full of cabinets in that time, but it's like he had to teach himself all over from scratch. Besides, he's teaching me, and that slows him down.

We plan to sell the birdhouses at Uncle Nack's farm stand when he opens up in June, splitting what we make fifty-fifty. We'll charge seven dollars for the bluebird houses and twelve for the painted ones. Poppi thought up a logo and made us a sign that says KATIE'S KRAFT KORNER with one big K. I can't wait.

The first week of June, it's so humid, it feels more like August. Sitting on the bleachers at the rec center watching Dennis pitch, the air feels like a soggy sponge. My hair must be one big frizz.

It's the ninth inning, and Dennis just struck out the first batter. The umpire stoops to dust off home plate. You can tell by the way Dennis tosses the ball in and out of his glove that waiting for the ump to finish irks him.

It's weird that Ursula just pulled her van into the parking lot. She should be at her restaurant, prepping dinner. Something about how she brakes sharply and the way the van slips backward when she shifts into park makes the hair on the back of my neck stand up. She leaps out, never glancing over at Dennis, shading her eyes with her hand, and hurrying toward the bleachers. Her face is pinched up. Her hand goes right to her heart when she spots me. I quickly turn away.

The batter hits a grounder. Dennis catches it and throws him out at first. I look back at Ursula coming at me, shaking her head. Her eyes are flat and watery. She chews her lip. I want to scream at her to stop looking at me like that and go away. I stand up and jump off the bleachers. Everything around me fades into the background—all I see is her standing in front of me. With all my might, I want to shove her away. I know she's going to say something I *do not* want to hear. In my brain, I'm yelling my head off to God. Do *not* let it be Poppi.

"Something happened," she says sadly.

"My mother?"

"No, honey."

My legs are so weak they cannot hold me up. I slump back down on the bleachers.

Then her arms wrap around me, rocking back and forth. "I don't know how to tell you. Poppi had another stroke. An ambulance took him and Uncle Nack to the hospital. Uncle Nack was still there when he called me."

I put my hands over my ears to block her out. She just holds me tighter.

Chapter 18

Somewhere outside our house, another car door thuds closed. The parade of neighbors with casserole dishes and cakes started right after we got home from the hospital last night and has not stopped. From where I crouch in the corner of the divan, Poppi's friends crowd the room like too many shadows until Uncle Nack turns on the glass-shaded lamps.

Why didn't I come right home from school yesterday instead of going to Dennis's stupid game? Poppi would've met me at the mailbox. I could have called 911 if I had come right home, or maybe it wouldn't even have happened if I was there. Instead, the last time I saw him, I was rushing out the door, late for school. On the way past his chair, I pecked him on the head. My lips barely touched his hair.

"Air ball," he said.

I should have gone back and hugged him, given him a real kiss. But I was afraid of missing the bus, so I dashed out the door.

Ursula stoops down in front of me and hands me another tissue. Behind her, Dennis paces back and forth.

"How about if I go in the kitchen and get you something to eat," Ursula says.

"I'm not hungry."

"You need to eat something, honey."

"I just want my Poppi."

She places her glass on the end table next to Poppi's empty pipe and holds my face in her hands. Her fingers feel cool and smell like Ivory soap. "I know, sweetheart."

Rain pounds on the windows. Uncle Nack rushes around closing them as if that can keep out this storm.

Last night's rain washed away the humidity. Today is so chilly for June, my arms are covered with goose bumps. Uncle Nack and I sit at the kitchen table while the man from the funeral home shows us pictures of caskets.

"Most folks are partial to the metallic bronze one called Kensington, our best seller," he says.

I reach across the table and flip the page to the ones made of wood, point to one that looks like cherry.

"Ah, the Brigadoon—top of our wood line." His manicured nails touch my wrist when he turns the page back to the bronze one and slides the book right in front of Uncle Nack. "The Kensington is our most popular."

"Poppi worked with wood," I say defensively. I do not like this guy.

"Yes, of course." He forces one of those fake smiles grown-ups make at kids right before they pat you on the head. His eyes shift back to Uncle Nack. "I'm sure you'll find the Kensington meets your needs without adding unnecessary expense."

Uncle Nack shuts the book and pushes it across the table. "We'll take the cherry one," he says.

After the undertaker leaves, the house is so quiet. You can hear the hall clock ticking all the way upstairs. Poppi's only suit is laid out on his bed. I sit next to it and run my fingers along the sleeve, pick up the jacket, and bury my face in the lining. There's not a hint of Poppi in there, no Old Spice or wood chips. The smell of dry cleaning and hot iron fills me with the worst pain, and all I want is Poppi humming his song and hugging me until it goes away.

When I look up, Uncle Nack stands in the doorway. The skin under his eyes looks loose and paper-thin. If he was Poppi, he would come in and sit with me, rub my arms or my back, but Uncle Nack stays put, wringing his hands. It's miserable sitting alone on this bed, but I'm grateful he doesn't come in here trying to be Poppi.

"What are you doing in there, honey?"

It's impossible to answer, so I just shake my head. After a minute, he gently lifts the jacket from my hands, smoothing it back down on the bed.

"Did you tell my mother yet?"

"She's not answering the phone. I drove over and left a note, but the neighbor lady says she hasn't seen her."

"Am I going back to live with her now?"

He stares up at the ceiling, massaging his shoulders and neck. The lines near his eyes deepen. "Poppi fixed it so you can stay here. He made me your guardian."

"Isn't Mama my guardian?"

"He had her sign a paper."

All of a sudden, the room feels too small—even sitting down, it feels like I might bump into something. He reaches for the box on the nightstand, plucks a tissue, and hands it to me. After I blow my nose, I fold my hands together and squeeze them between my knees. "What kind of paper?"

His whole body goes up and down when he sighs. "Look. Poppi left a good pension from the Carpenter union, and I can cook for Ursula if we need extra. We'll be okay, you and me, Number Two."

It comes out sounding like a question, like maybe he doesn't believe it any more than me.

I don't want to be in the house when the undertaker comes back for the suit. I ride my bike to the beach and hunker down on the jetty. It's cloudy and windy and the beach is deserted. The jetty is cold against my legs, but I just sit here shivering because there is nowhere else I feel like I belong. Tears drip off my face.

A bunch of seagulls pick at something near the water's edge. One of them grabs whatever it is in its beak and carries it over the water. I close my eyes, wishing one of those seagulls could carry me out to sea and take me to wherever Poppi is now.

"I've been looking all over for you."

I open my eyes and rub my sleeve across my face. Before Dennis can sit down, I shoot up and head for my bike. "I'm going to the Villas to look for my mother."

"Do you know where she is?"

"No."

"So where will you go?"

I straddle my bike, and flip up the kickstand. "Are you coming or not?"

By the time we bike the six or seven miles to Wildwood Villas, my thighs burn and it feels like something keeps slamming inside my chest, but I don't care. We ride up and down street after street looking for her VW or Ray's truck. In the parking lot beside the fishing club, I hop off my bike and flip down the kickstand.

"You can't go in there," Dennis says, all bossy.

I ignore him and walk to the door.

"The sign says members only."

"I don't care."

"Their cars aren't even here."

"The bartender might know where to find her." I throw the door open. Inside is dark and smells like greasy fish and full ashtrays and stale beer. An old guy in a flannel shirt with the sleeves cut off smokes at the far end of the bar. The bartender has his back to us, washing glasses. He looks up in the mirror behind the bar when Dennis clears his throat. "What are you kids doing in here?"

"My grandfather said you know my mother."

He turns around and picks up a rag on the bar to wipe his hands.

"Her name is June," Dennis says.

The bartender checks me out. "You Lou the carpenter's grandkid?"

I nod. He shifts the toothpick he's chewing to the other side of his mouth. "Like I told your uncle, best I can do is tell her when she comes in."

Dennis spins around and heads for the door. There's no other choice but to follow him.

"Hey, sis," the bartender says.

I pause. "Yeah?"

"Sorry about your grandpop. He was a good man."

Later that night, I wake to the sound of a tree limb scraping the house. I have had the same dream three nights in a row. In it, Mama and me are locked in the cellar, but it's like we don't care. Like we both know if we go up the steps and try the door, there's something terrible on the other side, and we're better off just staying down there with Uncle Nack's wine. Every time we start up the steps, I make myself wake up before we get to the top.

The night of Poppi's wake, the limousine pulls up at the funeral home under an awning in the center of the circular driveway. Uncle Nack gets out first and reaches in for my hand. I wear a new gray jumper with a black sweater. Earlier today, it was Ursula who rushed me to Dellas when she realized I didn't have anything dark to wear. There wasn't much to pick from, so we settled on the jumper. Ursula says at my age the gray is okay, that because I'm just a kid, I don't have to wear black.

In the vestibule, the undertaker stands behind a podium in his stiff black suit, white shirt, and dark tie. He hands me a holy card with Poppi's name on the back and a picture of Saint Francis feeding birds, a rabbit, and a deer on the front.

It's early, and we are the only ones here. I try not to look at the casket in the front of the room. My head feels woozy, my stomach hollow. The pink and green swishes on the rug get blurry.

It's an effort to take even baby steps, but I keep going, past the empty chairs lined up in rows. Uncle Nack holds both of my arms while we walk up to the kneeler. My eyes are glued to a candle flame reflected in the casket's dark wood.

Near Poppi's hand, I touch the white satin. My fingers move over it until they brush his. His skin doesn't feel real. When I finally look at his face, his hair is all wrong; parted at the side and combed down over his ears, the way Ronni did it, the way he *hated* it. My mirror and change purse spill out of my shoulder bag when I grope in it to find a comb.

"What do you need?" Uncle Nack asks gently.

"I have to fix his hair," I say frantically.

He pats my wrists. "It's all right."

But it's not.

I dig deeper into my bag for the comb, and more stuff spills out. My breath wheezes in my ears. My head feels like it's getting pulled into a funnel.

All I know is that I *have* to fix his hair.

Uncle Nack picks up my lip gloss and tissues, tossing them back into my bag.

"Maybe we should sit down."

"He hates his hair that way." I furiously blink back tears.

Uncle Nack slips his comb out of his back pocket, combing it through Poppi's hair. Breathing gets easier when he gets it right.

The undertaker stands behind us. "Can I be of assistance?"

"All taken care of," Uncle Nack says wearily. He holds my elbow. We both kneel in front of the casket. Every time Uncle Nack shifts his weight beside me, the kneeler puffs under my knees. He makes the sign of the cross repeating, "Ah, Lou" under his breath.

Yellow roses shaped like a rosary drape across the top of the casket. The ribbon on them says Loving Grandfather instead of Poppi. A basket of red roses and baby's breath near his feet says Beloved Brother, and the tangerine ones near his head say Beloved Father. I know they are really from Uncle Nack because I heard him order them. There are lots of others: carnations, gladiolus, daisies, mums; NEPHEW, BROTHER-IN-LAW, COUSIN, FRIEND. The flowers smell so sweet, you can taste them.

When we finish praying, Uncle Nack sits in a high-backed chair, and I sit on a loveseat. He puts his head way back and closes his eyes, but mine are wide open, searching as people start to come in. Ursula and Dennis get here first. Cam and her parents are in the line that snakes beside the rows of chairs up to the casket. After they pray, Mr. and Mrs. McKee hug me and murmur how sorry they are. Mrs. McKee smoothes my hair off the side of my face and Cam grips my hand tight. We stand quietly for what feels like a long time until the winding line of people starts to back up. "We should find seats," Mrs. McKee says.

"I'm staying with Katie," Cam says, squeezing my hand so I know she won't let go.

"Okay. We'll be in the back," her mother says.

Just as Cam and I sit down on the loveseat, Mama totters right by the man with the holy cards. He taps her on the back to hand her one, and she crumples it into her pocket without looking at it. Her legs wobble in her high heels. She has to hold onto the back of the chairs as she makes her way up front, brushing right past the other people waiting. Instead of kneeling to pray, she stands in front of the casket, staring down at her folded hands. She comes over to the loveseat and leans down like she might kiss me on the lips. I quickly turn my head, getting a whiff of her breath as her cheek brushes mine. "Take off your sunglasses," I jeer, not even trying to hide how much I want to reach up and rip them off her face.

She looks surprised and touches her face, thrusting the glasses in her pocket with the holy card.

"Couldn't you not drink for one night?" I hiss through gritted teeth, hoping Cam can't hear.

Mama mumbles something I don't understand.

"Just forget it." I ball my fists in my lap.

She gawks at me with watery eyes. "I hope you never have as much to forget as me."

Later, leaving the funeral parlor, Mama surprises me and gets into the limousine to come back to the house with us. She has not left the kitchen, swigging down her second drink as if she has more reason to hurt than me.

Dennis and Cam follow me around from the kitchen to the living room. Everywhere we go, there are people eating and talking and drinking beer. Some of them laugh. I want to scream at them all to shut up and be respectful or just go home.

The cellar light flickers when I turn it on. The first few stairs creak on our way down. Dennis and Cam sit on the bottom step. After pacing back and forth near the barrels, I pick at the waxy cork with my thumbnail.

"What are you doing?" Dennis asks nervously.

I ignore him and work my nail under the cork, slip the straw into the hole, and fill up a glass right to the tippy top.

Dennis stands with his hands on his hips all bossy. "We should go back upstairs."

"You go." I gulp down half the glass.

"Let me taste." Cam takes a little sip and makes a big face like she wants to spit it out.

I refill the glass and hold it to my lips with both hands. Dennis looks like he might try to pry the glass from my hands, so I chug it before he has a chance. It burns, but even before it hits my belly, it starts dulling the pain in my head.

"This is so wrong." Dennis pries the empty glass from my hand.

"Oh, shut up."

Like he knows anything about what's right or wrong. What do any of them know? Like all those people at the funeral home with their sweaty palms and limp-arm hugs saying, "It hurts right now, but it'll get better."

Poppi is gone forever, just like my father. If I live to be a hundred, it will always be true. Beneath the hush and sniffling, I heard them say, "Poor thing" and "time heals," but I know better.

I know loss adds up, it stays and swells, and time has nothing to do with it.

Part 11

Chapter 19

C am and I are under the railroad trestle near the canal celebrating my seventeenth birthday—drinking Coke with rum she snuck out of her parents' liquor cabinet. She's in one of her moods because last night, her new boyfriend broke their date for the Halloween dance. He called at dinnertime and said he had a temperature of 102 degrees. It might be true, but you can bet he'll pay. He's the quarterback, and his football teammates call him Cannon Arm. Cam has a hissy fit when I call him that, so to her face, I call him Rick. No matter what you call him, I feel sorry for the guy. He may be a hunk and captain of the football team, but nobody gets away with canceling a date with Campbell McKee.

Hazy light from the yellow moon leaks through the bare tree limbs overhead. All you can smell is train oil and wet dirt. I dig my hands into the carpet of crunchy leaves and toss fistfuls into the air. They look like shadows floating down over Cam's legs.

"I can't believe Dennis didn't come home for my birthday weekend," I sulk.

"Guys suck." She holds out a gift bag. "Forget the snake and open your present."

I peek into the bag and pull out layers of tissue paper. Nestled inside is a set of hair combs—perfect for holding back my long hair. It's been almost a year since my last haircut. I decided to let it grow after Dennis mentioned—like a hundred times—that he likes girls with long hair. In the moonlight, the combs look like real silver. The stones are smooth and look pearly.

"They're opals," Cam says.

"My birthstone."

"Did I surprise you?" she asks eagerly.

"For once." I roll my eyes.

She whacks at the air, pretending to slap me, throwing back her head and laughing that cottony laugh that makes you feel wrapped up in flannel.

I like presents to be a surprise, but Cam usually can't keep a secret. Like when we were fourteen and I said how much I worshipped Karen Carpenter. A week later, Cam blurted out that she bought me a Karen Carpenter tape for my birthday. Even though she ruined the surprise, I loved that tape. The day Karen Carpenter died, Cam and I stayed up all night in her bedroom listening to it, lighting candles and crying, obsessed by Karen's voice on Cam's stereo. I never told Cam that Karen Carpenter's sunken cheeks and big dark eyes reminded me of my mother.

Uncle Nack and I have not seen Mama for over three years. Uncle Nack says if she comes around now, he won't give her the time of day. I'm not sure I would either, but I'd like the chance to find out.

Cam takes the combs from me. "I'll put them in for you." She lifts my chin and laces them into my hair. "If that lizard Johnnie Verne could see you now, he would beg you to take him back."

Johnnie is history and we both know it. We met last June at the indoor roller rink in Wildwood—I was skating backward, doing the moonwalk with Cam when I bumped into him and knocked him down. Turns out, he was visiting his grandmother for the summer, working on the boardwalk at a custard stand. We went steady in July and August. He stopped calling the week after he went home to New York in September. Mostly, I went out with him to make Dennis jealous. That worked about as good as growing my long hair.

I hug Campbell. "Thanks for surprising me."

The next afternoon, I slowly close my trigonometry book, pretending I'm not beyond ecstatic when Dennis unexpectedly pulls his Mustang into the driveway. After he got a baseball scholarship to college, Ursula used the saved-up tuition money to buy him the Mustang as a graduation present. His car radio is so loud, you feel the vibrations from Bruce Springsteen booming "Rosalita" up here on the porch. Getting out of the car, Dennis glances at the smoke curling up to the sky from behind the shed. Uncle Nack is burning leaves even though he knows he will get fined if they catch him doing it again. The smoke smells earthy and sweet. Dennis strides up to the porch and hands me a box wrapped in comic strips. "Happy birthday."

It looks like he's doing his part for my birthday after all—I almost feel bad for trashing him last night. Almost.

His kinky hair is combed straight back in a way that looks sort of James Dean with a cowlick. Sandy-colored stubble covers his chin except for the small scar from a slide into home plate during last year's state championships. I have a recurring daydream about running my fingertips over his dimple and that scar.

He stands in front of me. His body blocks the sunlight trickling through the clouds. He has on his lucky red Converse hightops, the only style sneakers he wears since he pitched a no-hitter and a shutout in back-to-back games the week after he bought his first pair last year.

He touches the box on my lap. "Open it."

He used newspaper instead of tissue paper inside the box, too, but it's not the funnies, it's the Life section. Right on the front page is a headline about alcoholism. It seems like you can't pick up the newspaper or a magazine these days without seeing one of those stories. They say it's hereditary, but I don't buy it and have already decided it will not happen to me. I scrunch up the newspaper and toss it aside. Tucked underneath is a Glassboro State College sweatshirt. I want to put it right on and pretend I'm his girlfriend wearing his jersey.

"I got large. I know you like things big."

I hug it to my chest. "It's perfect."

He rocks in the glider opposite me. "Did you go to the Halloween dance?"

I know what he really wants to know is whether Cam went with another guy. A few weeks ago, she told him she might go to the dance with him even though she never actually keeps a date with him. Like always, she reneged when Cannon asked her out. Part of me wants to be mean and tell Dennis about Cannon, but he looks so defenseless sitting there chewing his lip, his Adams apple bobbing every time he swallows. Everything is so right about him—I cannot bring myself to hurt his feelings. "The DJ sucked, so we hung in the yard most of the time." The yard is what we call the clearing between the tree line and the dumpsters in the back of school where seniors smoke and drink beer. "You didn't miss much. Cam didn't even go."

He cracks his knuckles. "I figured she went with somebody else."

I could be heartless and tell him the whole story, but instead I blurt out, "Maybe one of these dances, you should ask me." The words aren't out of my mouth before I want to take them back. I snort, hoping he'll think it's a joke.

His head jerks up like he knows it's no joke. "You mean like a date?"

"Whatever." I make a production out of folding the sweatshirt back into the box, shaking it out, and painstakingly folding it again. "I guess," I say, sneaking a sideways glance at him.

He rubs his hand over his chin hard enough that he might rub a bald spot in his stubble, as if maybe he's actually considering the possibility. He doesn't look at me when he says, "You know I can't get serious. I have to finish college, and I want to play ball."

This is not the first time he has said that about *not* getting serious. It must make sense to him, but I have no idea what it means.

"Then why do you keep asking Cam out?"

He shifts from foot to foot, looking up at the treetops. "It would be different with you."

I want to shake the fool. I mean, isn't it being different with me exactly the frigging point?

The next Saturday is the second time I candy-stripe at the White Briar Nursing Home to earn the fifty volunteer hours seniors need to rack up before graduation. I like the way I look in my red-and-white pinafore uniform, so instead of going home to change at the end of my shift, I let the bus pass my stop and go right up to the beach where the local guys play touch football every weekend.

A couple of nor'easters in late October redeposited the sand. It covers most of the jetty and makes the beach look much wider. Today, the sun is bright and the lighthouse in the distance looks like a painting against the gray-blue sky. Except for Cannon, Joe and John Raymond, and their nerdy friend Charlie Tee, I don't know most of the guys here today. The rest of the guys playing must work with John at the fish cannery. The Ocean Drive Cannery pays good money for a high school graduate, and Joey and Charlie plan to work there after graduation in June, too. Of all the guys we hang with, Dennis is the only one who goes to college.

As soon as I walk up, Charlie Tee takes off his glasses—which are as thick as Coke bottles—and asks me to hold them so they don't break while he plays. I take them from him and don't bother asking how he'll see the ball without them because Charlie has had a crush on me since our first slow dance when we were twelve. I have to be careful he doesn't read something into a simple question like *how will you see?* I sit down beside Cam on her beach blanket. We talk more than watch, but I can't help noticing when a dark-haired guy I don't recognize shows up. The guys make a big fuss, slapping him on the back. Cam elbows me in the ribs so hard, I almost tumble sideways into the sand.

"That's Jake Rossi."

"The guy who made your fake ID?"

He wears a forest green V-neck sweater that shows a triangle of black curly hair below a splotchy, purple birthmark on his neck. If I had a birthmark like that I would wear a turtleneck, but with that V-neck it's like he's proud of it and trying to flaunt it.

The sleeves of Jake's sweater are pushed up to his elbows, showing his muscular arms. He has this way of snatching the ball from the air and darting around on the sand that makes me think he's probably a good dancer.

After the game, we all cluster around the guys' cars. Cam and I sit on the edge of the promenade with our legs dangling near the bumper of Jake's jacked-up Chevy Impala. He passes out beers from a cooler in his trunk. You can tell he really takes care of his car because every few minutes he leans down and buffs a mark off the cherry red fender or one of the spoke-studded hubcaps with his sleeve.

"Introduce me to your cute friend, Reds," he says to Cam.

"Like you're too shy to introduce yourself."

"Don't break my balls."

"I'm Katie," I say boldly.

Jake holds out a beer but pulls it back when I reach for it.

"How old are you?"

"Old enough."

"You just missed her seventeenth birthday," Cam says.

"If I knew, I would have sent you a dozen roses." He hands me the beer. His thick-fingered hand reminds me of Poppi's. "What's with the costume?" he asks, narrowing his eyes in a lustful way that gives me goose bumps and makes me wish I went home and changed.

"It's a volunteer thing for school."

He keeps eyeing me, so I decide to chug half my beer.

"Not bad for a girl." He smiles a sexy smile and actually looks impressed.

Later, after Cannon drops Cam and I at her house to do our homework, all I can talk about is how romantic Jake is.

"Romantic?"

"You know, what he said about sending me roses for my birthday."

She looks at me like my face is covered with hives. "Get a grip. Saying he'll send flowers is just BS. Romantic is when he coughs up the bucks and sends them."

Last Saturday, I ended up on Uncle Nack's shit list for not going right home from candy striping, so today I stopped home and changed before coming to the beach. Lately, you never know what might tick Uncle Nack off. I try to remember he's doing the best he can, but even though the house has always seemed too big for just the two of us without Poppi, he's on my back so much, it's like every time I turn around, we bump into each other.

I brought my school book, *A Separate Peace* with me to the beach because I still have to read the last chapter and write a book report before Monday. It's hard to read between half-watching the game, listening to Cam, and surreptitiously glancing around for Jake—who is the real reason I went home to change clothes.

When Jake finally shows up, he salutes Cam and me without bothering to stop and talk, waves the guys off when they ask him to play, and goes off by himself to sit on the jetty. I angle my head to watch him out of the corner of my eye. It's hard to tell for sure from here, but it looks like he's writing in a book.

Maybe he's writing a poem about the water or light-house. It would be so dreamy if he turns out to be a poet. I close *A Separate Peace* and tuck my fists under my chin with my elbows on my knees, trying to observe him without gawking.

When the guys finish playing football, Cannon is in a big rush to get Cam home to watch the Army-Navy game. Jake strides up to his car, opens his car door, and tosses his book under the front seat. Just as I'm giving up on Jake paying any attention to me, he turns around. "Need a ride?"

"I guess," I say, trying to sound nonchalant.

"Call me later." Cam jiggles my arm, digging her finger-nails into my wrist.

Jake drives along Beach Avenue. There isn't much traffic in the off-season. All the overhead stoplights blink yellow.

"What do you do at the cannery?" I ask.

"General maintenance." He parks in front of the arcade, pulls a cigarette from the chest pocket of his leather jacket, and offers it to me.

"I don't smoke."

He lights it for himself.

"What were you doing on the jetty?"

"Drawing."

"Can I see?"

The way his lip curls makes me think he'll say no, so I'm surprised when he reaches under his seat, pulls out the book, and flips it open. The picture is like a cartoon, mostly head with lots of wild, curly hair and a slender face with expressive eyes and a Roman nose sitting atop a tiny, well-built body. Damn if it's not me!

Looking at it feels a little like being undressed. "You drew me?"

He shrugs like it's no big deal, but it feels pretty big to me.

"Who taught you to draw?"

"I taught myself."

"Why do you work at the cannery if you can draw?"

"I'm saving up to go to art school."

He stares out the side window. Tunnels of sunlight pour through puffy clouds onto the ocean. Since he isn't watching, I go back to studying the little fake me. After a few minutes, I tap his arm to hand him the book. He takes it and tears out the page. "Keep it," he says coolly.

"Wow. Thanks." I tuck it inside the back cover of *A Separate Peace*.

His expression is part cocky and the rest uneasy. "Want a soda?" he mumbles.

The only open snack counter is the one next to the fudge store. A few seagulls dig into the smelly trash barrel out front. While Jake goes to the counter, I stand near a few tourists, watching a gangly kid with pimples stir fudge in a copper kettle in the candy store's open front window. I thought about applying for a job at the fudge store last summer until I saw the goofy apron they make you wear and heard this routine the fudge guy recites now.

"Do you know why I'm pouring this sugar into the kettle?" Fudge guy asks.

"To make it sweeter," a little girl in the crowd pipes up.

Jake walks up beside me and hands me a can of cola. My favorite is birch beer, but he didn't ask. I say thanks and take a sip.

"And why am I putting in all this chocolate?" The fudge guy stirs with both hands on the wooden paddle, pushing his glasses up on his nose with his forearm.

"To make it taste gooder," the same little girl says. A few people around us chuckle.

The fudge guy's glasses slip down again. He pushes them up with the back of his wrist. "And why is it my job to stand over this kettle all day stirring and stirring the fudge?"

"Because you never finished high-school?" Jake says it so glibly, he cracks up the entire crowd.

Fudge guy's face turns blotchy red. His eyes cloud up and twitch with the kind of worthlessness you feel waiting for your turn in the government cheese line. I think Jake's wisecrack is funny too, but the look on fudge guy's face feels too familiar, and I just can't laugh at him.

Chapter 20

C am's bed is littered with college catalogues—University of Miami, Florida Southern, Central Florida. I pick up a few and fan them out in my hands, "Aren't you applying anywhere close?"

"I want to go somewhere warm."

"Florida's so far away."

She gives me the duh eye roll. "That's sort of the point."

All of the nursing brochures I requested from the League of Nursing are for South Jersey schools because I want to go to school near Dennis. Besides, Uncle Nack says we can handle the tuition for an Associate degree program even if I don't get a scholarship.

"I think I'll be a librarian," Cam says flipping through one of the catalogues.

"No way." In the last hours, she has said she wants to be a journalist, make-up artist, public relations consultant, movie producer, and a newscaster.

"But I'd look so kick-ass in a bun and those half glasses." She tries to keep a straight face, but she cracks up. After a minute, she says, "I can't believe you want to be a nurse."

"Why not?"

"Bed pans, bathing old people. *Gr-ross.* It's like penance, like you're still trying to make up for not being there when your grandfather died."

I throw my pen at her and snort out loud so she knows how crazy that sounds. She swats the pen, and it rolls under the bed.

Sometimes I hate what she thinks she knows about me.

The next Saturday afternoon, after the touch football game, Jake takes me for a ride along Sunset Blvd to Cape May Point. In the distance, the murky clouds at the rim of the sky look like a mountain range.

Jake parks across from the beach beside a closed-up pink cottage. Across the street, seagulls fly low over the choppy ocean and dried-up beach grass on the dunes. Jake slides his arm over the back of my seat, tangles his hands in my hair, and tilts my face to kiss me. His tongue tastes smoky, probing between my teeth. Johnnie, my boyfriend from last summer, thought he knew how to French kiss, but it was nothing like this. Jake's tongue doesn't dart in and out. He kisses so good, it makes me dizzy, but I don't know if I'm doing it right when I kiss him back. He moves his hand out of my hair to turn off the ignition. In the distance, a foghorn blasts. The ferry must be just coming in or leaving. Before I realize what Jake is up to, he slides his hand under my sweater, tugging the edge of my bra. His eyes look as fiery as his fingertips feel on my ribs.

"Um, no," I say, embarrassed.

He covers my lips with his, his fingers inching up. "Relax, babe."

I clutch his wrist, but his fingers keep going.

"Jake." I push his hand away even though part of me wants to keep going. Uncle Nack will ground me for life if he finds out I went parking. The way Jake looks at me when he leans his head back goes right through me. His hand roams again, and again I push him away. Without a word, he starts the car and is stone quiet the entire ride back. Instead of pulling into our driveway, he stops at the curb, shifting into neutral like he's waiting for me to get out, so I do.

I duck my head through the window, but he doesn't lean toward me. There's no way to kiss him goodbye. "See you next week." I try to sound upbeat, but it comes out more like a plea.

He shrugs and guns the motor. The tires squeal. I watch the car zoom up the street, wishing he would stop, back up, say how sorry he is, and ask me for my phone number, but he just keeps going. On the porch, I smooth my hair and tug down my sweater before opening the door.

"Why are you late?" Uncle Nack doesn't look up when he says it, just keeps forking eggplant parm into his mouth, gripping the jar of grated cheese as if someone might steal it if he lets go. He shakes on more cheese between every bite.

For a split second, I can't think up a lie. "I had to stop at the library to drop off a book."

"Who were you with?"

"No one."

He points his fork at me. "How many times do I have to tell you? I want to know where you're going and who you're with."

"I just went to the library."

"Well I hope you got a good book. You're in for the rest of the weekend."

"Jeez." I plop down in the chair across from him and scoop some salad onto my plate.

I want to ask him why he has to make it into such a big deal, but the way he slams the cheese shaker on the table warns me to button it. Lately, he's so bossy. Like, what is the big deal if dinner isn't right at six? And why is it a crime if you like burned toast, or mushy ice cream, or showers so hot, you fog up the mirror? You would have thought I burned the house down when he had to move the smoke alarm away from the bathroom because my steamy hot shower kept setting it off.

He carries his plate to the sink, scrapes it, and turns to go outside with his cigar. "Do the dishes when you finish eating." Halfway out of the door, he turns back. "And don't pick the radishes out. Eat what you put on your plate."

The Saturday of Thanksgiving weekend is the first Saturday in weeks that Dennis comes home from college. Waiting on the promenade for enough of the cannery guys to show up to have a touch football game, he pretends to smile when I introduce him to Jake, but you don't have to look close to see his eyes narrow judgmentally. To spite him, I squeeze in beside Jake to shower him with attention, but he acts like he barely knows me, joking with some girls I haven't seen here before.

Rather than be ignored, I get up and trudge along the sand out onto the jetty to watch two fishermen in rubber coats and hip boots cast their rods. Icy salt beads spray my face. A huge wave crashes against the black rocks. I jump back and my foot skids, arms flapping in the air to catch my balance. A hand steadies me from behind.

My heart feels like a loose propeller thumping in my chest, hoping I'll turn around and see Jake, but no, it's only Dennis. "Why are you here?"

He shoves his hands elbow-deep into the pocket of his hooded sweatshirt. "There aren't enough guys, so the girls are filling in. I thought you might want to play."

I jump off of the jetty and stomp across the sand. It has already been decided that those other girls are on Cannon and Jake's team, and I'm with Cam, Dennis, and Joe and John Raymond.

After a few plays, Dennis passes the ball to me. I tuck it under my sweatshirt, zigzagging across the sand until Jake catches me near the water's edge. Instead of touching me with his two hands the way you are supposed to, he grabs me around the waist and pulls my whole body into his. In the December chill, his warm, sturdy body is impossible to ignore. He sneaks his hand up under my shirt to take the ball. His fingers cup my breast. When the nuns say never to let a guy touch you like that, they act like it only feels good to him. Wrong. I shiver and lean into Jake.

He presses his lips to my ear. "First down."

After that, it's impossible to concentrate on who has the ball. Thank God some of the regular cannery guys show up. I quit playing to walk to the lighthouse to calm down my insides. I'm only a little beyond the jetty when I hear the flap-suck of sneakers in the wet sand behind me.

"Wait up," Jake says.

My heart pounds non-stop. I open my mouth to say something. Like an idiot, nothing comes out. We walk quietly side by side.

Jake kicks a long hunk of nautical rope attached to a torn piece of netting. "Fishing sucks," he says.

A little further up, there are two broken wire crab cages a few feet apart. "I like crabbing," I say.

"Bor-ring." He walks up to the dune and flips a piece of driftwood over with his foot.

I study it for a moment. "A raccoon," I say playfully.

He gives me a look that's part encouraging, but mostly mocking. "Come again?"

"Dennis and I do that, say what the driftwood looks like."

"And this piece looks like a raccoon?"

I kneel down and point. "These are the paws and these dark spots are the eyes."

"A raccoon?" He touches his hand to my forehead as if I'm feverish. "You sure you want to stick with that story?"

I go to whack him on the arm, but he catches my hand and holds it. We walk holding hands like that around a small tidal pool littered with open clamshells.

"Did I tell you I applied for art school?" he asks.

"Where?"

"You never heard of it—a little college near Roanoke with a really good program in animation."

"You're going to Virginia?"

"First I have to get in and come up with the dough."

"When did you graduate high school?"

"Three years ago."

"Can you still get student loans?"

Jake shrugs and picks up a clamshell so huge, it covers his entire hand. He stoops and scoops up some foam from the shoreline. In the setting sun, the bubbles look like iridescent marbles: pale blue, aqua, pink, and gold.

"I love how beach foam shimmers," I say.

"I never noticed."

"Didn't you grow up around here?"

"Wildwood."

Wildwood is about five miles up the coast from here. It's a Doo Wop beach town with neon sighs, fake palm trees, and a touristy boardwalk.

"You grew up in Wildwood and you hate fishing and crabbing and never saw beach foam?"

"I saw it, just never gave it a physical."

He blows on the foam, and droplets spray my face. The stink reminds me of our old clamshell path in front of the trailer—and that makes me think of Mama.

If you can believe next-door Lucy, Mama stayed in bed for four months after Poppi died. When she finally got up, she sold the trailer and now we never know where she lives or what she did with the trailer money. Uncle Nack says she pissed it away or drank it. He's probably right, but you can't talk to him about it. He says Poppi bought the trailer for the two of us, and that Mama should have given me my half of the money for college.

Christmas is just a few weeks away. Jake has acted more like my actual boyfriend since that Saturday we walked on the beach, so Cam and I have been in and out of every store on Cape May's Washington Street mall, looking for a present for him. She bought Cannon a sterling silver ID bracelet engraved "Rick" to replace the one he wears that says "Cannon," but it's too soon for me to buy jewelry for Jake.

"Get him a sweater," Cam says assertively.

"Clothes seem like something your aunt gives you." The only thing I know for sure he might like is drawing stuff, and I don't know where to get that in Cape May.

"How about this key chain?" Cam asks.

"Too cheap."

"Gloves or a wallet?"

"Too stuffy."

"A book?"

"Too intellectual."

"You're making me frigging nuts. Pick *something*. How about car stuff?"

"What, like floor mats? That's so impersonal."

She gives me a look that makes it clear she can't take this much longer. I pick up a leather belt with steer horns on the brass buckle.

"Perfect—it says interested without being mushy." She may be humoring me, but I decide to put an end to her misery and buy it for him.

Back outside, we get a few stores away when she reaches into her pocket and pulls out an eye shadow compact, the bigger-than-normal size with at least a half-dozen colors.

"Look what I picked up at the general store." I know from the triumphant glint in her eye she literally means *picked up*.

We were ten the first time I caught her shoplifting a Baby Ruth candy bar. I was so mortified, I went to confession and didn't talk to her for a week.

"I don't believe you. It's not like you can't just buy what you want."

"This way's more fun."

"What if you get caught?"

She rolls her eyes and plucks another compact out of her other pocket. "Got you one, too."

"I don't want it." I say in my high and mighty voice.

"Yes you do," she scoffs and tucks it into my coat pocket.

The truth is I do want it. I just wish I had the guts like her to take things for myself.

Chapter 21

*I*t was Uncle Nack's idea to start my own Christmas Eve tradition and invite my friends over to decorate the tree tonight. At first, it seemed lame, just a way for him to know where I am, but trimming the tree and going to midnight mass with Jake grew on me. It's as close as we've been yet to having a *real* date.

While the Raymond brothers and Dennis wrestle the tree into the stand, Cannon and Cam help me cart the decorations down from the attic. Uncle Nack waited around to meet Jake until almost eight-thirty, but he'll be late picking up Ursula for their date if he waits any longer. On the outside, I pretend I don't care that Jake is more than an hour late—inside, I'm borderline crazy. Every time I go into the kitchen to get sodas or snacks, I sneak a huge swig of wine.

Thank God I didn't brag to Dennis and Cam about my big Christmas Eve date with Jake.

Finally around nine-thirty, Jake's souped-up muffler roars outside. I'm hardly breathing when I open the door. He didn't ask if he could bring friends, but there are two guys with him. One of them is a head shorter than Jake, with long blond hair. The other one looks a lot like Jake but with lighter hair and glasses. They nod and smile and walk right in when I open the door.

Jake smirks and hands me a bottle wrapped in silver paper and a green stick-on bow. "Merry Christmas, babe." The bottle has a wire thingy and gold foil paper on top with a strip around it that says Bath Bubbly. If he bought me Bubble Bath, the belt is probably all wrong. Should I have gotten him soap-on-a-rope?

On the way into the living room, Jake's short blond friend takes off his jacket and tosses it into the open closet. He turns to me. "Hey, I'm Doug." His short-sleeved tee shirt has the sleeves rolled up so it looks sleeveless and shows off his tattoo—like he came here right from a tryout for "Grease." I've never seen a guy with his *own* name tattooed in a heart on his *own* arm before. The other guy, the one who looks like Jake, leaves his jacket on but it's open so you can see his U of Penn sweatshirt.

In the living room, I point at the shirt. "You go to U of P?"

"First year of med school."

"Tim's my cousin from the brainy side of the family." Jake plops down on one of our antique chairs. The dubious expression on Dennis's face says he can't believe you can be in med school and be related to Jake.

Jake takes a new pack of cigarettes out of his shirt pocket, thumping the unopened pack on his palm. After he lights up, he raises the volume on the radio when John Lennon comes on singing "Happy Christmas." The entire time, Dennis keeps crawling under the tree to loosen and tighten the bolts in the stand, getting up to walk around the tree in between each adjustment. Except for the music, there's an uneasy quiet while we all watch until Dennis pronounces the tree perfectly straight.

Cannon helps Dennis untangle and string the lights. Tim joins in with Joe and John to make a little assembly line handing me ornaments. From the loveseat, Cam fires orders about moving whatever ornament I just hung to a better spot, and Jake and Doug stuff fistfuls of popcorn into their mouths and tell jokes.

Jake tells one about a lady who goes into a hardware store to buy a hinge but sees a toaster she wants. "So the clerk yells from behind the counter, 'Lady, do you wanta screw for this hinge?' And she says 'No, but I'll blow you for this toaster.'" Jake leans back laughing so hard at his own joke, the front legs of his fragile chair lift up off the floor. The back legs creak. I laugh at Jake's joke with the others.

Dennis sneers disapprovingly. "You might want to put all four legs on the floor so you don't break that chair."

Jake glares but doesn't snap back, shifting forward so the delicate chair legs thud on the floor. He stands up slowly. "Where's the head?"

I point the way to the bathroom. When he's out of earshot, I snatch a Santa ornament from Dennis's hand. "You don't have to be rude," I gripe.

He just about rips my finger off, grabbing the ornament back from me. The entire time Jake is gone, Cam and Cannon make out on the corner loveseat. Without asking, Jake's friend Doug gets up to change the radio station to rock instead of carols. On the way back, he trips on Cannon's stretched-out legs. "Hey man, get a room," he taunts them.

This night is not working out the way I imagined.

Jake finally comes back carrying three beers. The last thing Uncle Nack said before he left was no drinking, but

I'm not about to say anything. I stare Dennis down to make sure he doesn't even think about blurting out something else to humiliate me. He ducks back under the tree to plug in the lights. Jake tosses Tim and Doug each a beer, and twists the top off his own. He takes a big swig and pats his stomach. "Out with the old, in with the new." He licks his top lip and winks at me.

By the time we finish decorating the tree, it's time to leave for midnight mass, and I still haven't found a good time to give Jake his present. Everybody piles outside. Jake drapes his arm over my shoulders to walk out to his car. He unlocks the door and pulls me close so fast our teeth click when he kisses me. "Bye, babe."

"Aren't you coming to mass?"

"Only church I go to is Saint Mattress, when I can't get up in the morning." Tim and Doug find this hysterical; they both bend over in fits of laughter.

"But it's my Christmas Eve tradition."

"My Christmas Eve tradition is to do some serious drinking."

Tim and Doug howl again, like he's Bob Hope with the one-liners. Joe and John Raymond pull away. In the front seat of his car, Cannon kisses Cam, his hands coiled in her hair. I'm so jealous, I would twist off her ponytail if I could reach it from here.

Jake runs his hand down my back and pats me on the butt. He pulls me closer and kisses my nose. "Say a prayer for me." He gets into his car and revs the motor.

I don't turn around until his taillights are blurring little spots on Green Turtle Creek Road.

Dennis stands by his Mustang. "You okay?

"Perfect," I say in a deliberately snotty tone.

He opens the door of the Mustang for me to get in. I do, and he closes the door and trots around to the driver's side. He puts the key in the ignition and turns sideways in his seat. "He's not good enough for you."

"Do. Not. Start."

He goes to say something else, but I thrust my open hand in front of his face to cut him off. "Can you just shut up and drive?"

He's the last person I need telling me about who or what is good for me—like he has *ever* had a clue.

The day after Christmas, when I get home from returning the belt I never gave to Jake, Uncle Nack stands in the kitchen looking all-serious, one hand on his hip.

"One of your friends left his jacket in the closet."

I reach to take it from him. He pulls his arm back and opens his hand to show me an almost-empty baggie of dope and some rolling papers.

"This was in the pocket."

"You shouldn't have looked."

"It fell out when I picked up the jacket. Is it yours?"

"How can it be mine? It's not even my jacket."

"Is it that Jake's?"

It really pisses me off the way he says *Jake* as if he just ate a bad clam. "No."

"Who else was here?"

"Just some guys he knows. They're not even his friends. We'll probably never see them again."

Uncle Nack runs his fingers through his hair. He has taken up chewing the inside of his cheek the way Poppi used to when he worries. He makes a loud sucking-in sound. "Do you use drugs?"

"No."

"You come with me."

He looks really pissed, so I stay a few feet behind and follow him to the bathroom, standing out in the hall while he empties the bag and flushes it. He rips the papers into shreds, tossing them at the trashcan. Most of them miss and float down onto the floor.

"I won't have drugs in this house."

"I told you they aren't mine."

"And who drank the beer?"

"How should I know?"

He shakes his head, grunting like a rhinoceros. "You'd think you'd know better after watching your mother."

"I said I didn't drink it."

He looks at me funny but I stare him down, holding my ground. I'm good at this, so he has no idea how much I lie.

None of them do.

Chapter 22

Sister Genevieve Mary is at the front of the classroom writing our American History homework on the blackboard. She's the kind of nun who keeps you for detention if she catches you talking but hardly notices when you pass notes. She missed the one I passed to Dot Byrne asking her how to write "jerk" in shorthand. Most of the girls in my classes are in honors academic, but Dot is commercial because she wants to get a job, make money, and get married right after graduation. She might be the smartest girl in our class, but just because she's not academic, some of our classmates snub her. I'm the only person who knows that she's secretly engaged. The nuns would never let you wear an engagement ring, but they don't know the garnet ring on her finger is more than just her birthstone.

Dot flicks her thick, straight hair over her shoulder and squints at my note. We write in our smallest handwriting because Sister wears coaster-thick glasses. Just in case she does see the notes, she won't be able to read them. Dot wears glasses, too, which is another ridiculous reason some of the girls don't talk to her, but hers aren't half as thick as Sister's.

At the beginning of the semester, Dot showed me how to write I love Dennis in shorthand. When I told her about Jake, she showed me how to write his name, too. Most people think I'm just doodling, so I can write all over my book covers without anyone but Dot knowing what it says. Since she told me her secret, I trust her with mine.

It's Friday afternoon, last period, and every minute drags. As soon as Dot passes my note back, I scribble the symbol for jerk anywhere there is a squiggly Jake on my book covers. This is what I'm doing when I look out the window and see what could be Jake's car. It's hard to tell for sure because it's parked way up the street near a line of school buses. It can't really be Jake, it's not even three, and he works until four. But then he gets out of the car, leans on the fender, and lights a cigarette. There's no mistaking it. That is definitely Jake.

Crap. Cam is on the Prom committee and has a meeting after school. I can't walk to the bus alone. I jot a new note; Jake's here. You have to walk to the bus with me. Dot's whole face lights up, like she can barely wait to meet him.

As soon as the bell rings, we rush to our lockers, then to the bathroom to check my hair and hike my uniform above my knees. Dot slips her glasses into her pocket even though without them, she will hardly be able to see what Jake looks like. Outside, the sun glows behind a puddle of clouds. It's really cold, but I shove my knit hat into my pocket—better to freeze off my ears than let Jake catch me wearing that hat.

I haven't seen Jake in the three weeks since Christmas Eve—no New Year's Eve or Happy New Year. Nothing. My plan is to ignore him, heading straight for the bus like we don't see him. I make myself walk briskly, hanging onto Dot's arm as if we are best friends engrossed in conversation, having the time of our lives.

Dot squints in his direction. "He looks really cute from here," she whispers.

Unable to control my jitters, I laugh too loud. Jake calls out my name. I suck in my breath and try to make my face look surprised.

"Jake. What're you doing here?"

"What does it look like?"

I grip Dot's arm so tightly, I'm probably cutting off her circulation. She shakes me off to put out her hand. "Hi. I'm Dot."

Jake flicks his cigarette to the curb and shakes her hand, barely touching her fingertips before pulling his hand away. "It's frigging cold out here." He zips up his leather jacket and rocks back and forth on the balls of his feet. "Let's get in the car."

"Can we drop Dot off in Court House?"

Jake jiggles the change in his pocket, glancing up at the sky like he wants to say no. "Yeah, get in."

Thank God Dot babbles about nonsense until we drop her off. The car is noticeably quieter until Jake pulls up at the corner of our block so Uncle Nack won't see me getting out of his car. That is when it happens.

"Do you want to see a movie tonight?"

A *date?* Is he actually, finally, unbelievably, asking me out on a genuine, honest to God, freaking date?

"They're showing retro movies this month—*The Deer Hunter* is playing."

Through sheer force of will, I make my voice sound indifferent. "What time?"

"I'll pick you up at nine."

Of course I just close the car door without mentioning I have already seen *The Deer Hunter*. I put one foot in front of the other, trying to appear nonchalant instead of giddily sashaying up the block.

All during dinner, Uncle Nack lectured about not necking in the theatre and how far away to sit in the car. He wasn't happy when I told him we're going to the late show. I sucked it up and for once kept my mouth shut—at least he's letting me go. He left for Ursula's a half hour ago, so he doesn't know Jake is outside honking, not coming to the door to pick me up the way a real date is supposed to.

On an unlit street around the corner from Cape May's only movie theater, Jake pulls to the curb, letting the car run. You can smell the steamy heat blowing out of the vents. He passes me a quart bottle of beer in a brown bag. "I got accepted," he says with a hint of proud disbelief in his voice.

"To art school?"

"Got the letter yesterday. That's why I blew off work today." We pass the beer back and forth. "Honky Tonk Woman" booms so loud from the car radio it feels like the car is shaking. No one but us hears it because all the bed and breakfast inns on the street are boarded up for the season.

By the time we settle into our seats in the back row of the movie theater, the cartoons and coming attractions are almost over. Jake starts right in, gently blowing in my ear. I giggle. There are maybe ten people in the entire place, but an old guy a row up shushes me. That makes me laugh more. The guy throws us a dirty look and moves up a few more rows.

It's is a good thing I saw *The Deer Hunter* with Cam and Dennis because I'm too busy tugging down my sweater and trying to keep Jake's fingers out of my waistband to watch it tonight. It's like he's trying to get his money's worth and squeeze every kernel of popcorn he paid for back out of me. The only time he stops groping is during the Russian roulette scene. I nibble my popcorn with my eyes closed because watching that scene once was plenty for me.

After the movie, Jake wants to go parking, but it's after midnight. I can tell he's pissed that I have to get right home. I give in and agree to stay a little longer when he opens another beer. It's after one by the time he pulls into the driveway, lets the car idle, and nuzzles my neck in a way that makes me so light-headed, I can't figure out how he got my bra unhooked. He sucks right through my sweater, sending shock waves down to my belly. Part of me wants him to keep doing it, but the part that knows Uncle Nack would blow a gasket pushes him away.

"I have to go." But then I just sit still, catching my breath.

He sits up and grips the steering wheel with both hands, shaking his head. When I get out, I don't know if it's from the beer or the kissing, but I'm so woozy, it's a challenge to walk straight. I sneak in the back door and go right up to bed.

In the morning, I could have over-slept and missed my driving lesson with Dennis if the phone wasn't ringing off the hook. I shove my pillow over my head to block out the racket, waiting for Uncle Nack to answer, but it just keeps ringing. I drag myself out to the hallway and lift the receiver.

"Is this the Drennen residence?" The voice is formal and unfamiliar.

"Who's this?"

She says something that sounds like Betty White. "I'm calling from Memorial Hospital about June Drennen."

At the sound of Mama's name, my hand tightens on the phone. Suddenly, I am wide-awake. "Who are you?"

"A social worker in the Emergency Department at Memorial Hospital—I'm trying to find June Drennen's family."

I lean hard against the doorjamb to keep my balance. "What happened to her?"

"To whom am I speaking?"

"Her daughter."

"Is your father there?"

In the mirror across from where I stand, I watch myself shake my head no like an idiot. "What's wrong with her?"

"She's confused."

"How did she get there?"

"Someone dropped her off without talking to anyone."

That chicken-livered son of a bitch Ray, I figure.

As soon as I get off the phone, instead of taking the time to look for a tee shirt, I tuck my nightshirt into my sweatpants, yelling for Uncle Nack at the top of my lungs. In the bathroom, I splash water on my face, slap a finger full of toothpaste in my mouth, swish, and spit it out. I race down the steps, calling out to Uncle Nack again.

A note on the kitchen table says he went antiquing with Ursula. They always take her van to antique shop. I grab his car keys off the hook near the back door.

I don't know how to adjust the seat and have to sit way up to reach the pedals. The car stalls right away. I turn the car key again and pump the gas like crazy. There's a grating screech until I let go of the key. I shift into drive. The car lurches forward a few feet. I swerve and slam on the brakes to avoid hitting Dennis pulling into the driveway. He rolls down his window. "What the hell are you doing?"

"My mother's in the ER."

He gets out and opens my car door. "Get out. We'll take my car."

He parks Uncle Nack's Caddy and climbs back into his driver seat, shooting me the once-over. "You reek like booze." He pulls a comb out of his pocket. "And you might want to comb your hair."

I snatch the comb from his palm. "Can you just shut-up and drive?"

At the ER, the nurse leaves us in a cubicle to wait for the doctor. I pace—four steps, pivot, and four steps back, setting my foot square in the tile blocks, careful not to step on a crack. Dennis is up the hall somewhere at a pay phone, trying to call Ursula and Uncle Nack. All you can hear is the quiet turmoil of hospital noise. Everything smells metallic.

"I left a message with our maintenance guy at the restaurant." The little worry lines near Dennis's eyes and mouth make it clear he would rather be anywhere but here. The plastic chair squeaks when he sits down. I can feel his eyes follow me back and forth. "Sit down. You're making me nuts," he says, tensely.

"I can't stay still."

The doctor opens the curtain, peering from me to Dennis and back at me.

"Where's my mother?"

"How old are you?"

"Twenty-one." I can whip out the fake cards Jake got me to prove it if I have to.

Dennis lets out a whoosh of air but doesn't rat me out. The doctor raises his eyebrows and doesn't really look at me when he says my mother had a psychotic episode.

"What does that mean?" Dennis asks.

"She's disoriented, hearing voices, and seeing things. Her blood test shows a high level of alcohol and lysergic acid."

"LSD?" My brain feels like it broke loose and is boomeranging around my head.

A chubby black woman comes into the cubicle carrying a file. She introduces herself as the social worker who called, shaking my hand, but I miss her name again, because in my head I am shouting, *Holy shit, my mother took LSD!*

"Does your mother have a history of mental illness?"

"No."

The social worker hands the file to the doctor and leaves. He flips through the pages. "Well, she had an admission six years ago in our detox unit."

I detest the tone of his voice. Like it isn't bad enough that Dennis is hearing every mortifying detail without this guy acting as if drinking is mental illness, and I purposely lied. "Can I just see her?"

The doctor snaps the chart closed and says he'll get the nurse.

All I can think about is that time Mama was in rehab, when the counselor told us alcoholism was hereditary. After Poppi explained what hereditary meant, I asked who Mama had caught it from. He said that it wasn't something for me to bother about. I believed him then, and I still believe him. Whatever is wrong with Mama cannot be from drinking—it has to be the LSD.

The nurse pulls back the curtain and motions for us to follow her. "Be prepared. She probably won't recognize you."

We pass some empty cubicles and a few with patients on stretchers. I hope they don't catch me gawking. One guy with a tube in his nose makes rasping sounds; another has his eyes closed tight while a woman clutches his hand. A toddler peeks around the edge of a curtain to play hide and seek. She holds a smiley face balloon that bobs in mid-air. I want to smile back at her but my face feels numb. With each step, my body gets a little stiffer.

In Mama's cubicle, the best I can do is stand at the bottom of the bed, watching her head thrash around on the pillow. She looks like a mummy, her arms crisscrossed over her chest. I have to remind myself to breathe in and out.

"The straitjacket is so she doesn't hurt herself," the nurse says.

It's been a couple years, but Mama doesn't look anything like I remember. Her uncombed hair is streaked with gray. She frantically tries to get her arms loose, pleading, "Help me" in a tiny voice. It gives me the chills and reminds me of the part-fly-part-man trapped in the spider-web in the movie *The Fly*. Until this second, that movie was the scariest thing I had ever seen.

Mama's eyes seem to focus for a few seconds and I think she might recognize me, but suddenly her voice changes, shrieking like she's possessed.

"Get-the-walls-off-me-start-over-1-2-3-too-many-legs-1-2-start-over-slant-eyed-bitchinbastards-Jesuskook-rifle-killed-1-2-3-keep-them-off-no-legs-I-count-sonsofbitches-I count it all. . ."

Her eyes are wild and scared—big craters in her face, like Poppi that first time I saw him in the hospital. A rush like gushing water fills my ears. My lungs cannot get any air.

Somewhere in the distance, there are noises and voices and the pungent stench of ammonia. I twist my head away from that smell and open my eyes. We're back in the little cubicle. Ursula rubs my arms. I push the nurse's hand with its reeking little brown bottle away from my face. As soon as I can stand up, Uncle Nack tells Dennis to take me home.

On the drive home, the wipers chase each other back and forth across the windshield but can't keep up with the heavy rain coating the glass like Vaseline. Dennis hunches over the steering wheel, pulling the sleeve of his sweater over his palm to clear a round spot in the fog—a hazy orb I wish I could disappear through. In front of the house, I want him to reach across the console, take me in his arms, and hold me until the fear goes away. Instead, he grips the steering wheel. "You need to stop drinking," he whispers gravelly.

"What the fuck does that have to do with anything?"

"You want to end up like your mother?"

Who the hell does he think he is, preaching to me? "I would *never* take LSD."

He comes around and opens my door, but I sit here ignoring him, letting rain drip through his hair and down his face. When he's good and wet, I get out and slam the door hard enough to rattle the window. "Your father's an alcoholic. Why don't you stop drinking?"

He wipes the rain from his eyes. "That's different." He looks so sure of himself, I want to get back in the car and make him stand there dripping, or better yet, punch the smug off his face.

I poke him in the chest. "Well, good for you." I turn and splash right through a big puddle to get to the porch. His sneakers make squishy sounds behind me.

I turn abruptly on the porch. "Good. Bye."

"I'll come in with you."

I yank the screen door and give him a look I hope says just leave. "No thanks."

"I don't mind."

I stamp my foot and spin around. "Well, I do."

He jams his hands into his pockets. "Fuckin' A."

I watch him walk with deliberate slowness back to his car, rain running down the back of his bare neck. When he pulls away, I slam the door and go right down to the cellar.

The siphon tube isn't where Uncle Nack usually keeps it. I search for it in the utility cabinet. It's not in there, but Poppi's old macaroni guitar is on the bottom shelf. Greasy dust sticks to my fingers when I lift it out. A cool draft comes through the old block window in the corner. My clothes are damp and I can't stop shivering, rocking here on the floor, hugging the guitar to my chest.

Chapter 23

Every time I visit my mother in the psych unit, it gets harder not to obsess about whether I come from a long line of people who drink, die young, or go nuts. I sit across from her in the lounge where the psych patients are allowed to smoke, careful not to get too close. A patch of hair at her crown is turning prematurely white like Poppi's and Uncle Nack's. Her lips move as if she is deep in conversation.

"Are you talking, Mama?"

"Counting," she says in a robot voice.

"What?"

"Have to count." Her tone of voice creeps me out. She leans in toward me.

I lean back to keep my distance. "What are you counting?"

The dull gray half-moons under her eyes twitch. "Moved my finger and foot. Have to count. Keep it even." Her eyes dart around the room. She points down at her feet. "Moved this toe, have to move this one. Keep it even."

Maybe the counting explains the repetitive rhythm to her chain smoking. Two short puffs and a long one, she taps the cigarette four times on the edge of the ashtray and starts the cycle again, over and over, always doing it exactly the same. "Where's Ray?" She plays taps for a while with her cigarette, her lips moving a mile a minute. She asks again, "Where's Ray?"

I look into her eyes and nothing stares back at me, making the hair on the back of my neck stand up. I'm so sick of her asking about him again and again every time I visit. "Why do you keep asking? He doesn't care. He isn't coming."

She flings the cigarette into the ashtray, bunches her hands into fists, and pounds the sides of her head, rocking back and forth, baying like an injured animal.

I chew the inside of my cheek, feeling like crap, moving just close enough to pat her elbow until she stops hitting herself. She has enough real stuff to miss in her life so I will never understand why she misses *him*, but being mean to her fills me with guilt. "I'm sorry, Mama. I didn't mean it." I gently touch her wrist. "He can't come because he's working, that's all."

She slants her head to squint at me, unclenches her fists, rubbing her hands up and down on her thighs. I gently put my hand on her knee, listening to her count until she settles down.

On the bus ride home, I press my cheek to the cool window, staring blankly out at the red-violet streaks in the late-afternoon sky. Visiting my mother really puts me out of sorts. On the spur of the moment, I get off the bus down the street from Ursula's restaurant. It's hours after lunch and probably too early to be prepping tomorrow's breakfast. She just got the outside of the building repainted a pale shade of pinky-beige. The windows and doors are trimmed in maroon and outlined in navy. It seems like she picked those colors to match today's sky. I walk around back and knock on the door.

"What a nice surprise," Ursula says warmly, taking a step back to let me in. She cocks her head to the side. "You know Dennis isn't home this weekend, right?"

"I came to see you."

Her brows knit in concern "What's up?"

"Nothing." I follow her into the kitchen and lean back in a chair. She pulls up a chair across from me.

"I went to see my mother." I shift around as I say it as if a tack is poking me in the butt.

"How'd that go?"

I shrug and run my fingernail over the flamingo embossed on one of her new Sunday brunch menus, wondering how much Ursula knows about heredity. "Did you know my mother's mother?"

"I remember her from the neighborhood growing up."

"But, did you *know* her?"

"Not really."

I worry the edge of the menu with my fingertip. "Did she seem like, nice?"

She holds her coffee mug near her lips but doesn't drink it. "What are you trying to ask me, honey?"

How do I ask her if my grandmother was a drunk who passed it to my mother, who maybe passed it to me?

I sigh. "Nothing, I guess."

She tilts her head to the side, slightly raising her eyebrows. We sip in silence for a few minutes.

"Did you know Uncle Nack's wife?"

"Nettie died a few years before we got friendly."

"Nobody in the family ever talks about her."

She slowly centers her cup on the saucer. "People get ashamed when someone dies like that."

"Like what?" I stare straight into her eyes. "Didn't she accidently fall off a bridge and drown?"

She pauses so long, her eyes glued to mine, I think I might finally get to the bottom of the Aunt Nettie family secret. "Is that what Uncle Nack and your Poppi told you?"

I bob my head.

A flush bathes her face. She lowers her eyes. "You should probably have this conversation with your uncle." She walks to the sink, turns on the water, and feverishly scrubs the inside of her cup, reminding me so much of how Poppi always got overly interested in cleaning his pipe whenever I asked him about Aunt Nettie. By the time Ursula turns to face me again, her color is back to normal and it's clear I totally blew my chance to get her to spill any family secrets.

"Dennis mentioned you have a new beau," she says a bit too cheery.

"What did he say?"

"Not much. I got the feeling he doesn't know him well."

I study the coffee grounds in the bottom of my cup, wondering if she's covering for him or if he really hasn't told her he thinks Jake is a jerk.

An hour later when I get home, I'm still unsettled and decide to call Cam. Between candy striping and visiting my mother on weekends, I hardly get to see Cam outside of school anymore. The last time we talked at her locker on Wednesday, she was in such a big rush to meet up with Cannon, I barely had time to tell her about getting acceptance letters for two more nursing schools, bringing me to three out of four so far.

This late on a Saturday afternoon, she's probably out with Cannon again—they are always together–but I decide to call anyway. It's a longshot, but just maybe they'll invite me to go out with them tonight—all I have planned is eating a quart of ice cream and starting the paper that's due Monday for my advanced placement English class.

"Don't tie up the line," Uncle Nack grumbles from the living room as if he has radar and detects my hand on the phone. I know he has to call in his bets on tomorrow's college games to Tony the Barber before it gets late, but I don't care. He has watched nothing but basketball on TV for the last week and personally, I'm sick of March Madness. I turn my back like I don't hear him and lift the receiver.

"I mean it," he warns.

"Tough shit." I mean to say it under my breath, but it comes out a little louder. Uncle Nack doesn't hear it, but when I put the receiver to my ear, instead of dial tone there's laughter. "Is that Italian for hello?"

My heart beats in my eardrums. The phone didn't even ring. "Who is this?"

"So, now you don't remember my voice?"

With my eyes closed, I can see the smug tilt of Jake's head that matches his cocky voice. I try to sound nonchalant. "You have to admit I haven't heard it much lately."

I want him to say he misses me and how sorry he is for not calling and for dropping me off two blocks from home the last time we went out, because he was pissed about *not getting any.* That night, I walked along Shun Pike in the dark at midnight without gloves or a scarf, wondering if staying a virgin was really worth being cold and alone.

"You busy tonight?" Jake asks.

"Going to the movies with friends."

"My cousin Tim's here. Want to go to Wildwood with us?"

Did he not just hear me say I have plans? I should tell him to shove it. "What time?"

"We'll honk about eight."

Later, when the horn blows, Uncle Nack frowns and sucks in some air. "He should knock and come in."

Ursula looks up curiously from her *Better Homes and Garden* magazine but doesn't say anything.

I grab my coat and stop on my way by Uncle Nack's chair. His white hair is still thick and wavy where I peck the top of his head. I know he's thinking, is he really the best you can do, but for once, he doesn't say anything, which is good. I don't have to defend Jake in front of Ursula.

Tim is in the back seat, rolling a joint. He salutes me when I get in. Jake drives to the same bar called Pacific Blue in North Wildwood where he took me once before. The bouncer knows Jake, so he hardly looks at my fake cards. I like the way Bernie the pointy-faced bartender knows Jake's name and says hello to me like he remembers me. He wipes the bar in front of us and slaps down three coasters.

Jake and Tim order drafts. Bernie shifts the toothpick he's chewing to the corner of his mouth. "And for the lady?"

They keep the mugs on ice here, so the drafts look frothy and tempting, but I know I shouldn't get a beer because to prove to myself I am nothing like my mother and can stop any time I want, I gave up drinking for Lent. "Do you have birch beer?"

"You gonna order a burger and fries with that? This ain't Burger King." Jake takes a deep swig and wipes the foam off his lip with the back of his hand.

He's got a point. I can go to Burger King with Cam and Dennis—I only get into places like this with Jake. Besides, Lent is more than half over. That's long enough to prove my point. "Give me a draft," I say bravely to Bernie.

After our date at Pacific Blue last Saturday, things with Jake might be looking up. This week, he actually called two days ago on Thursday to ask me out for tonight. After I took a chance and told him Uncle Nack doesn't like him honking and waiting for me outside, he came to the door and rang the bell. While I get my coat, he and Uncle Nack stand in the foyer and shake.

"That's a nice looking Cadillac," Jake says.

"There's no car like a Caddy for the money." Uncle Nack isn't exactly making eye contact with him, more like giving him the evil eye. "Katie says you work at the cannery."

"Yep, three years."

Uncle Nack nods. You can tell he's adding up Jake's age to twenty-one in his head.

Instead of taking me *out* somewhere, Jake drives down the winding dirt road behind the ranch that gives riding lessons to kids. He parks in back of a dilapidated shed and turns off the car. We make out in the pitch black until his elbow thumps hard against the steering wheel.

"Shit, my crazy bone." He gets out and moves his sketchbooks off the back seat. "Let's get in back."

When I don't move right away, he leans down and sticks his head through the open door. "Pretty please," he teases.

I know it's a bad idea, but I slide over and let him help me into the backseat. In the bigger space, his hands are all over me. I let him take off my sweater, but not my jeans, gripping his hand tight every time he tries to pull down his zipper or unhook my bra. His body is heavy when he presses his groin against mine. His hips move slowly at first, his fingers grope the snap on my jeans.

Even through the denim, his zipper digs into my pelvis. He presses harder and moves faster. He's sweating and breathing hard. When he gets out of the car, rearranging himself, he keeps grumbling about being too old to come in his pants. I pull on my sweater. In a way, we didn't do anything, but it's the first time we went that far, and it makes me want to go home and take a steaming hot shower.

The car is so quiet on the ride home, I can hear my watch tick. I keep buckling and unbuckling my watch band. He pulls up out front and stares out the windshield.

"I thought you liked me," he says bluntly.

I touch his wrist. "I do."

"You have a funny way of showing it." I wish he would turn the car off, say he still likes me, and kiss me goodnight. When he doesn't, I get out and lean back into the car. The look he gives me makes me feel like a big cheat.

"I don't get you," he says, drumming his fingers on the steering wheel.

"I just don't feel ready," I say uncertainly.

For a second, he reaches over and touches my hand, jiggling my pinky, shaking his head.

When he lets go, I straighten up and close the door. "Well, bye," I say too brightly.

He revs the motor and pulls away before I'm on the porch.

The next day, I'm studying when Cam blasts into my bedroom, bouncing up and down on my bed so hard my books fall all over the floor. She waves her hand right in my face, showing off a new ring—one jet black and one snowy pearl perched high on a swirly gold band. My hair is still wet from my shower, and it falls across my eyes in a big clump. Hopefully, it hides the envy burning my cheeks.

"Cannon took me to the Washington Inn last night for my birthday and after dinner, the waiters brought out a birthday cake with a sparkler in it. Everyone in the restaurant sang Happy Birthday," she gushes, twirling her hand in the air. "The ring was tied to the sparkler with a glittery ribbon." She sighs all dreamy-like. "It was *so* romantic." She leans in closer. "After dinner, we went to his house, and no one was home." Her eyes are steady and so content like when we were younger and she always had the better secret. "We started fooling around in his bedroom— and we went all the way," she adds breathlessly.

I bolt upright so fast, my head slams the headboard. "*All the way?*" I try to hide it, but I know I'm eying her like I'm not sure I like her and her swan-necked posture and smug poise. I look away from her beaming face and push at the cuticle on my pinky with my thumbnail. It might kill me but I have to ask, I need to know. "*How* did you know it was time?"

"I just did."

"But *how?*"

She sits up so straight, it feels like she has to look down to see me. "It just felt right."

I hug my pillow to my chest. Right this second, I detest her graceful gestures, loathe her self-assurance, despise her blissful glow.

I utterly and completely hate that she has done another thing first.

Chapter 24

Drenched from walking home from the school bus without my umbrella, I duck around the rain pouring through the back porch gutters, scoot into the mudroom, strip off my soggy shoes and socks, and kick them under the bench next to Uncle Nack's mud-caked boots. All week, he's been plowing weeds under in a field he hasn't planted for years, because the Silver Dolphin, a fancy new restaurant on the promenade in Cape May, wants to buy all their Jersey fresh produce from him this summer.

The phone rings just as I enter the kitchen. At the sink, Uncle Nack stops peeling carrots to reach for the dishtowel and wipe his hands, but I'm faster, snatching a carrot and getting to the hall phone before him. My tacky feet stick to the hard wood floor.

"Hey there," Dennis says on the other end.

The grandfather clock chimes quarter to five. He never calls before dinner on a school night. "You're calling early."

"I only have a few minutes. I need to get to the library to study for a test."

"What kind of test?"

"Business Law."

"Bor-ring," I say to be funny, but he ignores me.

"My mom said you got another nursing school acceptance—you're four for four."

"And yesterday, I found out the Carpenters' Union is giving me a thousand dollar scholarship."

"Way to go, Ace."

"Uncle Nack still thinks I'll get something from the V.A. since Poppi was a veteran."

Dennis clears his throat like he didn't hear me. "I've been meaning to ask you something."

I nibble the end of my carrot.

"Are you eating?" he asks.

"Just a carrot. Is that what you called to ask me?" I think my joke is hilarious, but he grunts.

"Very funny."

I pop the last nib of carrot into my mouth and crunch loudly in the too-long space of silence.

"Is Jake taking you to your prom?"

Something in the way he blurts it out makes me swallow too fast. The carrot feels like sharp pebbles going down. I keep swallowing to clear the sting in my throat. I don't want to tell him Jake said he is too old for a prom because I haven't given up. He'll hopefully say yes when I plead with him again. "I guess."

A long hiss of air whistles through Dennis's teeth. There's a drumming sound like he's tapping his fingers on the mouthpiece.

This is a weird conversation. I'm not sure what to do with all these quiet spaces. I change the phone to my other hand and scratch an itch on my elbow.

"Do you want to do something this weekend?"

"Jake might take me to Wildwood."

There's a pop and a few seconds of rustling static. "Sorry, I dropped the phone. I should probably stay here and work on a paper that's due next week, anyway."

For a long time after we hang up, I stare at the phone, wondering if what I'm thinking could be true. Was he asking me to hang out, or was he asking me for a date?

On Saturday, Uncle Nack is over Ursula's, and Jake and I have the backyard to ourselves. Jake leans back in the lounge chair with his hands behind his head. I like this time of day when the sun's shadow makes the side of Poppi's old woodshed look stenciled with tree branches. All these years, Uncle Nack and I have left everything inside the shed just how it was the last time Poppi worked there—as if nothing changed when everything did.

I pull my chair up close so my knees touch Jake's. "Please?"

"I ain't the prom type," he says aloofly.

I want my senior prom to be special, not like the junior prom with Cam's cousin from Philadelphia who didn't talk to me most of the night. I want to giggle with Cam while we try on strapless chiffon gowns, spend the day at the salon having my nails painted and my hair swept up in a French twist. I want to walk down the stairs and see the awe on Jake's face when he gazes up at me, to gush over the corsage he buys me, pin on his boutonniere, line dance at the post-prom, go all night bowling, and eat pancakes at the diner at sunrise.

"I really want to go," I whimper.

"I really *don't.*"

Uncle Nack's new bug zapper zings bugs left and right, so maybe Jake doesn't hear my breath catch in my throat. The shadows on the shed are fading and hopefully it's too dark to notice my eyes brim, but just in case, I turn my face away. He reaches over and tugs on the Saint Jude metal around my neck until I have to lean into him.

"Hey, don't break the chain."

He lets go. The medal was a Christmas present from Uncle Nack. It bothers me that he thinks I need the patron saint of the impossible hanging from my neck, but I wear it rather than hurt his feelings.

Jake rubs my arms. Even though I try to resist, he pulls me onto his lap and reaches up to snap a magnolia flower from a low branch. "Don't pout." He tickles my chin with the blossom. "I'll take you to that new Silver Dolphin place for dinner instead."

It's Sunday morning, and I should have waited until after church to tell Cam about Jake. She hasn't stopped whispering since mass started. The lady in the pew in front of us keeps turning around and making a be-quiet sign with her finger to her lips. The altar bells chime and the priest holds up the host. We stand up with everyone else as if we're going to communion, but sneak out the side door instead.

A priest I don't recognize smokes on the rectory steps. His collar is undone. He raises his eyebrows. "Leaving early doesn't fulfill your obligation, girls."

"Yes, Father." The possibility of me acting anything but contrite to his face is remote, but Cam puffs up her cheeks like she might say something smart. I link my arm in hers to drag her down the path.

"Like smoking outside church makes him a role model," she snorts.

I pull her further out of earshot. She frees up her arm and slips a new lip gloss out of her pocket, coating her lips and handing the tube to me. When I get it near my lips, the cloying smell of sweet oranges engulfs me. I change my mind and hand it back to her.

"Spite the sucker and ask Dennis," she says smugly.

A trash truck rumbles through the intersection filling the air with the stink of garbage. Cam is the only person I know who can pick up a conversation midstream after you think it's over. She has pushed the *take Dennis to the prom* idea all morning, but there's no way I can ask him because instead of asking me to his prom last year, he took a girl he hardly knew. Besides, I'd have to make up some story about why I'm not going with Jake. "He won't go."

"How do you know if you don't ask him?"

"I know Dennis."

A few weeks later on prom night, Cam prances in front of her bedroom mirror. My short black halter dress, bought for my dinner date with Jake with the money I had saved up for a prom dress, looks drab next to Cam's watery-pink off-the-shoulder gown. At least the fringed shawl Cam talked me into buying dresses up my outfit.

Downstairs, Cam's mom wears Birkenstocks and an ankle length flower print dress. Her long braid is tied with a shoelace and hangs down almost to her waist. She snaps pictures with her 35 mm camera. Cam's dad's hair is pulled into a short ponytail at his neck. He drags out his video camera, the kind with a voice-over, and keeps making goofy statements like, "Here's our stunning Campbell and her handsome beau going to her prom," and "We're delighted her best friend Katie is here to witness this grand event."

Cam touches the pink crystal heart necklace—a prom night gift from Cannon—with her perfect, French-tipped fingernails. Her hair looks exotic, swept to one side and pinned with an orchid near her ear. I have to keep reminding myself to smile, pretending it's not killing me that Cam gets to go to the prom and I don't.

"Get some pictures with just me and Katie." Cam slides my shawl down off my shoulders so it drapes around my upper arms. "Show off the halter, girl."

"Flash me those knock-out smiles." Mr. McKee makes us turn in circles to get the full effect.

When I've been here long enough to be polite, I peck Cam on her flawlessly roughed cheek and say goodbye.

"I wish you were coming." She jiggles my hand. Her lips crease into a pout. I shrug and force a smile, waving her off, knowing if I do not leave this minute, I might start to cry.

My new pumps rub the back of my foot on my three-block walk to the Queen Street Bed and Breakfast Inn where I'm meeting Jake. Uncle Nack would have one of his fits if he knew Jake didn't pick me up at Cam's, but it was my idea to meet here instead. The last thing Jake needs is being the center of Mr. and Mrs. McKee's gush-fest.

I lean on the Inn's gatepost to slip off my shoe and knead the stiff back of it with my toes. To pass the time while I wait, I read one of the brochures from the basket on the gate.

By the time Jake pulls up, I have memorized the room rates. Just as I open my mouth to bitch at him for being late, he makes a low wolf whistle. "You look *really* good."

Feeling my cheeks flush, I press my lips together and forgive him.

As I get into the car, my dress rides up my leg. Before I can shimmy it down, Jake lays his hand above my knee. "Pretty sexy," he says, squeezing my thigh.

Heat bathes my face again, goose bumps quiver up and down my arms. While he drives, I sneak peeks at him out of the corner of my eye. Being with dressed-up-Jake is a little like being with a stranger. He looks older, handsome in a navy sport coat and blue pinstriped button-down shirt. The collar is open, showing off his gold chain with the Italian horn. His blotchy purple birthmark shows too, but you can tell he doesn't care.

Jake parks up the street from the Silver Dolphin Restaurant. Instead of coming around to open my door, he stops near the front fender to light a cigarette, gazing across the street at the ocean while he smokes. In my head, I can hear Uncle Nack saying, "You can dress him up, but you can't take him out," but I'm thinking if he cleans up this good, he still might change into someone more considerate.

I get out and walk over to Jake. My stiff shoe is rubbing a blister onto my heel. Jake finishes his cigarette as the sun melts into a lemon puddle on the horizon.

He touches my elbow to steer me into the restaurant. Waiting for our table, something about being dressed up and sitting at the bar makes it hard to find things to say. Thankfully, the bartender comes over and rescues us from our clumsy small talk.

"What can I get you?" He has bushy gray eyebrows that go up and down a few times when Jake orders us both Manhattans. "Got ID?"

It's nerve-racking the way he looks right at me when he asks. This is my first time using my fake driver's license at a fancy place. I have to force myself not to look at Jake when I slide it across the bar, staring instead at the engraved pin on the bartender's shirt that says his name is George.

"Twenty-one, eh?" He looks from me to the card and back at me. "You look younger."

"Yeah, George, I get that a lot."

He gives me a squirrely look. I almost tell him to forget it and give me a cola, but then he hands me my license and starts mixing our drinks. I have to will my hand to stop shaking when I stuff the license back into my bag.

By the time our table is ready, I'm sipping my second Manhattan. The maître d'—his name pin says his name is

Larry—asks if we want a table near the window or at the banquette.

"We'll take the window seat, Larry," I chirp before Jake has a chance to answer. It might be the Manhattan talking, but I like this lofty feeling that I'm the one in control.

Larry carries my drink to the table in front of the picture window. While we sat at the bar, it got dark outside. I hear the waves crashing into the beach across the street, but I can't see them. It feels elegant when Larry pulls out my chair, shakes out my napkin to place on my lap, and tucks my chair in after I sit down. He hands me my menu.

"What's in a Manhattan?" I ask him.

"Whiskey and vermouth, Madame." Larry bows, smiles, and glides away.

After picking the cherries out of my empty glass to suck the juice out, I stand to go to the bathroom. My legs feel like Play-dough. I sway against the table and drop back into my chair.

"Tilt," Jake teases. The way he grins at me makes me want to reach over and touch him. When I do, he takes my hand in his, kisses my fingertips. "Isn't this better than a silly prom?"

He's right. My brain must be sparkling inside my head from the magic in that drink.

It's a good thing there's a brass railing along the dance floor to help steady me on my way to the ladies room. Inside, there are two old ladies in polyester pantsuits—one lime green and the other the color of an over-ripe peach. The whole time I pee, they complain about only getting two olives in their salad. They're still out there clucking after I flush and go to the sink. "For four dollars, they should give you the whole jar," the peach says. It strikes me so funny, I laugh right out loud. "The whole jar," I mimic. Crap, did I say that out loud?

Their backs stiffen; they roll their eyes at me and march out. I almost bust a gut trying to stop giggling long enough to put on more lipstick. With the biddies gone, I have the bathroom to myself. Standing sideways in front of the mirror, I can see my whole back and the way the dress flows over my hips. It feels like I'm watching myself from outside of my body, checking me out from somewhere far away. Damn if I don't look good.

I'm only back at the table a minute when the waiter brings a carafe of red wine and two wine glasses. I put my hand over the top of my glass.

"I'll take another Manhattan."

"I thought we'd switch to wine," Jake coaxes.

"No thanks." I tip my empty Manhattan glass at the waiter. "And put extra cherries in my next one."

By the time our entrees are served, my tongue feels numb. I can hardly taste my flounder. The room is out of focus. Maybe Jake was right and I should have switched to wine.

The band plays disco and a few couples hop around on the dance floor. I know Jake is talking because I see his lips moving, but the music is so loud, I can't hear a word he says. My head feels like a bobble-head doll head rolling around on my neck. Just as I raise my voice to tell him to speak up, the music stops. I know people are staring, but who cares. I giggle and Jake shushes me, but you can tell by his eyes he thinks it's funny, too.

When the waiter brings the dessert menu, Jake orders us stingers. A drink for dessert? I am *so over* caring about the prom.

The lead singer announces the next song is a ladies choice. I hardly feel my legs when I jump up and grasp at Jake's hand. I miss and almost fall into him, but he catches me. The band starts playing "The Great Pretender."

"Let's dance."

"I can't dance."

"You have to. Ladies choice." I start singing along.

He gets up, puts his fingers over my mouth, and whispers in my ear. "I'll dance, if you promise not to sing." We're both laughing out loud.

He pulls me close and takes jerky little steps. His breath tickles my neck. He wasn't kidding, he can't dance, but my cheek feels so right pressed to the thick hair where his collar is open, I don't even care. My head fills up with his woodsy cologne as we move in a slow circle at the edge of the dance floor.

When we go outside after dinner, the air feels like cool water on my skin. I lean against a lamppost while Jake lights a cigarette. Everything is blurry with soft edges. I rest my head against the post and close my eyes. When I open them, Jake stands right in front of me, his cigarette between his teeth. He puts both hands on my waist and pulls me close. I take the cigarette from his mouth to take a drag, but it slips from my fingers to the ground.

"Oops." I try to crush it with my toe but miss. It rolls to the curb. "Damn worthless shoes." I kick off one, then the other, and cha-cha a few steps in my stocking feet.

"Whoa." Jake picks up my shoes and props his arm around my waist. We shuffle like that to the car. He bends down to put the key into the lock. I run my fingers through his hair, pull his face to mine, put my tongue in his ear.

"Feeling frisky, babe?"

I rub my whole body up against him, suck on the skin below his ear. "I'm giving you a hickey."

He purrs. "That's not all you're giving me."

"Let's go parking."

The car bumps up and down on the dirt road that leads to the canal. I let myself fall sideways against Jake. He pulls me close the way he likes to until I'm almost sitting in his lap.

I keep trying to undo his belt buckle.

"You're crazy," he says, laughing deep in his throat.

When we get out at the canal, my legs tingle like I just took off roller skates. I do this dance, sort of a shimmy with my shawl while Jake spreads an old beach sheet from his trunk on the ground. As soon as he pulls me down beside him, his hands are all over me, near the hem of my dress, then inside my pantyhose. My arms feel weightless when I wrap them around his neck. We kiss and my head swims, swirling in spongy circles.

We should stop.

His tongue probes deep into my mouth. My brain is putty. My whole body feels unhinged.

I should tell him to stop.

It's really dark, too dark to see. His breath feels balmy on my face and smells like sweet, smoky candy canes. Music from a passing party boat drifts over us. Water from the boat's wake laps the shore near our heads. Jake's hard body covers mine, and the ground feels damp and marshmallow soft, and my body melts down into it, sliding deeper and deeper, as I tumble with Jake into the dark, floating, liquid night.

Chapter 25

The next day, my head feels like I slept under the boardwalk with a tramcar parked on top of me. To keep Uncle Nack off my back, I told him the reason I've been sick in bed all day is from eating bad clams.

What got into me? I had it all under control until I drank that stupid stinger. My leg is draped over the side of the bed to see if putting one foot down on the floor stops the spinning like Jake said.

It's not the first time Jake has been wrong.

Last night is fuzzy, but parts of it aren't fuzzy enough. It's sore down there between my legs.

Oh. My. God. *I did it with Jake.*

If only that part could be a bad dream.

Every time I doze off and wake up, I realize all over again that Jake hasn't called. I'm not even sure I want to talk to him, but at least he could call. As if God just heard me, the phone rings. With the pillow over my head, I pray, let it be him. *Don't let it be him.*

Uncle Nack calls up the stairs. "Cam's on the phone."

I pretend to be asleep just like when Dennis called earlier this afternoon. Listening to her blow-by-blow saga of the prom is the last thing I need.

Sometime around five, for the third time today, Uncle Nack tries to make me eat. He places the tray right on the bed.

"Jake called about an hour ago. You were sleeping."

I must have really been asleep that time. I didn't hear the phone. "If he calls back, tell him I'm not here."

His disapproving look says *I am not lying for you.* He repositions the tray closer to me. The reek of the escarole soup almost makes me puke. At least the oatmeal at breakfast and the chicken broth at lunch didn't smell. "I don't want it," I protest weakly.

"You have to eat something." He rests his palm on my forehead. "It doesn't feel like you have a fever."

"You don't get a fever from eating bad clams." Why can't he just leave me alone? I roll over and pull the covers up to my chin.

The next time the phone rings, it wakes me from a dream about being seasick in a rowboat.

"It's Jake," Uncle Nack shouts up the stairs.

I lie here with the covers over my head, pretending I don't hear his voice getting closer, hollering my name.

The whole room spins when I get up. "I told you to tell him I'm not here," I screech, jerking the door open. Uncle Nack stands right outside my room, holding the receiver from the hall phone in midair. Damn. It's my own fault for buying that extra-long phone cord to use the phone in here. I yank the receiver out of his hand. "Thanks for nothing," I mouth.

He marches to his bedroom and slams his door closed.

I bang mine too and press my back against it. "What?"

"Why don't you want to talk to me?"

"Like you don't know."

"As a matter of fact, I don't."

"You *knew* I didn't want to do it."

"You could have fooled me."

"At least tell me you used something. You used a condom, right."

He draws in his breath. "I figured you took care of it."

My legs start trembling. I slide down to the floor. "How could you think that?" If I don't lower my voice, Uncle Nack will hear. "I can't believe you. Do me a favor and leave me alone. Do. *Not.* Call me again. " I slam down the phone.

The next time I wake up, sunlight slices through the blinds. My alarm clock says it's almost eleven o'clock—I must have slept sixteen hours straight through the night. I take my time sitting up and lowering my feet to the floor. My whole body feels wrung out. It's a good thing Uncle Nack always has Sunday breakfast at Ursula's café. I have the bathroom to myself for at least another hour.

After my long, hot shower, I almost feel human, wrapping myself in a towel and brushing my hair, stopping midstroke when I hear a car. At the window, I pull back the edge of the lace curtain, watching Dennis park between two weeping cherry trees. He gets out and stares at the house, shades his eyes, and looks up at my window. My towel slips a little when I let go of the curtain to step back, hoping he didn't see me.

He knocks and, after a minute, pounds harder. This is all I need. He obviously knows I'm here.

I call through the open window, "I'll be down in a few minutes."

I put on a tee shirt and overalls and tie my wet hair into a loose ponytail. The room still spins if I move too fast. I tread softly on the stairs. At the bottom, I stand back from the screen door to watch him before he sees me. He hasn't been home in a few weeks, and his hair looks longer, brushing his shirt collar at the back of his neck. He turns when I step out onto the porch.

"I didn't know you were home this weekend," I say with an edge of annoyance.

"I called yesterday."

"I thought you called from school."

He takes a few steps closer and like a reflex, I step back, nearer to the door.

"How was the prom?"

I look away and pull dead petals off a potted tulip. When I run out of dead petals, I pinch the ends off brown leaves. "I didn't go." Without looking up, I know he's staring at me.

"How come?"

"Just didn't, that's all." I try to sound indifferent as I sit on the edge of the bench Poppi made when I was seven years old. After all these years, the weather has turned it gray, but you can still see the letters where he let me carve my initials into the seat. My hands are clasped between my knees.

Dennis sits down beside me. "Did Jake punk out on you?" he asks skeptically.

"It's no big deal." From the corner of my eye, I see him shake his head.

"I would have taken you," he says guardedly.

"Right."

"I would have."

I look straight into his eyes. They are true blue and so full of pity, I ball my hands into fists and hammer his chest.

"Hey." He holds my wrists to make me stop, but he doesn't squeeze; his fingers feel gentle. "What's your problem?"

I jerk my arms away and turn to avoid his gaze, digging my thumbnail into the carved K on the bench. He reaches like he might touch my hand. I pull away too fast, catching my nail in the wood.

"Shit, shit, shit." A thin line of red spreads under the nail. I suck on it to stop the stinging and then poke my thumb in front of his faces. "Look what you did."

"Why are you so pissy?"

I squeeze my eyes shut. There's no way I will cry. "Why did you wait until now?" I ask, glumly.

"What do you mean?"

"To say you'd go."

"You said Jake was taking you."

This time when I look into his eyes, the pity is gone, replaced by surprise and something that might be regret.

I swat a tear with the back of my hand. "I really wanted to go."

He heaves a big sigh. "You should have asked me." There's no missing the apology in his voice.

For the next few weeks, I search all over the house for that book about girl stuff Ursula bought for me when I was eleven or twelve, but I can't find it anywhere. I keep trying to reassure myself.

There must be a million reasons for a girl to miss a period.

How did I let this happen?

Jake never gave me his phone number, but when we first started going out, I had looked it up in the phone book. I didn't know his mother's name, because when he talked about her at all he called her the queen, but there was a Carmella Rossi on 26th Street in North Wildwood that seemed like the right address. I dialed the number a few times last winter when Jake hadn't called for a few weeks, but always hung up if someone answered.

Last Tuesday, I dug that paper with his number on it out of my jewelry box. Until today, every time I called, the phone just rang and rang. I'm so surprised when he answers that my arm doesn't move fast enough to hang up.

"Hello."

His voice sounds nicer on the phone when you can't see the conceited way he slants his head or the cockiness in his eyes. Or maybe it just sounds good because I haven't heard it for so many weeks.

"Hell-oh."

I clear my throat wishing that could clear my head. "Jake?"

"Yeah?"

"It didn't sound like you."

"Katie?"

"I'm sorry I yelled and hung up on you." I switch the phone to my other hand and wait for him to say something. I wait a while. "Are you still there?"

"I've been meaning to call you."

Really?

"But this is a bad time. I'm on my way out."

"Oh." I realize I'm holding my breath and let it out in a gush. "Will you come to my graduation next week?" I sound so lame. I bite my tongue.

"Let me call you back when I can talk, okay?"

"Okay."

We say bye and he hangs up before I do. The dial tone sounds so shrill, it hurts my eardrum.

Every day waiting for Jake's call feels like penance. I have the house to myself tonight. Uncle Nack and Ursula went to Atlantic City on a casino trip with the church. The liquor cabinet in the bottom of the china closet has always been off limits, but tonight, I fill a juice glass with whiskey, adding some water to the brown glass bottle so you can't tell any is missing. After a few swigs, I dial Jake's number, determined to let the phone ring a hundred times if I have too, but after a few rings, a woman answers. She has one of those raspy voices that make you picture a cigarette hanging from the corner of her mouth.

"Can I talk to Jake?"

"He's out."

"Can you give him a message?"

"Who's this?"

"Katie." It comes out like some big excuse, like if it were written it would all be lower case letters.

You can hear the question in her tone when she repeats my name and clucks her tongue.

"Can you remind him my graduation is Saturday and I'm saving a ticket?"

"Got it," she says and hangs up.

Over the last few days, it's been one drama after another. The first was Cam springing the news that in a couple of weeks, she and Cannon are driving to California for a six-week-see-the-county-while-we're-young road trip. Like it's not enough that Jake vanished into thin air, or that Dennis spends half of the summer at baseball camp, now she's splitting for six frigging weeks.

The other commotion has been whether Mama would be too nervous to come to my graduation, but unlike no-show-Jake, she's here. After the ceremony, she stands in the aisle between Ursula and Uncle Nack, wearing a dumpy dress she probably got from the Salvation Army. The group home found her a job there sorting the donated clothes. Her pay goes right to the group home and they give her a small allowance. The Salvation Army lets her take clothes for free—which is good because she keeps putting on weight. Her face and the bags under her eyes always look puffy.

As soon as the ceremony ends, Cam and I hug like she's leaving tomorrow instead of in a couple of weeks. We walk arm and arm up the aisle before she hugs me again and splits off to find her parents. I head for Uncle Nack and Mama, who immediately picks up a bouquet of blue-tinted carnations that were lying on the empty seat that should have been Jake's. She hands them to me shyly. They smell like wet weeds and funeral parlor and remind me of Poppi. Dennis clicks away with the camera he gave me this morning for my graduation gift. I hold the flowers in front of my face to hide from him.

"Do you like them?" Mama asks. You can tell the way her lips keep moving after she asks that she's worried and counting.

Most of my classmates have roses in deep red or soft yellow to match our school colors. Across the aisle, Cam's bouquet is three times the size of mine, with long gold ribbons and sprays of baby's breath, but Mama probably spent her whole allowance for the week on the carnations. I cradle them in my arms, sniffing them again even though the smell turns my stomach. Mama looks down and picks imaginary lint off of her dress. I pat her on the arm. "Carnations are my favorite."

It's only a little white lie.

The Friday after graduation is the anniversary of Poppi's death. I know Uncle Nack knows it too, but neither of us says anything. We never do. Some years, we go to the cemetery a week or two before the day to put flowers on his grave, but with my graduation last weekend, we didn't go this year. Today, we work at the farm stand like it's any other day, like we are both afraid of what might happen to us if we admit what day it is.

Uncle Nack picks through the tomatoes, separating the ones that are getting soft to put them on the bargain table while I work the register. He doesn't know yet that I put off sending the deposit for nursing school when I missed my second period last week. He left the papers and the filled-out check on the kitchen table for me to take to the post office. Instead, I stuffed them under my underwear in my top bureau drawer.

This is the first day all week it hasn't rained. Everything feels soggy and smells damp. There are puddles everywhere and the mosquitoes are fierce. Now that Uncle Nack supplies produce to a few local restaurants, he cut back the hours at the farm stand during the week. That left me nothing to do all week but sulk around the house and listen to Jake's phone ring endlessly every time I called.

He finally answered the phone last night, and now it stopped raining today. It feels like a sign, like everything still could work out.

Hearing his voice last night made me so hopeful, I didn't even say hello. "I really need to talk to you," I blurted out.

"I've wanted to talk to you, too."

"Can you come over tonight?"

"How about tomorrow?"

"What time?"

"Seven-thirty. I'll meet you the same place as last time."

"Okay, see you there," I said, trying to sound more encouraged than I felt.

That means tonight. And the sun came out today. He has a decent job at the cannery. He could use the money he saved for art school and do the right thing.

After dinner, I walk across town to the Queen's Inn and lean against the fence with my thumbs hooked in the waistband of my shorts. My waist is so thick, these khakis are the only shorts I can fit into, but even they bite into my skin.

The Inn looks the same as it did when I waited here on prom night, except the garden is full of pink primroses and lavender. It makes the place look more romantic and feels like another good sign. The wicker basket on the gate is still damp from all the rain, and the brochures all have water stains along the edge.

My stomach churns like crazy. It's definitely too soon, but every time I sit still, it feels like something moves inside me. I try to never stay still. The sun starts to go down. I pace back and forth in front of the Inn, checking my watch so often I have to make myself put my arm behind my back and leave it there while I walk to the corner to look up the street. To keep from going nuts, I make a rule not to look at my watch until I am back in front of the Inn. Eight-thirty. I'm tired and I want to sit on the curb, but I'm afraid Jake won't see me. Something must have happened. I feel like someone out of an old heartbreak movie, the kind where he waits for her on top of the Empire State building but she gets hit by a car and never shows up. This cannot be happening. I check my watch again.

How did I let myself get into this mess? With all my might, I shake off the thought that he might not come.

By ten, I have to admit it. I walk home in the darkness, staying off the main streets where someone I know might see me.

Uncle Nack and Ursula sit on the porch rockers, drinking the sun tea Uncle Nack brews for hours outside in a glass jar.

"How was your night?" Ursula asks.

"Fine."

"Pull up a chair and I'll get you some tea."

There's no way I can sit here with them acting all honky-dory, drinking tea. "I'm kind of tired. I'm going up to bed."

Inside, I want to go right down the cellar, but the door always squeaks. They might hear it from the porch. Instead, I go to the fridge and pour a half glass of juice.

I tiptoe into the dark dining room, open the bottom of the china closet without turning on the light, pour from the first bottle, not even sure what it is.

In my bedroom, I lean my hands on the vanity and stare into the mirror for a long time. I look the same, but I know I am different, that my whole life is different now.

What made me think Jake would bail me out?

It seems stupid, but all I can think of is that prom night bartender, George. I wonder what my life could have been instead of this if he had looked harder at the small print on my fake license, held his ground, and refused to serve me.

But this is not his fault. It's mine. I screwed everything up. And all because I was too proud, or know-it-all, or just plain stupid to ask Dennis to the prom and drank that last stinger with Jake.

Chapter 26

It's mid-August, and I've made a million excuses to avoid Dennis since he returned home from his college baseball camp last week. Usually at this time of day, the only action at the farm stand is a straggler stopping on the way home from the beach to pick up corn on the cob, tomatoes, or onions for dinner, so I'm surprised to look up from settling the cash drawer to see Dennis's Mustang pull up. The tires kick up dust in the empty gravel parking lot. Like a reflex, I untie my change apron so it hangs loose in front.

"Hey there," he says shyly.

I nod my head in his direction, trying not to lose count. He looks so tan and muscular, it's hard to concentrate and I have to start over. He picks up a tomato, puts it down, examines the corn, fidgeting as if he's as uncomfortable as I am. Or maybe he's annoyed that I'm not paying attention to him.

"Need corn?"

"I'm here to talk to you," he says matter-of-factly, as if he didn't hear my mocking tone.

I rubber band the bills, write the total on a slip of paper, and tuck the paper into the rubber band.

"I'll finish up if you want to go with Dennis," Uncle Nack says.

They both look at me like I'm supposed to say something, but the only thought in my head is how do I get into his car without him noticing my belly bump?

Dennis opens the passenger door for me, walks around to his side, and buckles up. "You haven't returned my calls," he says.

Since it's not a question, I don't respond, just keep studying a crushed bug on the windshield—its guts smashed on the glass reminds me a lot of me.

Two fantasies got me through this summer. In the first one, Dennis gets down on one knee when I tell him. He can't stop saying he loves me, makes me promise to marry him, and be a family.

In my other fantasy, the doctor tells me it's all a big mistake. There's no baby, just a tumor, and they can probably cut it all out and save my life.

Dennis glances over at me when we catch the red light at Sunset and Broadway. "What's with the apron?"

"My shirt is stained with berries." There's no way I'm taking off this apron. I start humming along to Elton John on the radio to avoid saying anything else.

Dennis turns off Sunset Blvd. onto Sea Grove Avenue. I close my eyes, wishing I could undo all of it, go back to riding our bikes here, building imaginary houses.

Dennis parks near the old red-and-white convent where a few women, probably nuns, in dark skirts and white blouses rock on the porch. Their world looks so simple and serene. I envy them. Dennis makes small talk about heading back to school in a couple of weeks.

All summer, I have convinced myself that as long as no one knows the truth, my thickening body is just an obstacle, not a pregnancy; a problem, not a baby, but as my feet follow him over the shifting sand, each step makes it harder to pretend.

Wild beach flowers and weeds prickle my legs on the path through the dunes. Near the water's edge, people scour the beach for shells and Cape May diamonds. I sit in the sand in front of the dunes. "Let's stay back here," I say. A light breeze ruffles the beach grass beside me. I pull my knees up and squeeze them to my chest.

Dennis kicks off his sneakers, digging his toes into the sand. "Why are you avoiding me?"

A cloud blots the sun and turns the water dingy gray. I hug my legs tighter and lean my chin on my knee.

"What's wrong?" he presses.

"Who says something's wrong?"

"Is it because you stopped seeing Jake?"

"Who said I stopped seeing him?"

"Are you seeing him?"

"What's with the sixty-four questions?"

His neck turns blotchy red. He picks up a stone and skims it across the sand to the water. Even sitting down, he can skim a stone better than anybody I know. It bounces and makes little circles on the water's surface before it disappears into a wave. If only it could be that easy to toss away what's inside of me.

"I've missed you this summer." He stretches his legs straight out in front and picks up a handful of sand, opening his hand to let the sand sift slowly through his fingers before picking up another fistful. "Being apart made me realize how sometimes, when something is right in front of you, you can't see it. Do you know what I mean?"

I shrug skeptically. "Not really." My tone makes it clear I'm in no mood to figure it out.

He rubs his hands together to clean off the sand. "Do you want to go out? I mean, do you want to like, try dating?" The shy urgency in his voice breaks what is left of my heart.

My mouth drops open but nothing comes out. Then, as if I'm someone else, I start to laugh, a shrill loud noise that sounds like a frantic seagull. As suddenly as I started, I stop laughing and hide my face between my knees. The tears drip down my legs; my body won't stop shaking. The smell of greasy fried food in the air from the snack shack down the beach makes me queasy. When I finally look up again, Dennis's face has a look with no expression.

"I'm sorry." My voice sounds panicky and too loud in my ears.

Dennis scoots up to sit right in front of me. In the fading sunlight, the skin around his eyes looks drained of color. "Would you please tell me what's going on?"

Something inside me cracks wide open. "I'm pregnant."

Beyond his head, a cloud blots the sun. His eyes turn as dark as the water. "Holy shit. Holy frigging shit!"

I put my chin down on my knees. He rests his hand on my hair and moves my bangs back and forth with his thumb. "Are you sure?"

"My last period was April."

"Does Jake know?"

I want to say not yet, but I have to admit it's time to give up hope. I plunge my hands into the sand. "You must think I'm the world's biggest idiot."

Air whistles through his teeth. You can see in his eyes he's disappointed in me, but the thing I love most about him right this minute is, he doesn't say it. He doesn't say I told you so either.

I blow my nose on a wadded up tissue from my pocket. "I don't have the money for an abortion." I roll my lips together.

"Is that what you want?"

What I want is to know my father and have a mother who isn't nuts, to go back to before Poppi died and crawl into his lap. I want to never meet Jake, go to nursing school, live off campus, and party every weekend with Dennis.

"I wish I asked you to my prom," I say, sorrowfully.

He brushes my bangs out of my eyes. "I'll get you the money for an abortion if that's what you want."

A few mornings later, Dennis drives me to the abortion clinic in Camden. Planned Parenthood made the appointment for me the day before yesterday when they did the official pregnancy test. They said I really cut it close, and if I'm going to do it, it has to be this week. The air inside the car feels thick with humidity. I scrunch against the door, my cheek pressed to the glass while nothing passes before my eyes outside the window. We have hardly said two words during the eighty mile ride.

In the clinic parking lot, Dennis comes around to my side to open the door. I can't make my legs move to get out of the car.

"I can't go in," I whimper.

He reaches for my arm, but my hands are folded so tightly in my lap, my fingers throb. Tears run down my cheeks. I drop my chin to my chest. "What am I going to do?"

He squats down so we are eye level, but I can't look at him.

"I can't have a baby."

He gently strokes my wrist for what seems like a long time.

"Uncle Nack will kill me."

Dennis rummages through the glove compartment and hands me a fast food napkin. I cover my face with it. "How will I take care of it? I can't go to nursing school if I have a baby."

"It's after nine. You'll miss your appointment if we don't go in now."

"I don't think I can do it."

He heaves a long sigh. "Are you sure?"

The hiccups in my chest shake my whole body. I can't remember the last time I was sure about anything.

On the way home, Dennis plays a tape of strange music. There are no words, just chords that are hopeful and hopeless at the same time.

"What is that?"

"Alto flute. Do you like it?"

The music is so sad. There's no air in the car and after crying so hard, my eyes burn and feel puffy. I close them, and it's like I'm dreaming. There's Poppi, singing me to sleep in a voice so clear, I hear it like it's real. I love you truly, truly, I do.

It should make me happy to hear Poppi, but it just makes me feel more alone.

An hour later, Dennis pulls into the driveway in front of the house. "Do you want me to come in with you to tell Uncle Nack?"

I heave a sigh so huge, I feel emptied out. "I need to do this alone." I close the car door, take a few steps, and turn back. "Thanks anyway, Dennis." I watch him drive away before I walk into the house.

After dinner, Uncle Nack and I are in his car at Ferry Park. It surprised him when I asked if I could go with him to watch the new three-tiered ferryboat dock. It's still really humid. On the way here, I stuck my head out the window and let the air rush into my face. It made me breathless and reminded me of Sunday afternoons the summer after Poppi died when Uncle Nack used to put down the convertible top on his white Coupe de Ville caddy with the red interior to take me with him and Ursula on their Sunday drives. On the days Dennis didn't come with us, I had the entire back seat to myself. I would stretch my legs out on the seat, bend my neck way back against the armrest, and watch the world overhead rush by—telephone pole, telephone pole, treetop, telephone pole, birds on a wire, never-ending blue sky. With Frank Sinatra blaring from the radio while the wind gushed over me, I'd forget about Mama and Poppi for a while, just like I tried to forget about Jake and being pregnant this summer.

Uncle Nack stares out the windshield at the ferry when I blurt it out. His face goes flat, eyes shut, shaking his head. He grips the steering wheel with both hands and turns to me. Amazingly, he doesn't look angry

"It's not the end of the world," he says, haltingly.

"It's the end of mine."

"Worse things happen."

"What could be worse?"

He presses his palms into his temples, laces his fingers on top of his head, squeezes until his elbows almost touch in front as if he's trying to keep his skull from exploding. The way he mutters under his breath sounds like he might be praying.

After a few minutes, he turns sideways in his seat. "Some women, like your Aunt Nettie, can't have babies at all." He holds my hand firmly in his, looking into my eyes. "That's what's worse."

He pats my wrist and rests his hand reassuringly on my shoulder. "A baby," he whispers huskily, nodding his head a few times. "I can't say this is the way I'd pick. But we got this far, you and me, Number Two. We'll make this work out, too."

He sounds so full-hearted and self-assured. For the first time in months, I feel a flicker of hope that what he says about working this out may actually be true.

Chapter 27

My due date was six days ago. Since yesterday afternoon, there's been an ache in my lower back that might be the start of labor, but I do my best to ignore it. After all these months of following the doctor's order to not touch a drop of alcohol, I could really use a drink. I know I can't chance taking even a sip, so after a late lunch, I decide to distract myself by hanging a new shower liner in the upstairs bathroom. My hands are lifted over my head, feeling for the hole to stick in the shower hook when the first pain grips me—sharp and quick as a paper cut. I gulp a mouthful of air. The plastic liner smells like ripe fruit and reminds me of brand new dolls at Christmas.

When I was little, no matter what other present I got, I loved the baby dolls best. My favorite had a frilly white dress with lace at the neck and waist and a soft plastic head full of new doll smell and rust-tinted curls. She came with a pinwheel taffy, so I called her Lollipop Molly.

It's been years since I thought about Lollipop Molly. Remembering her today feels like some kind of sign.

I let go of the half-hung shower liner to hold my belly and sit on the edge of the tub. This cannot be happening. The pains have to stop. I'm not ready.

Massaging my belly, I stare up through the skylight. The clouds look like exhaust against the wintry sky.

Hiding my bulging body in the house all winter has felt like exile, but it's still better than what comes next, so completely unknown and never-ending. I sit on the edge of the tub, rubbing and gasping and willing the cramps to stop so the baby can stay put inside me. I sit for so long that the sky is dark the next time I glance up.

The doctor and Ursula both warned me about my water breaking, but I'm not ready for the wet trickling down my legs, either. I stuff a towel between my legs and creep back to my bedroom to change into dry sweatpants, calling downstairs to Uncle Nack to say I'm too full from lunch and I'm skipping dinner. I curl under the covers in my bed until one spasm hardly stops before another one starts. I try to stand up. The pain doubles me over and I know I can't wait any longer. I yell for Uncle Nack.

At the hospital, I start to finally understand what they mean when they say *I didn't know what hit me.* A nurse helps me out of the car into a wheelchair. Inside, people wearing green push and probe and poke things into me, gently scolding me for waiting so long. They wheel me away from Uncle Nack onto an elevator, down a hallway into a bright, shiny room, propping me on a table with my knees in the air. My doctor ducks under the green sheet draped over them.

"The baby is crowning," he says.

"It's what?" My voice sounds frantic.

A nurse strokes my arm. "It means he can see the baby's head." Another nurse jabs a big syringe into the tube in my arm, pushing the plunger. Warmth spreads up my vein and into my neck. All the green people running around start to look like giant artichokes.

"The baby's almost here," somebody tells me.

Shove it back in. I. Am. Not. Ready. Did I say it out loud or just think it? The room turns squishy and the lights seem so bright, it gets harder to keep my eyes open. Someone off in the distance keeps urging me to push. If she says it one more time, I might rip her lips off. My body feels torn in two.

"One. More. Good. Push, Katie."

"I can't," I screech.

"You can. Take a deep breath. Come on, honey, deeper. Now push."

I shriek and grunt and push until from that same far-off place comes a whimper and someone says she's beautiful and here, take a look. There are no words to describe the feelings in my chest and head when I peek at her. She is beautiful.

She really is.

I don't know how long I was in the recovery area yesterday, but I was exhausted when they wheeled me back to my room. Except for the hour when Uncle Nack was here and the few times the nurses brought Molly from the nursery, I slept most of the day.

After dinner, I called Mama to tell her she's a grandmother, but she didn't seem to grasp that it's me who had the baby. It was too hard to explain it to her without my roommate overhearing.

My roommate had a baby girl too, but her baby's daddy visits them. I pretend to be asleep when he's here, but

I watch through the slits in my eyes as he checks his new daughter the same way I checked Molly the first time they brought her in to me. He gingerly lifts the soft blanket like the baby is a delicate present in a layer of tissue paper, his fingers light on her ears and eyebrows before they travel down her shoulders, arms, and legs. Like me when I cuddle Molly, he seems mesmerized by the perfect pink nails on his baby's miniature fingers and toes. When he kisses his baby's fuzzy head, I roll on my side and focus on the silver threads of a spider web shimmering in the sunlight outside the window, not sure who or what I miss more—Poppi or a normal mother, my own father or the absence of Molly's.

The next time a nurse comes in, I ask her to pull the curtain.

A little later, there's a light knock on the door. You can hear the joy bubbling in Ursula's voice when she says, "You-who-hello."

I sit up. Everything below my waist throbs. Uncle Nack peers around the curtain, inching it open. Behind him, Ursula carries a bundle of pink roses and baby's breath.

Uncle Nack salutes from the bottom of the bed. Ursula hands the flowers to him to hold and pulls me into her arms for a comforting hug.

"How are you, sweetie?"

"Sore."

"I bet." She pouts her lips in sympathy and smoothes back the hair that's stuck to my cheek.

Uncle Nack hands me the flowers. They're wrapped in a receiving blanket instead of the usual cellophane and clipped with a diaper pin. It looks so special. You can tell Ursula took her time arranging it herself.

"Dennis sends his love. He would have come, but there's some big to-do going on at school."

I swallow my disappointment. What could be bigger than me having Molly?

"Did you get to see her?" I ask eagerly.

As if on cue, the nurse materializes, carrying Molly. "Grandparents get special privileges. They can visit the baby in your room." She winks and nestles Molly into Uncle Nack's waiting arms.

With no real grandparents in sight, it doesn't seem worth the trouble to correct her. Besides, it's a relief to be labeled a normal-looking family, even if that couldn't be further from the truth.

Right after Uncle Nack and Ursula leave, a different nurse comes in with a bottle. She casually asks me if I'm sure I don't want to change my mind and try breastfeeding.

I'm not about to admit to her that I nixed breastfeeding after reading in their brochures that you might hurt the baby if you have even one measly drink.

I shake my head. The way she presses her lips together, you can tell she doesn't approve of my decision. She hands over the bottle and lifts Molly onto the bed to show me how to swaddle her tight in her receiving blanket. She says it's supposed to make Molly feel like she's still inside of me, and it might fool Molly, but it doesn't fool me. Deep in my tissues, I already miss the memory of her curled-up body. Her kicks and nudges are imprinted on me, as much a part of me as I am a part of her. It feels like half of my heart is living outside my body now. This instant love, this knowing her from the inside out, terrifies me.

Did Mama feel this way about me when I was born? And if she did, how did she let me go?

Every time I'm alone with Molly, I recheck every inch of her body to make sure I didn't miss anything. Once I reassure myself her teeny body is perfect, I study her closer for signs of Jake, even though I don't really want her to be like him.

With her round brown eyes and tiny Nacaro nose, Molly resembles a sweet, shrunk-down Poppi. Uncle Nack claims the soft auburn-tinted fuzz on her head and her rosebud mouth come from Nonna's side of the family. Good, no Jake there. But, even at two days old, she is a child with her fists up. The way she presses them to her cheeks and raises them in thin air, you just know she will always get her way.

That must be the part she got from Jake.

On Saturday, we finally get to go home. Even though I can walk on my own, the nurses make me sit in a wheelchair to ride down to the lobby, where Uncle Nack picks us up. The nurse shows us again how to strap Molly into the carseat the hospital donated to us. It's nerve-wracking to think about taking Molly home. In the hospital, it was like I didn't really have to be a mother, no matter what happened, there's always someone who knows how to handle it. But at home—at home, it will be just Uncle Nack, and me, and Molly on our own.

Uncle Nack pulls slowly into the driveway, trying hard not to bump over the curb and unsettle Molly. Dennis's car is parked between the weeping cherry trees. My heart triple beats in my chest. Dennis sits on the porch, jiggling his leg up and down. Beside him, a life-size pink Flamingo wearing a maroon Glassboro State baseball cap sits on a rocking horse, the wooden kind, with a velvet seat and a red yarn tail. As soon as I see that hobbyhorse, I decide to name it Cheatin' Arthur after Poppi's favorite horse.

Dennis dashes down the steps and opens my door to help me out. I lift Molly from the carseat. The way Dennis grins down at her makes him look like he might bust wide open. He bounces from one foot to the other, trying to peek inside the blanket as we walk back up onto the porch. He picks up Cheatin' Arthur and follows us inside. I sit gingerly on the couch to take off the snowsuit Uncle Nack bought Molly. Dennis squeezes in beside me.

"Can I hold her?" he asks anxiously.

His face glows but you can tell by his deliberate movements when I place her in his stretched out arms he's afraid she might break.

"Like this," I say, carefully moving his hands so one of them cradles her neck and head and the other props up her back and butt the way the nurses showed me. He holds her like that, with his elbow on his knee, and gazes into her face for the longest time. It makes me a little jealous that the look is for Molly, not for me, but it makes me proud, too. "Will you . . ." I stop and swallow. "Do you want to be her godfather?"

"Damn straight." His eyes never leave her face. He gently stokes her cheek with his thumb, kissing her forehead. "Hey there little Molly. I'm your godfather."

The first week Molly and I are home, I leave messages for Campbell every other day to ask her to be godmother. Since she left for college last fall, I have only seen her one time, for like two hours over her Christmas break. She didn't say it, but I think she was still pissed at me for telling Dennis I was pregnant before I told her. Maybe she still is. Just when I decide to give up, she calls me back.

"Sorry it took me so long to call back. Between drama and my sorority and cheerleading, there's hardly time to study." She sounds breathless.

"I've been busy myself." I was going for nonchalant, but it comes out more self-pitying.

"God! Here I am talking about my school stuff and you have a baby. I can't believe you really have a baby." She says baby like it's a third world disease. My palms are sweaty. My heart thumps in my ears.

Across the phone line, something buzzes in the background. "Hold on a minute, I have to get the door." There's a rustling sound like she's pressing something over the receiver, then muted giggling, and she whispers, "I'll be ready in a minute, just have to get off the phone."

I feel totally dismissed, like talking to me is a great big hassle.

"I'm back," she says.

"Do you have to go?"

"We have a basketball game tonight. The Hurricanes could go all the way."

"Hurricanes?"

"Miami's basketball team. You must have heard of us. We're N.C.A.A."

I want to fire back *I'm M.O.M.* But I don't.

It's harder than I thought to talk to her. I don't know what I'll do if she says no. Unless you count Ursula, which would be totally weird, it's not like there's a clear second godmother choice. "Can you, you know, be Molly's godmother?"

"Molly? I didn't know that's what you named her."

"Yeah." If she asks me why I named her Molly, I'll make something up rather than say she's named after a doll. I'll say it was my great aunt's name.

She doesn't ask.

"So, can you?"

"Would love to, but I can't take time off from school to come home."

"Uncle Nack says we can wait until your spring break."

"Then sure, that's cool." We talk a few more minutes, but then she so quickly says goodbye to rush off to her basketball game, I forget to confirm her spring break dates. Instead of hanging up the phone right away, I stand still until my heartbeat slows down to match the drone of the dial tone.

On the day of Molly's christening, Uncle Nack drops us off in front of church and drives off to park the car. Dennis and Ursula take Molly inside. I wait out here for Cam. She was supposed to come to the house for pictures, but she's running late, so she's meeting us here. The cold air makes my nose run. There's a crick in my neck from falling asleep in the rocking chair again during Molly's middle-of-the-night feeding. I roll my head way back to stretch it out. The leafless tree limbs overhead look like a twisted road map against the blue-gray sky. From inside, you can hear the organ playing "Ave Maria." What if she changed her mind? What if she really hasn't forgiven me for telling Dennis first? Just when I'm ready to meltdown, she pulls up in her mother's black Volvo. Her hair is shorter than it has ever been—like an inch from crew-cut short.

"When did you get your hair cut?"

Her cropped hair makes her features look chiseled and gorgeous. She's dressed completely in black except for a red silk scarf tied at her neck. Her unbuttoned black coat shows off a black calf-length dress and sleek black boots.

"You never wear black," I say warily.

"It's my new thing." She offers me her cheek when I go to hug her, and we both end up kissing air.

"I was afraid you weren't coming," I blurt.

"What made you think that?"

"I thought you might still be mad at me?"

"Mad? For what?"

"You know, for telling Dennis first."

"No." She tugs on my arm. "Where do you get these ideas?" Her expression is so sincere, I decide I'm out of my mind.

I snort to make light of it, shrugging my shoulders. "Just new-mother-me freaking out."

"God, Katie, you're a freakin' mother!" She circles my wrist with her thumbs and forefingers, waggles both of my arms, pulling me in close for a real hug and kiss. Just like that, it feels like old times. Arm in arm, we walk inside.

After the ceremony, Ursula takes a detour to pick up Mama at her group home while the rest of us go back to the house. I'm in the kitchen getting gin and tonics for Cam's parents when Ursula arrives twenty minutes later. Alone.

"Where is she?"

Ursula pats my arm. "Sorry, honey. She's having a bad day. Her housemother, or whatever you call her, couldn't talk her out of her room."

I turn my back and clunk an ice cube into a glass. "No biggie," I say, feigning indifference.

"I'm really sorry." Ursula puts her arm around my shoulders for a quick squeeze.

I shrug her off. "Really, it's no big deal."

As soon as Ursula leaves the kitchen, I pour three fingers of gin into another glass and down it in one gulp. Even though it's been months since I've had a drink, the familiar burn feels good—maybe a little too good—going down. I rummage in the junk drawer, pop a Lifesaver mint into my mouth, paste an I-couldn't-care-less expression on my face, and head for the other room.

After I give Mr. and Mrs. McKee their drinks, Molly starts fussing in the lace-skirted cradle Uncle Nack and Ursula found at an estate sale. When I bend down to pick her up, the sweet smell of baby powder mingles with the fruity brown sugar from Ursula's pineapple-upside-down cake on the table next to the cradle. I walk about four steps when Dennis reaches out for Molly. Unlike his first time holding her, now he confidently bounces her lightly on his shoulder. She instantly stops fussing and coos, like after his shaky beginning, he has suddenly turned into an old baby-holding pro. Taking advantage of being baby-less for a few minutes, I walk around, looking for Joe and John Raymond. This is the first time I've seen them since last fall when they moved to Philadelphia for better-paying jobs on the assembly line at a drug company. Lots of young people think Cape May is backwater and boring, with mostly dead-end jobs, and they move to the city as soon as they can save up enough, but I was surprised when Joe and John moved. They always struck me as the type who would stay.

Near the kitchen, I step back into a shadow when I hear John say, "You have to give her credit for keeping it. A lot of girls don't these days."

"I know there's no way I would have," Cam says empathically.

For a second, it feels like total crap that they're gossiping about me, but then Dennis fills in the silence. "Katie's the strongest person I know."

Me? *Strong?*

"I hope she's proud," he adds.

Amazingly, the others murmur their agreement.

Suddenly, it dawns on me that the indescribable sensation, the phenomenal wonder I've felt since the first second I held Molly in my arms isn't just new-mother love.

I actually do feel proud.

Chapter 28

*W*alking Molly in her stroller every day must be doing some good because my old clothes fit again. Lots of days when we walk, we go back and forth near the Queen's Inn. As if time stopped the night Jake stood me up there and suddenly he will check his watch, remember, and come to rescue me.

It was Ursula's idea to take Jake to Family Court to get child support. At first, I couldn't imagine doing it, but when I went to the Welfare Office to get Molly government medical insurance, they told me I have to at least try to get money from Jake or Molly won't qualify.

Today is our court date, and I'm a basket case. If I don't soon make up my mind about what to wear, I'll be late. Since Molly's birth, I haven't had time to pay attention to how I dress, but Jake will be there. I'm determined to look eat-your-heart-out-the-one-who-got-away good. I finally settle on a soft apricot sweater that turns my eyes honey-brown and a short navy blue skirt that shows off the new, buff shape of my legs.

Rummaging through my drawer for the sweater, I find four airplane-size bottles of Southern Comfort. Cam brought them over the night I told her I was pregnant. She had taken them from her parents' liquor cabinet at their bed and breakfast inn. The doctor had already told me I couldn't drink, so I hid them in the sleeve of my sweater and forgot about them. Finding them today feels like some kind of omen. I hastily shove them to the bottom of the drawer and close it.

Uncle Nack and Ursula wanted to come with me today, but they might make a scene with Jake. They're babysitting instead. It wasn't easy, but I convinced Uncle Nack to lend me his car to drive myself to the courthouse.

For a month, everything has looked pea-green and wa-ter-logged, but today on the drive over, the sun is the same bright yellow as the daffodils. My paralegal from legal aid got here a few minutes after me. We sit on a wooden bench in the courtyard to go over my case. When we get up to go inside, there are wet lines on the back of our skirts from the damp bench. Hopefully, Jake won't notice.

Right inside the vestibule, we go through a metal detec-tor. The guard points us to a hallway, where we have to wait to be called. My paralegal sits, but I pace, back and forth until, out of the corner of my eye, I see Jake. The guy with Jake looks like a real lawyer. They both strut down the hall wearing the same cocky expression. I quickly plop down beside my paralegal, shrinking into my chair.

As they strut by, my paralegal nods at Jake's lawyer, but Jake won't look at me. He wears a dark blue blazer, jeans, and sneakers. It's a relief when he stares right past me and keeps walking. My stomach is such a jumble of nerves, if he made eye contact, I swear I might puke.

Forty-five minutes drag by before they finally call us into the courtroom. There's enough anger in Jake's eyes to fill up the whole room. After a guy upfront reads a bunch of legal mumbo-jumbo, the judge sits down. Jake's lawyer starts saying we don't even know if Jake is Molly's father. My paralegal jumps up and asks the judge to order tests to prove it. The judge looks like he might. Jake nudges his lawyer with his elbow and they start whispering.

"May we approach, Your Honor?" his lawyer says.

My paralegal goes up front with him to talk to the judge. After an eternity, she comes back to tell me Jake will pay $173.00 a month if I want to just settle it now. Uncle Nack will probably say Jake got off cheap, but I want this to be over, so I agree to sign the paper.

My paralegal has another case upstairs. She says goodbye to me in the hallway. Back outside, the sun makes me squint after the dim light in the courtroom. I fish in my pockets for the car keys while my eyes adjust. Jake and his lawyer shake hands on the top step, and his lawyer heads down the side steps. My brain tells me to go to the car quick and get out of here, but my legs just stand here. As soon as Jake sees me, he puts his head down and lets his breath out. I'm standing right in front of him, blocking the way, and there's no place for him to go.

"You could have just asked for the frigging money. You didn't have to drag me out of school and take me to court."

"You wouldn't talk to me."

"I would have if you showed up that night."

"What night?"

"The night we agreed to meet."

"You stood *me* up."

"I was there."

"I waited for two hours."

"I sat at the bar until after nine."

"The bar?" I'm totally confused.

"The Silver Dolphin."

"You said to meet you where we met before."

Deep lines crease his forehead. "Right. The Dolphin."

Tears sting the corners of my eyes. I blink to keep from crying. "I thought you meant the Queen's Inn." Without thinking, I move to one side and put my hand on his arm. As soon as I realize I'm touching him, I pull my hand back like a twelve-year-old. "You were *really* there?"

He grinds his fingertips into his eye sockets. A vein pulses at the side of his neck. Maybe his heart feels like a race boat in his chest, too. When he talks again, the harsh tone is gone. "I was there." He lets out a lungful of air.

The breeze picks up and a flag beside us flaps and clangs against the metal flagpole. "Can we go somewhere to talk?" I feel lightheaded.

He looks like he might say yes, but then he digs his hand into his pants pocket and pulls out his keys. "I need to get back to Virginia for my class tonight." He starts down the steps.

I touch his sleeve near his elbow and he turns around.

"Do you want to meet Molly?"

He bites his lip. His keys dangle in the air.

"I know you don't have time right now, but sometime?"

He looks down at my shoes. "I live in Virginia."

The crickets in the grass behind us chirp so loud, it feels like they are inside my head. I stomp my foot. "How can you just up and abandon us?"

He finally looks at me, but his eyes are distant, like in his head he's already on the road going south. "Don't worry. I have a job down there. You'll get your money."

He's lucky I can't find my keys. If he didn't get right into his car and pull away, if he took a little longer to unlock it or linger by the door, I might have had to run him over.

When I get home, my only thought is those four bottles of Southern Comfort, but I know I can't take even a sip before Molly is in bed. After dinner, I dress her in one of the kimonos she sleeps in and bundle her into the stroller for a long walk to tire her out. She's asleep by the time we get home. I can't take a chance of waking her and don't bother changing her diaper. I settle her into her crib and head straight for the bottom bureau drawer.

I open the first bottle. It smells like burnt honey, and is so sweet, at first I just take small sips. Whose idea was it to make a bottle this tiny? What a great big waste. I gulp it down and open bottle number two.

The next thing I know, there's a cat howling in my dream. It gets louder and through the fog, it dawns on me. It's Molly. My arms feel weightless and my legs are rubbery. I feel around in the dark crib for her binky to buy me some time. My head is numb as I make my way downstairs. When I get back with the bottle, she's crying again, but I feel too wasted to lift her, so I lean into the crib to change her, propping my chin on the crib rail while I hold her bottle. My eyes won't stay open. She cries every time I nod off and drop the bottle. Finally, she falls back to sleep.

The next time I open my eyes, the room is filled with bleak gray light, and Molly is crying again. My head feels too heavy when I try to lift it off my pillow. "Shush, baby," I say, but her cries get angrier and louder.

Uncle Nack taps on the door and tiptoes across the room to her crib.

"I'll get her," he says, waving me back to bed. He slings her blanket over his shoulder, holds her to his chest with one hand while he gropes in the crib for her empty bottle with the other.

As soon as he picks her up, you can see the spreading wet spot on her kimono. Her feet poke through the bottom where I forgot to retie the strings.

"She's soaked." His voice has a sharp edge.

We both notice the empty bottles strewn around my bed at the same time. All four bottles are empty. I remember downing the second one, but I swear I don't remember drinking the other two. He shoots me a disgusted look. Without a word, he abruptly turns and marches Molly out of the room.

I roll on my side with my pillow over my head.

When I wake up again, the room is lit with sunshine. I get right up, brush my teeth, stuff the empty bottles into a bag at the bottom of my trashcan, and head downstairs. At the kitchen table, Uncle Nack reads the newspaper, his hand resting on Molly's back while she sleeps across his lap on her stomach. As soon as I walk in, his lip starts twitching, like he has something he can't wait to say to me.

"You slept *awfully* late."

"Molly had me up half the night," I lie.

He folds the paper and plunks it on the table. "You were drinking?"

I turn my back to pour myself some coffee. "I had a rough day yesterday."

"Drinking isn't the answer."

I throw him a do-not-start expression.

"I told you I would go to court with you."

"Give me a break, okay?"

"You see what happened to your mother."

"I. Am. Not. Like. Her."

"We've talked about this."

I scowl into my coffee cup, at Molly, at a spot on the wall behind Uncle Nack's head. I drank one frigging time in umpteen months. Why does he have to make every little thing into such a huge deal?

When I finally make eye contact, the worry in his eyes reminds me of how Poppi used to look at Mama. I have to shut my eyes.

"What do you have to say for yourself?'
"Look, it was mistake. It won't happen again."

My tone is earnest, but Uncle Nack's pained expression makes me question if like me, he somehow hears the taunting little voice in my head, wondering if it's true.

Chapter 29

Ever since Molly turned six months old, she has this wide-eyed, unblinking way of studying me. It's like she figured out I have no idea how to be a mother, and she has to be constantly on guard. I pick up the baby powder and a clean diaper and say, "I'm going to change you now," searching her serious eyes for approval. She chews on her fist or punches the air, unconvinced. Most days, I watch her right back. It's like all of the time, we both have to keep up our guard to see what the other one will do next.

Molly eyes me now as I tuck her into the stroller for our walk to the annual Tomato Festival. It's almost a mile walk to Wilbraham Park, and the air is clogged with humidity. Like it's not bad enough that by the time we get there, I'm already sweaty and crabby. The first person I see is Mama with a band of misfits who can only be her housemates. Crap, what are they all doing here? Even though we only live about seven miles apart, I've never accidently run into my mother anywhere in the neighborhood before today.

I tug Molly's stroller behind a tree, duck my head under the canopy, and pretend to tie Molly's shoe, keeping my eyes on Mama. Her hair looks uncombed. She wears high-heeled sandals and what might be men's navy blue dress socks pulled up to her knees. Her white shorts show all the veins in her pale legs. You have to wonder if they have mirrors in her group home, or if maybe the people in charge who let her go out dressed like that are as wacko as she is.

Nearby, two women wearing shirts with dancing stick-people tomatoes on the front stop their conversation mid-sentence to gawk. They cackle that Mama's crew looks like something out of Mad Magazine's fashion dos and don'ts. In my heart, I know I should defend Mama, but seriously, who can blame them?

I wait behind the tree until Mama is at the far end of the park before walking briskly in the other direction. In the middle of the square near the bandstand, Uncle Nack's barber, Tony, plays an accordion and sings, "On the Way to Cape May."

A few booths up from where Tony sings, Ursula sells homemade salsa and tomato-basil muffins. There are embroidered tomatoes on the collar of her white shirt. She finishes a sale, kisses me on the cheek, and leans right into the stroller to play with Molly.

"Can I pick her up?" she asks, her arms already stretched out like she's going to anyway.

Most days, I admire how Ursula juggles so many things at once, but after just seeing Mama, it gets on my nerves. There she is, giving away free samples of her special-recipe, black-bean-tomato salsa in pleated paper cups. She effortlessly makes sales while she bounces Molly on her hip. The paperweights she uses to keep the copies of her recipe from blowing all over are plump rocks she painted to look like ripe red tomatoes. Every time someone picks up a free recipe, they ask if they can buy the paperweights. That's how cute they are.

She probably stayed up half the night painting the tomatoes, embroidering her shirt, soaking beans and dicing tomatoes, onions, and peppers from her garden to make the salsa, but she makes it look easy. Not like my mother, who dresses herself like a Looney Tunes character, would probably set the group home on fire if she tried to boil water, and has never even once held her granddaughter.

An hour later, when I get home, Uncle Nack is still at the farm stand. After putting Molly down for her nap, I steal down the cellar to fill a tumbler with wine. Since I ran into Mama today, I think I've earned the right to make an exception to my rule about never drinking before Molly's bedtime. Besides, Molly is asleep, and it's only a glass of wine.

It's after five when Uncle Nack's caddy rumbles up the driveway. I chug my wine and rinse the glass with dish detergent before he gets to the door.

As soon as we finish dinner, Dennis stops over to take a walk. Like most nights when we walk, he pushes the stroller and I march alongside. The headache that hasn't quit since I saw Mama throbs in my temples.

Any time this summer when Dennis and Molly and I did things together like taking walks like a little family, I daydreamed about him deciding not to go back to school so he can stay with Molly and me. But tonight, the way he yaks on and on about moving back to college next week, completely oblivious to my feelings, makes it infuriatingly clear that staying home with us never crossed his mind.

When we get to the promenade, we walk to the west end called The Cove. The bottom of the hot-pink sun dips into the ocean. Light pours down in shafts from the rose-tinted sky. There are still a few clusters of people lounging in beach chairs near the jetty, and most of the benches on the promenade are taken. Amazingly, my favorite bench at the end that looks out on the lighthouse is empty. I plop down to watch the sunset.

Dennis locks the brake on the stroller before he sits down. Molly waves her bare arms in the air. For most of August, just like earlier today, the humid temperature has been in the high nineties. Tonight, for the first time in weeks, there's a soft breeze off the ocean.

"Do you think it's too cool for her?" I ask uncertainly.

The way Dennis looks at me like I'm talking in pig Latin annoys me. "It's 90 degrees."

"But there's a breeze."

I touch Molly's belly to see if she feels chilly. She wears only a diaper because she has prickly heat on her tummy. Nobody says it, but I know they all think I did something wrong, like not change her often enough, or dress her when she was still damp after her bath, or slathered on baby oil when I should have used cornstarch.

Molly's face puckers, showing her one-sided dimple, just one more thing I worry about. "Do you think it's strange she only has one dimple?"

He raises his eyebrows. "It's cute."

"But, like, do you think it's normal?"

"I don't know," he says indifferently.

"Does it make her look funny?"

Dennis wrinkles his brows into a comical face, glancing from me to Molly and back at me. It pisses me off that he's not taking me seriously. Like, would it be so hard for him to reassure me?

Instead of letting it go, I tickle her chin until she smiles again. "Look at her. You don't think it makes her face lopsided?"

Dennis makes circles on the side of my head with his finger. "You're the lopsided one."

I slap his hand away. He's making my headache worse.

"Maybe it would help to make some new friends with babies who can give you perspective." He says it like he thinks he's my shrink.

"What's that supposed to mean?"

"You know, meet other young mothers, so you have something in common."

"So, now we have nothin' in common?" I snap.

"I didn't say that."

I ball my hands on my lap. "And how am I supposed to meet these young mothers?"

"Maybe if you took some classes or got a job."

I twist sideways to glare at him. "I have a job at the farm stand." The fact that he knows that this summer, Uncle Nack cut back and only opens the farm stand on weekends makes me even madder.

"I mean a *real* job."

It takes all my energy not to call him an asshole. "And what am I supposed to do with Molly?"

"Other single mothers work. My mother always did."

Heat rises in my cheeks. I swear to God, even though just a few hours ago, I compared Mama to Ursula, I am beyond ticked off now that Dennis dares compare her to me. I cross my arms over my chest to hide the dried spit-up stain on my top. "Obviously, I'm not your mother," I bark.

Dennis slightly inclines his head as if to remind me there are other people milling around who might hear us.

"I'm just saying . . ." He gets up and stands near the railing, blocking the sunset.

"Just saying what?" I hiss through my clenched teeth.

"I'm saying Molly doesn't have a father," he whispers hoarsely, looking down at his shoes. "She needs you to stop drinking and step up."

I shoot off the bench, my nose inches from his face. "Drinking has nothing to do with anything."

He takes a step backward. "I can smell it on you." He wrings his hands. "And your uncle said you've been sneaking it."

I poke my finger into his chest. "You people talk about me behind my back?"

He shushes me again, taking another step back closer to the railing, which is a good thing because I'm seriously ready to kick him in his shins.

"It's just Molly needs . . ."

I cut him off, stamping my foot. "Don't tell me what Molly needs. I'm the one raising her all by myself."

"We're trying to help."

"Well, I don't need your help. I don't need your mother acting like she's grandmother of the year, or Uncle Nack pretending he's Poppi. And I don't need you telling me what's best for Molly. What about what's best for me?"

I kick the stroller brake to release it. Molly falls back on her cushion. She laughs as if it's a game. But it is no game. The wheels run over Dennis's toes when I cut my turn too close. His mouth hangs open. Good, speechless for a friggin' change.

"And for the record, Molly does have a father. And, it's *not you.*" I grip the stroller handle and storm down the promenade.

The next day, all day, I wait by the phone for Dennis to call. I put off taking a shower and bathing Molly. I don't hang her diapers on the line outside so I can hear the phone when it rings. Through the kitchen screen door, I watch Uncle Nack trudge up and down each row of overgrown plants with his wheelbarrow, picking peppers and tomatoes. I've had to go to the bathroom for the last hour, but I'm holding it, sure the phone will ring as soon as I get in there. But it never does.

After Molly is in bed for the night, I'm still waiting, hunched on the couch, watching the phone, hands clasped so tightly in my lap, my fingers are numb. I sit here alone in a room full of shadows.

I don't know what time I finally gave up and came up to bed, or what just woke me up, but my whole body is damp. My temples thump so much, it feels like my heart is in my head. There's not a sound from Molly's crib. I stumble from my bed to kneel beside her and make sure she's breathing. It's too dark to see her chest move up and down. I rest my hand near her ribs until her heartbeat pulses against my palm and her moist breath warms my fingertips.

Every time I wake up sweating and afraid like this, I crawl back into bed promising to do better, to never sneak a drink again. Then I fall asleep and wake up and the sun is coming up. In the light of day, promises made in the dark seem childish and blown way out of proportion.

Chapter 30

*J*f anyone had tried to convince me Dennis would go back to school without calling or stopping over, I would have told them they were dead wrong. Now it's mid-September, and we still haven't talked and made up.

Since Labor Day, the farm stand has been closed for the season. My days are too long with nothing to do but take care of Molly. Walking her in her stroller for hours every day is the only thing that keeps me from totally losing my mind.

Today, there's a craft show on the promenade, and we wander among the stalls checking out lawn whirligigs painted like cardinals, blue jays, and eagles, Christmas ornament angels made out of Styrofoam egg cartons, and wooden clothespins painted like toy soldiers. One stall has an assortment of sweatshirts stenciled with red-trimmed lighthouses, pink starfish, pearly seashells, and V-shaped seagulls flying across the sunset. The sign on the stall says prison inmates stenciled the pictures on the shirts.

I stroll by the last stall and pick up my pace to trek down to The Cove at the end of the promenade. The sky is so clear, the lighthouse in the distance looks newly painted, and you can count the windows in the red-and-white convent at Cape May Point, even though it's a couple miles away.

This is the first time since the night of the fight with Dennis last month that I've come back to this exact spot. After all this time, it probably shouldn't bother me. But it does.

The way missing Dennis sneaks up on me when I least expect it reminds me of when you walk on a quiet street and out of nowhere, a dog comes running at you, barking wildly. How fear beats in your ears until you see the leash and know the dog can't reach you. How you have to walk a few blocks before your heart goes back to normal.

Being back at The Cove fills me with remorse. I quickly turn the stroller around and head for home. I know it's way too early in the day, but my only thought is hitting the bottle of whiskey I snuck out of the liquor cabinet last week and hid in the canvas beach umbrella bag in the woodshed.

I go through the motions of feeding Molly her lunch of pineapple cottage cheese baby food. To me, the stuff tastes yucky, but she really likes it. As soon as she finishes, I put her down for her nap and head out to the shed.

I'm unzipping the umbrella bag when my eye catches the Katie's Kraft Korner sign Poppi made all those years ago when we were going to sell the birdhouses we made together. It's stacked against the wall with old odds and ends pieces of picket fence. I walk over to get a closer look, fingering the pickets. They are all different sizes, left over from jobs Poppi did over the years.

Maybe because we were just at the craft show and saw how people create things you'd never expect from odds and ends. I can't say for sure, but when I look at those pickets, I see crayons lined up in a box.

I pick up a span of five pickets and study it at arm's length. Wired together with those pointed tops, it does look like a bunch of crayons. A kind of excitement I haven't felt for a long time tingles inside me. I stride over to the canvas bag and re-zip it, shove it under the workbench, and trot back into the house.

At the kitchen table, Uncle Nack reads the newspaper. It's only three o'clock, but the table is already set for dinner.

"Can I borrow the car while Molly naps?"

"Why?"

"The craft show gave me an idea of something I can make for Molly's room." My voice has this breathless sound. He raises his eyebrows like he wants to know more, but he doesn't ask, which is good, because I haven't worked the whole thing out yet.

He nods. I rush upstairs to get my money, tiptoeing into the bedroom so I don't wake up Molly.

My money is in an old mayonnaise jar on my bureau. Uncle Nack thinks it's dumb keeping money out in the open like that, but I like the way I can dump the money out easily when I need it. I pick the jar up carefully, so the change doesn't rattle, and pull out three fives and a one-dollar bill. There might not be enough to buy new brushes, but there's a coffee can of old ones in the shed.

Back downstairs, in the end table junk drawer, I find an old box of crayons and stuff them into my pocket to take with me.

Pete at the hardware store is an old friend of Poppi's. After I show him the crayons and tell him what I want to do, he's nice about explaining how to prime the wood and the difference between enamel and flat paint. After helping me pick red, green, blue, purple, and yellow enamel that are good matches for the crayon colors, along with some flat black for the labels, he shows me some hooks.

"You can use these to hang your work of art on the wall when you finish," he says encouragingly.

It feels nice how he calls it my work of art, so I buy the pack of hooks.

Molly is still napping when I get home. Uncle Nack agrees to watch her when she wakes up, and I go back to the shed to clean the dust and dead bugs off the top of the worktable. I'm lining up my paint and brushes in a row when I hear Uncle Nack's footsteps.

"Molly's still sleeping," he says, observing me curiously.

"Our extra long walk this morning must have tired her out."

He paces in the muted sunlight while I explain what I'm doing. The look on his face is part skeptical and part pride.

"Can you show me how to use the power saw?"

"What for?"

"To cut the pickets down to eighteen inches."

"I'll cut them for you."

Back when Poppi and I made the birdhouses together, he did all the wood cutting. I don't want to hurt Uncle Nack's feelings, but this time, I really want to do it myself. "I'd rather learn, if you don't mind showing me."

He takes off his glasses. He's still not used to wearing them all of the time. He's always taking them off to rub the red spots on the sides of his nose. The penetrating way he looks at me when he puts them back on makes me wonder if being at the workbench is making him miss Poppi, too.

While he sets up the saw, I run inside to make sure Molly is still sleeping. She's scrunched on her stomach with her butt up in the air. I pull her blanket up to her neck and hurry back out to the shed.

"This isn't a toy."

"I know."

"If you're careless, you could lose a fingertip." He wags a warning finger at me. "Or worse."

"I'll be careful," I say fervently.

He lectures a little longer. We practice on a few pickets until Uncle Nack is convinced I can do this on my own. He leaves to go check on Molly, and I work in the shed until dinnertime.

For the next week, I spend every extra minute in the woodshed. The hardest part is copying the crayon label, with its squiggly edge and oval in the center, but I figure out how to make a stencil out of a brown paper bag. It works perfectly.

The day my *work of art* is ready to hang on Molly's wall, I'm bursting with pride.

"Damn if that doesn't look just like five crayons standing up next to each other," Uncle Nack says, rubbing his chin. "Where did you get the idea?"

"Just thought of it."

"You could start a little business."

At first I think he's just being nice, but then he shows it off to Ursula, and she agrees. After dinner, we clear the dishes and sit at the table, thinking up ways I can sell them.

"You can make a few samples for me to display in the café," Ursula says heartily.

"And in the summer, we'll sell them at the farm stand," Uncle Nack adds.

"How much should I charge?" I ask doubtfully.

Ursula chirps right up, "Twelve dollars."

"Twelve dollars *each*?" It sounds like a lot of money to me, but they convince me to give it a try.

Three weeks later, I'm amazed when I already have four orders, plus the one Ursula sold right off the café's wall. She says they are big sellers with grandparents and for baby shower gifts.

Sixty dollars.

Yesterday, even after buying a ton more supplies, including extra colors to match all eight colors in the crayon box, I had enough money to buy Molly a fancy dress for Christmas, green velvet with a lace collar and cuffs and a red satin sash. I got it at the second-hand store, but you can tell it was never worn because it still has the tags on it. There was enough money left to stop at the garden center and buy smaller-size pickets, the kind you use for edging, so now I can take special orders in different sizes and colors.

It's good having the woodworking to pass the time because my birthday is only two weeks away and Dennis still hasn't come home or called. Every once in a while, like now, I dial his number. I always hang up if anyone answers. This time, just as it rings, Molly starts to fuss and distracts me. Before I can put the phone down someone says hello, but it's not Dennis. It's a girl. There is no way to hang up now. She can probably hear Molly in the background.

"Is Dennis there?" I ask self-consciously.

"He's at work. May I ask who is calling?"

What is she, some kind of secretary? Who talks like that on the phone? I imagine Dennis's apartment crowded with books, a baseball bat in the corner against the wall, the phone on a table with his glove and a ball. Her in the midst of his stuff, standing there sounding prissy.

Who is she? And why is she answering his phone?

A few hours later, when Ursula comes over for dinner, I make my voice sound nonchalant when I casually mention a girl answered Dennis's phone. Her face turns pink; she looks down. You can tell she's trying to be diplomatic when she says maybe it's his friend, MarieEleana.

What kind of person has a name like MarieEleana? Wouldn't a normal person want to be called just Marie or even Mimi? It doesn't even sound like a real name. Uncle Nack is at the sink, running hot water over the spaghetti in the colander. His neck bends in our direction like he's trying to eavesdrop. He turns off the water and empties the colander into the big spaghetti bowl. "Is she the new girlfriend?"

I almost drop the butter dish. How has nobody thought to tell me Dennis has a girlfriend?

Ursula gives Uncle Nack a look that makes him clamp his mouth shut. She lowers her eyes, compulsively straightening her silverware and napkin. "It's nothing serious. She's just a friend."

Right. Just a friend. Like that's supposed to make me feel better.

Do not get me started on what I know about being *just Dennis's friend.*

Chapter 31

The afternoon of my birthday, I bounce Molly's stroller over pinecones and dry patches in the straw-colored grass, pacing the lawn in big, loopy circles while we wait for the mailman. The sun isn't as bright as it was this morning, and my nose runs from the chill in the air. My pockets are empty, but I find a tissue in the compartment behind Molly's headrest. There's a blanket in here too, so I tuck it around her legs.

I can't see it yet, but in the distance, I hear the rumbling sound of the mail truck. The mailman finally pulls up and makes Jerry Lewis faces at Molly when I push the stroller up to the truck to take the stack of mail from him. I'm itching to go through it, but I don't want to look desperate. The truck pulls away, spewing stinky exhaust. My hands sweat as I thumb hastily through the stack. Under a Penney's catalogue and drug store circular are some bills and a blue envelope. I rip open a funny card from Cam, with a few lines of gossip about her new semester, signed miss you, love, Cam. I'm happy she remembered, but I can't shake the feeling that this is what is left of our friendship—all space and no phone calls, no present, a card with tidbits about her life that's signed miss you, but doesn't say *I hope to see you soon.*

I stuff the card into my pocket and check the pile again to make sure I didn't miss anything, but there's nothing from Dennis. He must really be holding a grudge to ignore my birthday.

Pressure builds behind my eyes. I blink furiously, refusing to cry on my birthday.

An hour later, I'm thinking about going to the wood shed to cheer myself up by putting the finishing touches on a wall hanging when the phone rings.

"I've been meaning to call." Dennis's tone is sheepish and uncertain, like he's as befuddled as me about the right thing to say.

For weeks, I've practiced the perfect comeback to make him sorry, but now that I have the chance, my mind is blank. Mostly, I'm just happy to hear his voice.

"I just called to say Happy Birthday," he says gingerly.

"I thought you forgot." My tone is meek.

"No."

"Or might still be, you know, mad." My voice cracks.

It's so quiet, I can hear him breathe in and out. I try to imagine what he looks like sitting there holding the phone, the glow from his reading lamp bathing his face, reflecting the turmoil in his clear blue eyes.

"Dennis?"

"Um."

"That night, I wasn't really mad at you. I was . . ." I switch the phone to my other ear, as if my mouth will work better on that side. Wrong. "Crap, I don't know."

He sighs loudly. "I think I understand."

"You do?"

"I didn't for a while, but I guess I do now."

"Maybe you can explain it to me." It was meant to be funny, but neither of us laughs. In the silence that follows, for the life of me, I can't think of a single thing to say.

"Did you get my birthday card?"

"You sent a card?" It's only part question. Mostly, it's an expression of whole-hearted relief.

"Yeah. Sorry it's late."

"That's okay."

"How's Molly?"

The change of topic throws me off balance. I'm pretty sure we should have more to say to each other about the fight and that one of us should apologize, but talking about Molly feels like much safer ground. "She can clap her hands and play so big."

"When do babies start to talk?"

"I'm trying to teach her to say Mommy. Uncle Nack swears she calls him Na-Na, but I think she's just babbling."

Babbling feels a little like what I'm doing. It's reassuring to be talking to him, but the sense of being connected and disconnected from him at the same time is confusing.

A few minutes later, when we hang up, I can't shake the feeling there was a ton more we both needed to say.

The next Saturday, I'm folding laundry when the bell rings. I bunch up Molly's overalls, drop them back into the laundry basket, and head to the door. On the other side of the streaky glass, Dennis looks so good, it takes all my self-control not to swing the door open and kiss him on the lips.

He follows me back into the living room. I move the laundry basket off the couch so we can sit down. For a few seconds, we just gawk at each other. Instead of the comb-back he's worn for years, his hair is parted on the side.

"What did you do to your hair?"

His cheeks turn pink. "My friend took me to her stylist." He doesn't have to say her name for me to know he means his *just friends*, friend, MarieEleana.

I look him up and down. You have to hand it to her. It's understated, but you don't have to look that close to see the change, the button-down shirt and preppy sweater, chinos, and boat shoes. The funny thing is, all those years looking at him since we were kids in backward baseball caps, hoodies, and untied Chuck Taylors, to me, he always looked exactly like he should.

He takes off what just might be a designer jacket and folds it over the rail of Molly's playpen like he might stay a while. "Did you have a good birthday?"

"One Hallmark minute after another."

He puckers his brow and just, like on the phone the other day, my joke falls flat.

"It was fine," I say lamely.

He reaches through the V-neck in his sweater, pulls a tan envelope out of his shirt pocket, and hands it to me.

I try to undo the flap without ripping it. A piece of parchment paper slips out and floats to the floor. Dennis picks it up and hands it to me.

I read the large print on the gift certificate out loud. "The Cape May Arts Center?"

"It's for woodworking classes," he says earnestly.

I'm not sure what I expected from him for my birthday, but this is *so* not it.

"They just opened in the old candy warehouse off of Perry Street."

"I saw them renovating it on one of my walks."

"I thought . . . you know. My mom showed me the crayon things you've been making."

A thrill flickers in my chest, like Dennis noticing my hobby makes it count for something.

Even though I purposely kept it secret from everyone else, confiding in him feels natural, and I spill about my plans to build a few more shelves and set up shop this summer on the side of the farm stand. I repainted the Katie's Kraft Korner sign to spiff it up.

"Maybe in class, I'll learn to make more stuff I can sell, like picture frames, or jewelry boxes, or those bird feeders that look like little houses."

He grins and leans in a little in my direction. His cologne has an unfamiliar, peppery smell. "The class starts next week," he says.

I fold the gift certificate back into the envelope. For a few seconds, I clutch it to my chest and smile back at him. Then I tuck it into the end table drawer so I don't lose it. For an awkward minute, we both sit grinning at each other with our arms crossed over our chests. "How long are you home for?"

He tells me he's going back tonight because he's taking six courses this semester and has to study constantly. He talks about the history final he aced last week and a work-study job he might take. I tell him about the like-new jack-in-the-box I found for Molly at the secondhand store—how she was afraid of it at first, but now she jiggles the crank and giggles. He talks about wishing he had enough time to read Larry McMurtry's novel, *Lonesome Dove* and to see the latest Rambo movie. We talk haltingly about everything like two people who know there is something huge they should be talking about instead, but we tiptoe around and don't mention our fight or his friend, MarieEleana.

I wake Molly from her nap a little early so he can play with her before he has to go. At the door, I shift Molly to my other hip and reach to touch his arm when he steps out onto the porch. He turns around.

"Thanks. The gift certificate is perfect."

I've daydreamed for years that the perfect gift from him would be a friendship ring, so it surprises me how much I actually mean it.

The following week on the first night of class, I must stand in front of my closet for an hour trying to figure out what to wear. Inside her crib, Molly squeezes the rail, bouncing up and down, scrutinizing my every move. Getting ready reminds me of September, when you're excited to go back to school to see your friends but keyed up about meeting the teacher. Across the room in her crib, Molly starts whimpering and jostling the crib rail.

"Almost done, Molly."

To let me know almost isn't soon enough, she jolts the rail with more force, shaking the entire crib.

I hastily settle on jeans and a long-sleeved red tee shirt with a scalloped trim and a little bow at the V-neck, hoping the outfit says capable of swinging a hammer without looking like a lumberjack.

With one last look in the mirror, I pluck Molly from her crib and carry her downstairs. At first, I was afraid Uncle Nack might not want to babysit every Tuesday night for a few months, but Ursula sealed the deal when she said she'll come over and help out. I hug Molly tight and kiss her all over her face. She laughs when I lick her neck, but then it's like she knows something is up because she starts to sniffle as soon as I hand her off to Uncle Nack and put on my coat.

She's usually good with Uncle Nack, but lately, she's becoming a Mama's girl. "Don't cry, Sweetie." I reach out to take her back from him, but he waves me off.

"She's fine," he says, but now she's crying for real.

I run back upstairs and get her favorite stuffed animal. "Here's Chickie." I tickle her under her chin, but she bats Chickie away, reaching her arms to me. She's crying so hard, her face looks maroon. I really don't want to miss my first class, but I feel torn. "Maybe I shouldn't go."

Uncle Nack bounces her up and down on his hip. "I'll take her into the kitchen for a cookie."

"Remember to turn on the night-light when you put her to bed," I say.

"I'll remember."

"And tuck Chickie in with her."

"Right."

"There's yogurt on the top shelf if she needs a bedtime snack." Why am I being so neurotic? It's not like he hasn't watched her a hundred times before.

His glasses are slipping down off his nose. He peers over the top of them, raises his eyebrows. "You're not going to the moon," he says so patiently, it highlights his impatience. With an apologetic little wave, I head out the front door.

As soon as I open the art center door, the smell of varnish fills the steamy air. There's no one in the lobby, but a handwritten sign on an easel says pottery is straight ahead and woodworking is in the basement.

A bare bulb hangs from the ceiling in the stairwell. I squint going down the steps until my eyes get adjusted. When I get to the bottom rung, all I see are three guys. From where I stand, I'd guess two of them are about thirty years old. The other one has white hair and a bushy mustache. Do not tell me there are just three guys and *me* in this class. I'm seriously thinking about going right back upstairs and out the door until this syrupy laugh rings out from the other side of the room.

"Hi, I'm Sunny." She starts walking toward me. I venture off the bottom step, and we shake. It's impossible to tell how old she is because she has almost-white blonde hair pulled back in a ponytail. Her painted-on brown eyebrows are too dark for her face. They have this deep horseshoe arch that makes her eyes look like wide-open exclamation points. She talks in exclamations, too. She says everything in doubles, like "I'm *truly, truly* glad to meet you," and "We're *really, really* going to have fun." After we shake, we walk across the room together to where the guys stand.

"I'm Ed, the instructor," the white-haired guy says. He looks down at the paper in his hand. "You must be Katie."

I nod and he says, "This here's John and Wayne."

Up close, you can definitely see they are brothers. Wayne is stockier and looks younger, but that might be because he's wearing a backward baseball cap so you can't tell if his hair is as thin as John's on top.

"I'm not usually good with names, but I think I'll remember John Wayne."

They all laugh. It's not all that funny, but them laughing makes me feel clever.

"That's *really, really*, hilarious," Sunny says.

Ed clears his throat. "It's just the five of us, so we might as well get started."

At first I think he's joking when he tells us that over the next ten weeks of class, we are going to build a shed.

A building, ten feet by twelve feet with working windows, a door, and shingled roof!

I expected arts and crafts, lawn ornaments, or duck decoys. We're making a *frigging* building!

The whole idea scares me silly.

And, incredibly, I am jump-up-and-down giddy and itching to get started.

Chapter 32

$\mathcal{I}$ cannot believe that the first time anyone bothered to mention that MarieEleana is coming for Thanksgiving dinner was three days ago when Uncle Nack casually dropped the bomb at dinner.

"How long have *you people* known." I waved my fork at him and Ursula, shooting them my snottiest look.

"*You people?*" Uncle Nack frowned, peering over his glasses at me.

At least Ursula had the good sense to look contrite.

"Unbelievable," I sneered, stabbing a piece of chicken parm and flinging it down on my plate.

Like nobody thought that tidbit might interest me?

Today, every time I think about meeting her, I feel queasy and disoriented, like when you ride in a train sitting backward. I try to take my time bathing Molly and getting us dressed. She's such a pretty baby; everybody says so. Today we both have to look our best, so even though it was supposed to be for Christmas, she's wearing her new green velvet dress. Yesterday at K-Mart, I splurged and bought cream tights and satin shoes that look like ballet slippers. With her auburn curls tied up on top of her head in a thin red velvet ribbon, she's cuter than Pebbles Flintstone.

For the first time in ages, my hair is set in electric curlers. To show off the muscles in my legs, I'm wearing one of the short skirts I used to wear to high school dances. At the second-hand store where I bought Molly's dress, I found myself a periwinkle blue, Jones New York sweater that looks brand new and feels like cashmere, even though it's a polyester blend. It has a sweetheart neckline, so instead of my Saint Jude medal, I dig through my jewelry box to find my silver crucifix that Mama gave me years ago. I haven't worn it for so long that it's tarnished. I hunt though the bottom of my closet for the jewelry cleaner. I find it way in the back under the felt shoe bag where I stashed the bottle of vodka I sweet-talked Joe and John Raymond's old friend, Charlie Tee, into getting for me when I ran into him near the liquor store last week.

Thank God the group home called yesterday to say my mother wants to stay there for Thanksgiving dinner. Part of me wishes she wanted to be here with me, but when it comes to my mother, we might as well live in a place called Cape Maybe—maybe she'll show up and maybe she won't.

Just as well, meeting MarieEleana is weird enough without worrying about my mother acting out.

After cleaning up my necklace, I dry it and clasp it on. The scoop neck frames it perfectly. I tighten the lid on the jewelry cleaner and carry Molly down to the kitchen where Uncle Nack opens a jar of black olives and drains the brine into a juice glass.

"Need help?"

"All under control." He takes a sip of the brine, licks his lips, and holds the glass out to me, obviously remembering drinking the salty brine is a favorite holiday habit of mine, too. "Want some, Number Two?"

He hasn't called me Number Two for a long time. I wonder what made him think of it today. Maybe it's the olive juice reminding him of holidays when Poppi grumbled at the way Uncle Nack and me rolled it around our tongues as if it was fine wine.

Poppi always made the same face at us, bottom lip turned down, tongue out, chin crumbled in on itself. I took tiny, little sips to stretch out drinking it, just so he would keep making that funny face. I smile at the memory, but with my stomach tied up in knots today, a shot of brine is about the last thing I need.

"Mind if I take Molly out for a walk?"

Uncle Nack shakes his head and arranges the olives next to the eggplant on the antipasto platter. I bundle Molly into her stroller.

Outside, the clouds are the color of ink. Chilly wind blows them across the indigo sky. Instead of bumping over weeds and up and down curbs, it's easier to walk in the street since most houses don't have sidewalks. We're moving fast up one street, over and down another; I don't slow down until my shinbones start to burn. By the time I turn to go home, the air is purplish gray and my calves ache. I forgot my gloves, and my fingertips feel numb and look a little blue. I pull the cuffs of my sweater down to cover them.

Ursula's van and an orange VW bug are parked in the driveway. What kind of person drives her own car instead of letting her boyfriend drive to a house she's never been to before? On the porch, I take my time lifting Molly out of the stroller, watching through the kitchen window as the three of them watch Uncle Nack sharpen the carving knife.

Ursula touches MarieEleana's arm and says something that makes them both smile. Dennis stuffs a piece of crispy skin into his mouth, his Adam's apple bobbing up and down when he swallows.

I smooth my hair, straighten the seams in my skirt, pick up Molly, and open the door.

Dennis looks the same, yet somehow different. He wears a faded blue denim shirt and jeans, his hair is a little longer, his tan faded, but that isn't it. There is something I can't put my finger on, like he's standing up straighter and has to look a little over my head when he says hello to me.

MarieEleana is nothing like I expected. All those nights lying in bed, calling her the Madame in my head, I imagined her as everything I'm not; long frizz-free blonde hair, blue eyes, a peachy-perfect, Ponds Cold Cream complexion. In reality, she's a little chunky, not fat, but healthy-looking, with short, straight hair almost the same color as mine. I can't tell if her eyes are brown or hazel because she keeps demurely looking down. Her face goes pink and blotchy when Dennis introduces us, as if she's been next to the hot oven for too long.

I cannot believe she's actually standing here in our kitchen. Her voice is soft. She sounds really sincere when she says how happy she is to finally meet me, making me think she had more time to get used to the idea of me than the few measly days I had to get used to the idea of her.

For a few minutes, everyone awkwardly stands around making a big to-do over Molly so we don't have to talk to each other. MarieEleana tickles Molly's chin with a toy stuffed turtle. Molly grabs for it and laughs.

"I got this for her at the animal shelter. Is it alright for her to have it?" MarieEleana asks politely.

"MarieEleana volunteers at the shelter." Dennis's smile drips with admiration and makes me want to puke. "She's going to be a vet."

MarieEleana's neck flushes bright red. Veterinary school is almost like medical school—she must be seriously smart. You can tell she's not comfortable with Dennis bragging about her. Her blush makes her look so genuine. I try to reassure myself it's probably all an act. But how do you make yourself blush?

Every time she asks me something about Molly, she has this way of staring into my eyes as if my answer is really important to her. Shit. I didn't plan on liking her. By now, I should be asking myself *what could he possibly be thinking*, but instead, I'm thinking—*smart, a car, no baby, socially responsible*. No wonder he likes her more than he likes me.

Uncle Nack pours wine from a gallon jug into a carafe. He hands the full carafe to Ursula to put on a tray with wine glasses and carry into the dining room. Uncle Nack picks up the turkey and they all follow Ursula, but I hand off Molly to Dennis and hang back to wash my hands. When they are out of sight, I gulp a few mouthfuls of Chianti right from the gallon jug.

As dinner progresses, if anyone has figured out the reason I offer to go back to the kitchen every time we need something, like more gravy or ice cubes, they don't mention it. By the time I get back from refilling the gravy boat, I've swigged enough that when I try to follow a conversation, my head has that out-of-body feeling that's like watching a TV program on fast forward.

Right after dinner, the phone rings. Uncle Nack is Ursula's emergency contact with her alarm company. Apparently, the alarm went off in the restaurant. The cops are there and there's not a problem, but she has to go over and reset it. Uncle Nack leaves with her. Dennis is in the living room, giving Molly her bottle. That leaves MarieEleana and me clearing the table.

"I'll wash," MarieEleana offers.

"We can leave them until later," I say, not relishing the idea of being captive in the kitchen with her.

"I don't mind." She turns on the spigot and squeezes a healthy stream of dish detergent into the sink. I grudgingly shake out the dishtowel.

A few minutes later, MarieEleana is placing a platter in the drain board when her finger clinks against a wine glass. One good look at that ring and my heart breaks. How did I not notice it earlier?

Last August, Dennis and I were in the gift shop at Cape May Point when I scrunched over the glass case to drool over that ring. When he asked the sales clerk about the stone, she said it was citrine, November's birthstone. She said it had the power of the sun to brighten the darkest mood. As she lifted it from the display case, she winked and said it was the perfect friendship ring because it brought harmony to relationships. I thought most of what she said was bull, but the way it sparkled when I tried it on felt like wearing a little sunset on my finger.

I had danced my fingers in the air in front of Dennis's face. "In case you need an idea for my birthday."

I was only half-kidding.

"It's not even your birthstone." He said it like it's some kind of mortal sin if you wear a ring that isn't your birthstone.

"Nice ring," I say cynically to MarieEleana.

The way she beams and delicately touches the ring with her fingertip, I'm guessing she totally missed the nastiness in my tone.

"I love the stone," she says dreamily.

"Yeah, me too." I clamp my lips shut before I can blurt that the ring should be mine—that I loved the friggin' stone first.

Even though part of me doesn't want to know, I can't help myself and keep asking MarieEleana questions about their *friendship*, determined to not flinch on the outside no matter how crappy it feels inside.

"We met in biology class last spring and ended up being lab partners."

I do a double take. All summer long on his walks with Molly and me while I fantasied about us being a family, was Dennis pining over her?

The pies warming in the oven make the whole kitchen too hot and mist up the storm door. I walk over and wipe a circle in the glass with the dishtowel. Pressing my forehead against the chilly window pane helps to clear my head. My breath re-fogs the glass. I close the door and go back to the sink to finish drying the dishes.

We're just wiping up the counters when Ursula and Uncle Nack get back. Dennis strolls in from the living room with Molly sleeping on his shoulder. I carefully take her from him. She stirs against my neck, whines, and yawns, but doesn't wake up.

"Ready for coffee?" Uncle Nack asks cheerfully.

MarieEleana wipes her hands on a dishtowel. "Sorry. I promised my parents I'd be home for dessert by seven, and I'm cutting it close."

The clock says twenty of six. "Where do you live?" I ask.

"Cherry Hill. It'll take about an hour and a half." She pats my hand where it rests on Molly's back. "I'm so glad we finally got to meet." Her tone and smile are so heartfelt, in spite of myself, I reflexively smile back.

She shakes Uncle Nack's hand. The way Ursula comfortably kisses her on the cheek, you can tell they've hugged each other that way before.

I keep my distance, following Dennis and MarieEleana to the front hall. A burst of cold air blows in when Dennis opens the front door. I hug Molly closer so she doesn't get a chill. Dennis holds MarieEleana's coat. She slips into it and he closes the door behind them. In the living room, I settle Molly into the playpen and cover her with a blanket. Her playpen is close to the front window. It's not my fault I can overhear Dennis and MarieEleana saying goodbye and kissing on the porch.

After a few excruciating minutes, Dennis comes in, rubbing the cold from his hands.

"Why didn't you go with her?" I ask meanly.

"I'm getting up early tomorrow to go hunting."

"Since when do you hunt?" I cross my arms over my chest. The fact that he has a whole life I know nothing about pisses me off and makes my life feel even more one-dimensional.

"I thought I'd try something new."

"Anything else *new* you haven't told me about?" I mean to sound flip, but my voice cracks.

He jams both hands into his pockets, his chin almost touching his chest. "I should have told you about MarieEleana."

I hiccup and cover my mouth with my fingers. "Ya think?"

"It sort of all happened right before Halloween, and I wanted to tell you in person."

"Oh, well, that explains it." I snort and plunk down on the couch.

He rises up a little on his toes before he slinks down on the other end of the couch and stares at his shoes. I dig Molly's pacifier from between the sofa cushions. I slip the pacifier on like a ring, shove my hand right up near his face, wiggling my fingers so he has to look at them.

"By the way, nice ring."

"Katie." His voice is gentle, almost a whisper, nothing like the shrill tone in mine.

"What's her birthstone?"

"Don't, Katie."

I pound my fists on my thighs. "When's her birthday?"

He takes a deep breath. "May."

I try to remember May's birthstone, opal? Maybe emerald or aquamarine? Not citrine. *Definitely not citrine.*

"The ring is what? Friendship? Going steady?" I know *exactly* what the ring is, but I want to make him say it.

"Why are you doing this?"

From the kitchen, Ursula calls us for dessert.

He tilts his head toward the kitchen. "They'll come looking for us if we don't go in."

I stare him down. "We'll be there in a few minutes," I holler into the kitchen.

He studies his fingernails. "I should have told you I was going steady."

"Damn right you should have."

The room is dead silent except for Molly's breathing.

"Do you love her?"

"Katie."

I know I should stop, but I can't. "Do you?" My head spins when I jump up too fast. I grab the side of the playpen to catch my balance, and the whole thing shakes. Molly's eyes shoot open and she whines.

Dennis reaches out to help me, but I shoot him an if-looks-could-kill warning that stops him in his tracks. Molly waves her fists in the air, fussing and crying.

Ursula comes in from the kitchen. You can tell she knows something is wrong because her eyebrows make deep furrows. "Everything okay in here?"

I scoff at her. Blood rushes to my head when I lean down to pick up Molly. "Perfect." I charge for the stairs to take Molly up to bed. "Everything is perfect."

Chapter 33

The next morning, Molly reaches both hands over her head, fists punching the air to let me know she's ready to get up. When I finally drag myself out of bed to change her, she won't stop rolling from side to side. The only thing keeping me from going insane while I try to fasten her diaper is imagining all the things that might break Dennis and MarieEleana up.

Maybe a baseball scout will draft Dennis and he'll leave her to play in the minor league in Florida. Or MarieEleana could have an old boyfriend who comes to his senses, shows up at school, and begs her to come back.

Maybe she'll come to her senses if somebody tells her Dennis is a Mama's boy with a lifelong crush on Cam.

I run out of breakup scenarios and carry Molly downstairs.

Uncle Nack left a note on the kitchen table saying he went up to Smeltzer's in Courthouse to order fertilizer. As soon as Molly eats the last spoonful of cereal, I bundle her into her pink snowsuit even though I haven't bathed her yet because my thoughts are driving me crazy and I really need fresh air. With Molly balanced on my hip, I wrestle the stroller out of the door onto the porch. Tires crunch gravel behind me. Ursula parks and gets out of her van. Her ski jacket is unzipped, and you can see her apron. She smells faintly of smoke and onions when she helps me lift the stroller down the steps. Her eyes look squinty and serious, like she wants to talk. I shoot her a don't-start look to make it clear that I am so not in the mood.

"Uncle Nack's not here," I say curtly.

She flinches and holds up a piece of paper. "I just came to drop off this order for three wall hangings."

I eye the paper but don't take it from her. The rest of my life sucks, but business is booming.

Ursula hesitates for a second, biting her lip. "Dennis told me you had an argument." She rubs her hands together and blows on her fingertips. The pity in her eyes is so obvious, I want to smack it off her face. "He didn't mean to hurt you."

See—Mama's boy. Like, he has to send his mother to apologize for him.

I duck my head under the stroller canopy and make myself busy straightening Molly's blanket. "You don't need to make excuses for him."

"He's concerned about you."

"Good to know." I bolt upright and start to push the stroller, but Ursula's in the middle of the path.

She touches the stroller canopy. "You know you can talk to me, Katie."

I shoot her a can't-budge-me-expression. "It's really none of your business."

She winces, like when you slam your finger in a door. "I better get back. We're serving tea for a holiday bed and breakfast tour." She rolls her lips together, zips up her jacket, and holds out the order paper again.

I feel so guilty for making her feel bad, I force myself to say thanks when I take it from her.

It's not her fault her son loves MarieEleana instead of me.

She kisses Molly and walks to the van, turning around before she gets in. Her eyes are glassy. "If you change your mind and want to talk, I'm here."

"I know," I say contritely, blinking like crazy to hold back the tears until she drives away.

It's a good thing Ursula dropped off those orders yesterday, because the only thing keeping me from polishing off the vodka hidden in my closet shoe bag is the growing batch of gift orders I have to make before the holidays.

Uncle Nack is watching Sunday afternoon football when I come down from putting Molly in her crib for her nap.

"Can you listen for Molly so I can work in the shed?"

He stuffs a handful of peanuts into his mouth and nods his head without taking his eyes off the TV.

Somewhere nearby, someone is burning leaves. Even though the air is icy, I leave the shed doors open wide so the smell of smoky cedar floats in with the hazy sunlight. Doves in the rafters make a racket, flapping around and cooing.

I'm working on five wall hangings at once. Just as I drop the blue paintbrush into a coffee can of turpentine and crouch down to pick up my green one, a foot emerges from behind the shed door. There's no mistaking that red converse. Dennis appears like a mirage in the shadowy light, emerging in sections as I look up: first the sneaker and pant leg, then his beltline, chest, and neck.

The surprise of seeing him catches me off balance and I wobble backward. He grabs my elbow, catching me before I topple over.

"Didn't mean to scare you."

I don't have a clue what to say. Are we even talking to each other?

"We need to talk." He pulls the string in his navy hood back and forth.

I let out my breath. "Yeah, we do."

He waits in the yard, and I go inside to get a jacket and check on Molly. She's sleeping on her stomach with her knees tucked under her and little spit bubbles between her open lips. I leave the door open to make sure Uncle Nack will hear her when she wakes up.

"Do you mind if I take a walk with Dennis?"

"Jeez. You gotta block," he says to the TV.

"Can I?"

"Be home for dinner," he says, never taking his eyes off the screen. He reaches into the empty peanut bowl.

I pick up the bowl. "I'll get you more peanuts before I go."

Walking to the beach, Dennis and I hardly talk, like now that we agreed to, neither of us has a thing to say.

A heavy mist shrouds the lighthouse, turning it to a smoky silhouette against the dreary sky. In my head, I'm praying, please God, let him say he broke up with her to be with me. From the way his chin almost touches his chest when he clears his throat, I know he won't.

He fiddles with his zipper, pulling it up and down in short, jerky motions. "I used to think someday we could be more than friends."

My body surges with nervous energy hearing him say the words I've waited forever to hear.

"Then you met Jake, and it seemed like you wanted to be with him."

My chest tightens. I stare mutely at my thumbnails.

"When he blew off your prom, I figured you would wise up; that I could wait him out. Then you told me you were pregnant, and . . ."

I steal a sideways glance at him. His eyes are glassy. His Adam's apple bobs up and down. I wish he would just say it and get it over with.

"I want to finish school, try to play professional baseball, save some money. A baby is more than I can handle. It's not that I don't care about you and Molly. But, I have a plan."

I wish I was smashed so I could *not* feel this.

Nobody knows his plan better than me—the sprawling house on Sea Grove with a picture window, porch swing, and perky wife. "I always thought we might end up together." My voice is so strangled and low, I'm not even sure I said it out loud.

His eyes are forced wide open like if he blinks, he knows he'll cry. "It's not like I planned for this to happen with MarieEleana. It just did. And the thing is, she has a plan, too."

The rush in my ears makes me lightheaded. Right this minute, I hate MarieEleana. I hate his plan even more than I hate myself for screwing up so bad, I can't be part of it. It feels like I am underwater, trying to hold my breath for too long, but instead of my past life, my future passes before my eyes.

I will not let myself cry in front of him. "Can you leave me alone now?" My voice is a hoarse whisper.

"Don't be mad."

"I'm not mad. I just want to be alone."

"I'll walk you home."

"Please." Without looking up, the rustle of fabric tells me he's fidgeting with his zipper again. "Just go."

He takes a few steps. "I'll call you tonight from school."

All I can do is nod. You can still hear the thud of his sneakers on the cement promenade when the tears start. Way out over the water, a lone seagull flaps its wings, fighting the wind. Against all that colorless ocean and sky, it seems as lonely as me.

Chapter 34

hank God I have my woodworking class to look forward to every week. At least for those few hours, I don't obsess about Dennis and MarieEleana.

In class, we spend half our time building the shed, and the other half on projects that Ed assigns each week. A few weeks ago, he taught us to make picture frames, and I started making all different sized painted and shellacked frames to sell along with my crayon hangings.

At the end of our last class, Ed gave us each a word and said we had to come back next week with our own original idea of something to make that fits the word. My word is quirky.

For the last five days, I have walked Molly all over Cape May, searching for ideas, checking out every whirly-gig, noticing decorative touches in the tilt of the roof on a bird-house, or little nuances in the slant of the perch. I make rough drawings in a sketchbook, determined to keep walk-ing until I come up with something brilliant for quirky. And, suddenly, I do.

On the night of class, I'm so worked up about my idea that I get to the art center early. I keep taking out my sketch-book to look at the drawings again. When I hear footsteps, I shove the book back into my canvas tote and fling it over my shoulder.

"Hey," Wayne says.

"Where's John?"

"Working." Wayne sits down beside me on the step.

While we wait for the others, Wayne tells me about his in-teresting life. He has two part-time jobs. He presses clothes at a dry cleaning plant during the day. At night, he works at a twenty-four-hour Mini-Mart in an action-packed section of Wildwood. Before he got here tonight, he watched the police make an arrest.

While he talks, I think about his thick, stubby arms, and how you can tell he's strong when he picks up wood. The muscles bulge and make his veins pop up. It's been a long time since I thought about a guy that way. As if he's reading my mind, he asks me what I think of his new mustache.

"It makes you look older," I say.

"That's what my girlfriend thinks," he agrees.

A girlfriend? Pop goes the fantasy balloon in my head. I try to seem casual when I ask, "What did you do for your word?"

"Shit, I forgot all about it."

Maybe I took this whole assignment thing way too seri-ously. A few minutes later, when Ed asks Sunny what she came up with for her word, *determined*, she goes into this long story about how her live-in-boyfriend left her after six-teen years and she's taking the class out of spite, to show him she *really, really* doesn't need a man around to fix a doorjamb, or repair the outside shower stall, which, from the sound of it, was broken the entire time they lived together. She says she is truly, truly *determined* to get over him, so every time she smacks a nail, she whispers his name. Her story takes about ten minutes, but she never actually tells us what she is going to make.

Now, I'm sure I got the project all wrong. Still, I might try that smack-the-nail thing with Jake.

Ed nods at Sonny, scratching his head. He checks his clipboard and smiles hopefully at me. "What did you come up with for quirky, Katie?"

"I don't think I did it right." I finger the edge of my sketchbook with my thumbnail.

"Show us what you've got."

"Well." I nervously lay my sketchbook across my lap. "My idea is to make doghouses shaped like dog heads." I breathe in deeply and open my book to a sketch of a basset hound's head with long, droopy ears and sad eyes. I'm still holding my breath when I flip the page to my sketch. "It's supposed to be a Labrador," I say sheepishly. "In case you can't tell from my drawing."

I expect them to laugh, but when I look up, Ed has a big, proud grin on his face. "Go on," he says encouragingly.

I trace the drawing with my fingertip. "You probably can't tell from the picture, but each face would have a different shape. The mouth would be the entrance and I'd paint eyes and a nose, but I need help figuring out how to make the shingles look like dog ears."

"Dog-faced doghouses," Ed says. He pats me on the back. "You get extra points for quirky and clever."

"I *really, really* love it," Sonny says, clapping.

Ed rubs his chin, deep in thought. "I'll help you work out the ear thing."

"Seriously?"

Wayne gives me a thumbs-up. "Make a German Shepherd, and I'll be your first customer."

I close my sketchbook and hug it to my chest.

I know it's just a doghouse, but it feels like a second chance.

Before I can start working on my first doghouse, I get swept up in the whirlwind of holiday orders for picture frames and wall hangings. By the time I catch my breath, it is mid-January, and Molly's first birthday is a few weeks away. I get distracted again, planning her birthday party.

I know it's a lot to ask, but I really hope Cam can come home for the party. I really want Molly to know her god-mother, not be like me, with only one memory of Aunt Helena. She grew up with my mother but moved to New York when I was a baby. My only memory of her is when she took me to a park with a swimming pool and a few amusement rides somewhere in Clementon, New Jersey. We went on the merry-go-round and she let me sit side-saddle on a white horse with a wreath of painted flowers around its neck. She held my waist, so I could lean forward each time we passed the long metal arm with the brass rings. Those rings seemed so special, but my arms were too short and no matter how far I stretched, I couldn't reach one. I wanted to keep riding until I got at least one ring, but they closed down the whole park after a thirteen-year-old boy hit his head jumping off the diving board. I understand it now, but back then, it seemed so unfair for them to stop the carousel and make everybody leave before I got that ring.

Aunt Helena still sends me a birthday card with a twenty-dollar bill every year, which is nice, but it would have meant more if she visited and spent time with me again.

"Beep-beep, you know the drill," Cam's answering machine message catches me off-guard. She's the first real person I ever called who has an answering machine. Mostly, I've seen them on commercials and TV shows. Talking into it makes me so nervous that after the beep, I say my whole name and sound like some kind of idiot.

It takes her almost a week to call me back.

"We're having a birthday party for Molly's first birthday in February. I thought if it's spring break, maybe you could come."

"Spring break is in March."

"Oh."

"Besides, my new boyfriend, Ben, is taking me to Fort Lauderdale for spring break."

"What happened to Cannon?"

"Ancient history."

How ancient can he be? They were still together in December when she was home during Christmas break.

"Ben's a philosophy major, of all things. He's a teaching assistant."

"You're dating a teacher?"

"A graduate student. He teaches part-time."

"I can't believe you broke up with Cannon."

"The whole distance thing. Anyway, Fort Lauderdale is *the* place for spring break. Just about my whole sorority is going. All anyone talks about is this bar called the Frog Pond where they serve seven green beers for a dollar."

"Sounds fun."

"So, how's my sensational god-baby?"

"She plays peek-a-boo and she's starting to talk. She calls Uncle Nack Nah-Nah and says tu-ca-ca when I put her down for a nap."

"Tu-ca-ca?"

"Her nap time is two o'clock. I always say, "It's two o'clock, naptime." So when she's sleepy, she says tu-ca-ca. Uncle Nack says it sounds like she's saying shit in Italian, but I think it's cute."

Cam laughs. We talk for a few more minutes before she has to get off.

"I'm really disappointed I'll miss her party, but I promise I'll make up for it at the end of the semester. I promise to always come up with something extra special for her birthdays." She sounds so sincere; my worries about Molly having anything less than an adoring godmother start to disappear.

All morning on the day of Molly's party, there are snow flurries off and on. On my way to the bakery to pick up Molly's cake, I look up and stick out my tongue, catching a big, airy flake that fizzes as it melts.

Molly's cake is a coconut-covered concoction in the shape of a kitten to match the kitten-covered paper tablecloth and plates I found for half price at the Dellas General Store.

Even with all my planning, it won't be much of a party. Joe and John Raymond couldn't come down from Philly, so it's just Ursula, Uncle Nack, Dennis and MarieEleana—and Mama, if she has her act together. At the last minute, I invited Cam's parents. They haven't seen Molly since summer. Mr. McKee is out of town at an innkeeper's conference, but Mrs. McKee is coming.

I wracked my brain for other people to invite, but unless you count Poppi's old friend, Pete from the hardware store, nobody else really knows Molly.

Molly wears the birthday dress Ursula bought her—a cornflower blue smock embroidered with tiny pink roses. It was nice of Ursula to give us the present early so Molly can wear it today. She gave her matching tights with ruffles on the butt and black patent leather shoes to go with it.

As usual, Molly wiggles so much while I dress her that she almost falls head first off the bed.

"Don't you want to look pretty for Mommy?"

"Ummummumm," she coos, chuckling and punching the air. She scrunches her toes until her foot is a tight little ball.

I tickle the soul of her foot. "Please let Mommy put on your pretty shoes."

By the time I get her new shoes on her and carry her downstairs, I'm seriously thinking I could use a drink. Ursula is in the kitchen, warming up the food. Mrs. McKee sits at the kitchen table folding napkins and talking to her.

"Oh, let me see." Mrs. McKee jumps up. Last summer, she cut off her waist-length braid and donated her hair to a place that makes wigs for ladies with cancer, but even with short hair she still looks like a hippie in her ankle-length denim jumper and lace-up boots.

Molly grips my index fingers and takes wobbly little steps. Uncle Nack comes up from the cellar, carrying a jug of wine.

"Let's go into the living room." Ursula dries her hands on a dishtowel and hangs it on the oven handle.

As soon as we get into the living room, there's a knock on the door.

"It's open," Uncle Nack bellows.

Dennis holds the door for MarieEleana. He follows her in, carrying a box wrapped in clown-covered paper, tied with a sunny, yellow ribbon. Dennis holds the box out to Molly. "Come to Uncle Dennis." He puts down the box and stretches out his arms to her.

I waddle her across the room. He picks her up, swings her up over his head, lowers her to make raspberries on her neck, pumps her back into the air. Molly shrieks with joy.

I take MarieEleana's coat from her. Her perfume tickles my nose when she brushes her cheek against mine in an air kiss. "It was so nice of you to invite me." She says it as if I had a choice.

"Say Uncle Den-Den," Dennis says to Molly.

After he repeats Den-Den about a hundred times Molly says, "Daah."

"Did you hear that?" he asks smugly.

MarieEleana gets cozy between Ursula and Mrs. McKee on the couch. Dennis kneels down, clapping and trying to get Molly to walk on her own, but she won't let go of the side of her playpen. I sit on the hassock and stretch out my hands to see if she'll come to me. She might say Dennis before she says Mommy, but if he thinks for one second that I'll let her walk to him instead of me when she takes her first step, he better get his head examined.

For a while, everyone talks at once: Mrs. McKee wants to know all about Molly, Ursula asks MarieEleana about school, Dennis asks Mrs. McKee about Cam and then he asks me about my woodworking class. We're making so much noise that Uncle Nack has to put two fingers in his mouth and whistle shrilly to get our attention when he comes out of the kitchen and says, "Let's eat."

After we finish our meatball and sausage sandwiches, Uncle Nack sits back in his chair and lights a cigar. I clear the table and decide to make coffee while I'm in the kitchen.

I'm just scooping the grounds into the coffee filter when Dennis comes in from the dining room.

"Need help?"

We haven't been alone in months. I'm surprised how much his being in here with me unnerves me. I lose count of how many scoops and have to dump the coffee back into the can to start over.

"Should I put the cake on that platter?" he asks.

I nod and he lifts the cake from the box. A glob of icing sticks to the lid. He runs his fingertip through it and licks it off.

"Mmm, coconut buttercream." He swipes another dollop and walks over to me. "Taste." He slips his finger into my mouth.

Sparks shoot up from my belly. It feels like the room goes into slow motion. From the surprise in his eyes, I know he feels it, too.

"Missed a smidge," he says softly, stroking my bottom lip with his fingertip. His thumb makes little circles under my chin. He takes a step closer to me, brushing my cheek with the back of his fingers.

It's hard to tell if either of us is breathing.

It's such a tiny movement, I sense more than see his head lean closer to mine, his lips slightly open. Just as I reach up to touch his fingers, I see MarieEleana out of the corner of my eye. He must see her at the same time because he jolts up, ramrod straight. I pretend to pick lint off his shoulder, but it's like our eyes are locked, and we can't look away fast enough. In the silence, I can hear myself swallow.

"Do you two need help?" The accusation in her tone splinters what's left of the spell.

He steps back and shoves both hands into his pockets. I turn in a circle, babbling inanely about needing a knife to smooth the icing over the bald spot on the cake.

The expression MarieEleana throws me is half question and half warning.

Dennis slinks across the kitchen. "We're pretty much finished." He touches her shoulder.

She turns abruptly. He trails her into the dining room without looking back at me.

Hours after they have all left, the remnants of the party are cleaned up. Molly sleeps soundly in her crib. I toss and turn, replaying the near-miss-kiss over and over in my head. I can't stop imagining what would have come next if MarieEleana hadn't come into the kitchen. How Dennis would have held my face in both his hands to kiss me, gently at first, our lips barely brushing, then deeper as his tongue explored mine. To stop obsessing about it, I press my pillow over my face and try to imagine a big neon warning sign flashing on Dennis's forehead. Impossible—Off limits—Belongs to Someone Else.

But my light switch must have a bad fuse. My caution sign keeps shorting out.

Chapter 35

It's been almost a month since the near-miss-kiss, with not even a peep from Dennis. Did it even really happen? Did I make the whole thing up?

Night after night, sleeping is impossible, tossing in bed, imagining what might have been. Last night, still awake at two a.m., I got out of bed and felt around in the bottom of my closet for the shoe bag, tipping the vodka bottle to my lips and emptying it before climbing back into bed.

Nights like that when I can't sleep, it doesn't really count as drinking. It's not about drinking at all—it's just about getting some sleep.

This afternoon, while Molly takes an extra-long nap, I'm in the woodshed with the radio up high, painting the finishing touches on the front panel of my first German

Shepard doghouse. While I work, I am acutely aware of two troubling thoughts. I still haven't worked out how to make the dog's ears—and last night's shoe bag bottle was the last of my stash. If I want to sleep again tonight, I need to find an excuse to borrow Uncle Nack's car and go to the Liquor Store. There's a little one in Rio Grande where nobody knows me. I must look older when I go in there with Molly because they hardly glance at my fake driver's license when they card me.

I finish painting the eyes and step back to inspect my work, holding the picture I'm copying from at arm's length in front of the doghouse. Satisfied that the eyes match up, I drop my paintbrush into a can of paint thinner, rub a smudge of black paint off my knuckle, and unplug the electric heater that spews lukewarm air into the chilly shed.

In the kitchen, Uncle Nack stands at the counter, dredging paper-thin slices of eggplant in breadcrumbs. Each slice sizzles when he lays it in the frying pan. I make a show of taking scrap paper and a pencil out of the junk drawer and sitting down at the table to write a list of paint and other supplies I need.

"Need anything from the hardware?" I try to sound off-handed.

"Hum, maybe some Elmer's glue."

I nod and add it to the list. From upstairs, you can hear the unmistakable sounds of Molly jabbering, finally awake from her nap.

"After I change Molly and give her a snack, can I borrow the car to go to the hardware?"

He forks the last slice of eggplant out of the frying pan and layers it in a baking dish, dousing the whole thing with gravy from a pot simmering on the back burner. "I'm finishing up. You can leave Molly here."

I clear my throat. "I'm gonna take her with me."

"It's cold out."

"The fresh air will do us both good." To cut the debate short, I scoot up from the table and head for the stairs.

An hour later, my hardware store purchases are on the floor on the passenger side, packed in the canvas store bag Pete gave me for free for being such a steady customer.

Now, I'm in the checkout line in the liquor store. Right next to the counter, there's a bucket of different fruity flavors of airplane-size brandy bottles. On the spur of the minute, I decide to treat myself, picking five or six flavors and placing them casually on the counter with the quart of vodka. I bounce Molly on my hip, making small talk about the weather with the cashier, while he speed reads my driver's license, takes my money, and puts my bottles into a brown bag with scraps of cut-up cardboard between them so they don't clink when I carry them.

Back in the car, I buckle Molly into her carseat and slip the brown bag of bottles into the hardware bag.

The sun is setting, and I decide to take the long way home through Wildwood Villas to catch the sunset along the bay. I start the car and reach into the bottle bag, twisting the bottle cap off the blueberry brandy with my teeth while I drive. At the bay, I park in front of a guard rail and turn to Molly in the backseat. "Look at the pretty sun Molly."

She chews her fist disinterestedly.

As the sun starts to dip, I polish off the blueberry brandy. All around me, the sky is fiery orange. I reach into my brown bag and decide to try the peach next. The sun sizzles and disappears into the dark water. The sky turns pinkish-red, but with most of the houses behind me closed up for the season and no streetlamps, the air turns midnight gray. I drop the empty peach bottle back into the bag, open the bottle of apple, and turn the car toward home.

The next thing I know, there's a tree trunk framed in my headlights, coming at me too fast. I have a split second of absolute certainty that there's a 50-50 chance I'll kill us both if I slam into that tree. I jerk the steering wheel hard to the left. My head smacks the side window. The car bucks and suddenly stops. When I open my eyes, all I see is murkiness in the haze from the headlights. Molly shrieks, "Ma-Ma-Ma," as if she doesn't see me sitting right in front of her.

"Mommy's right here." I unbuckle my seatbelt and half-crawl over the front seat, groping my hands over her face, legs, and arms. "Don't cry, baby." My voice sounds thick and sluggish.

Molly wails louder, twisting and punching the air. I can't stretch far enough to get her buckle undone.

I shake my head, looking around, trying to fathom where I am. Did I frigging fall asleep? There are snaky shadows on the windshield. And what's with the light in my eyes?

I squint at the silhouette holding a flashlight outside the window on Molly's side. *Uncle Nack?* He yanks the back door open, shining the light on Molly.

How did Uncle Nack get to the bay?

"Are you both okay?"

I nod, touching the growing lump over my ear where my head slammed the window.

"What the hell happened?" His voice echoes in my throbbing head.

Molly pounds the carseat with her fists, screeching, "O*ut-out-out.*"

Uncle Nack shoves the flashlight into his armpit to unbuckle her. He lifts her out and shifts the flashlight back to his hand to shine it upfront on me. An open bottle on the floor glares in the light's beam. Even in the dark, it's impossible not to see the mingling of sorrow and disgust on his face.

It's when he lifts Molly out of her car seat and I get out and blankly gawk around me that it all begins to sink in. That's *our* weeping willow I almost hit. How'd the car get in *our* driveway? I shake my head, trying desperately to remember driving home.

Molly sobs so hard, she can't catch her breath. I stretch my arms across the car hood. "I'll take her."

Uncle Nack ignores me, striding around the car to reach in and grab the car keys out of the ignition. He straightens up and slams the car door. "You're turning into your Goddamn mother."

I open my mouth to scream *I am not* but he turns his back to me and marches across the lawn.

I wait to hear the thud of the back door before I creep into the passenger side to gather the empty bottles and drag my bag off of the floor, shutting the car door quietly behind me.

In the shed, I wrap the empties in old, paint-stained newspaper and bury them in the bottom of a trash barrel. Unzipping the beach umbrella bag, I stash my leftover bottles in between the spokes of the umbrella. I push the zipped-up bag all the way to the back on the bottom shelf under the worktable, stacking pickets and the old window frames I recently started refinishing in front of it.

I tread guardedly across the dark yard to the back door, standing statue still, rubbing my egg-sized lump, listening until I'm sure there's not a sound coming from the kitchen. Inside, the only light is from the oven hood. Standing in the shadowy darkness, I make myself a promise.

This time, I will show him once and for all how wrong he is.

For the next sixty days I will totally not drink. There's no way someone with a drinking problem could work in the shed right next to those bottles every day for two entire months and not open them.

In the next sixty days, I'll prove to him—*and to me*—I am *not one sorry bit* like my mother.

Chapter 36

In the morning, it takes me over two hours after lifting my aching head off of my pillow, to stop procrastinating, dress Molly, and muster the courage to slink out of my bedroom. In the dining room, the bottom cabinet doors are open and the liquor shelf is empty. When I finally creep into the kitchen, Uncle Nack furiously rants about "the *stunad* episode with the car." The entire time, he hammers a metal bolt on the cellar door.

I open my mouth to say I don't know what, but he points the hammer at me.

"I do not want to hear it."

I shrink back. "I was just going to say I'll pay if there's anything to fix on the car," I stutter.

"Damn straight," he booms, securing a padlock through the hook and turning briskly to give me the evil eye. "I've got an errand." He stomps across the kitchen and out the door.

I don't let my breath out until the car disappears up the driveway.

A couple of hours later, Molly and I are in the living room watching a Sesame Street tape when he returns. He knocks around in the kitchen for a few minutes and heads back outside without coming in here or saying a word to me. Through the picture window, I watch him hunching over the flower bed, doing yard work. Every so often, he straightens up, brushes the dark mulch off his gloves, and stretches at the waist with his hands on his lower back, looking up, his lips moving as if he's still raving to the cloudless blue sky.

I venture into the kitchen while he's still out there to hurry and make lunch before he comes inside. AA and Al-Anon pamphlets are spread across my placemat.

My first instinct is to rip every single one into microscopic shreds. With my luck, he'll find a scrap and go off on another tirade. Without so much as a glance at them, I huff upstairs and shove them into my nightstand drawer.

For most of the next week, Uncle Nack brooded and I kept my distance.

One morning, I woke up to find an AA meeting schedule slipped under my bedroom door. That was over two weeks ago, and Uncle Nack has not said another word about the pamphlets, or schedule, or the "*stunad* episode with the car."

To keep my promise to myself, and make sure my head and hands are too busy to get into trouble for sixty days, I throw myself into building models for my first doghouses. With Ed's help, I solve the dog ear problem by adjusting the length and slope of the roof and creating plywood dog ear patterns that I cut out and paint. At the library, I check out every dog breed picture book. At night, after Molly is in bed, I pour over the photos, studying every aspect of each breed's head so I can precisely copy them. I methodically record every measurement in a notebook to help me repeat the same design again.

Although the climate inside our house was frigid for most of March, we made it through the month without any snow. Unexpectedly, we got twenty-one inches the first week of April. Uncle Nack strained his back hitching up the snow plow, and he couldn't clear the driveway. To make things worse, the arts center lost power and Ed cancelled class. Between no class for two weeks and Uncle Nack and Molly cranky with cabin fever, being snowbound almost did me in. It didn't help that I never heard from Dennis.

Somehow, in spite of all of it, I kept my promise and did not take a drink.

Finally yesterday, the weather warmed up and started melting the snow into rivulets that flow through the gutters and down the streets to the culvert.

This morning, the temperature hit an unseasonable sixty degrees. Now, vapors rise off what is left of the snow mounds, creating a fog so thick and steamy over the front lawn, you can hardly see beyond the porch rail. Everything smells like wet dirt and the pungent mulch Uncle Nack spread before last week's snow, when he expected an early spring. The fog is so thick, you can feel it on your face, taste the salt on your lips. It puddles on the tree leaves and drips off, so if you didn't know better, you would swear it must be raining.

Molly makes a game of it, toddling to one end of the porch and hiding in the haze. She stays there until I say, "Peek-a-boo, where's Molly?"

She giggles and totters out of the mist to the other end of the porch. She is at that age when she can do the same thing over and over like two hundred times. Just when I think I'll scream if she does it again, headlights break through the fog.

Dennis schleps out of the mist onto the porch. I blink, like he's not real, just an illusion rising in the hazy fog after a two-month hiatus. Without a word, he picks up Molly and swings her though the air.

"Dah, Dah, Dah," Molly gurgles.

For a split second, I foolhardily relish that it sounds like baby-talk for Daddy. The next instant, sanity returns and my heart sinks.

"Hey there?" There's an unmistakable hint of strain in the lines near his lips and under the forced airiness in his voice.

"Hey yourself." I slouch back, trying to look casual, like it's no big deal that he just materialized out of the mist, but I grip the chair arms so tightly, my fingers throb.

Dennis swirls Molly overhead again, tossing her a few inches into the air. She squeals with the kind of sheer joy I might have oozed if only that kiss had been real.

Dennis nuzzles Molly's neck and puts her down, sitting rigidly on the edge of the bench. You can tell that he's observing her so attentively to avoid glancing at me. I know him well enough to know there is something on his mind and that he won't bring whatever it is up until I'm wound up enough to want to unmercifully shake it out of him. You'd think after all this time I'd know some tactful way to get him to tell me what he's thinking and feeling. But I don't.

We both mutely watch Molly dash across the porch. She jiggles my hand. "Pee-boo."

I lift her to my lap.

Her little fists pump my arm. "No, no. Pee-boo." She twists and squirms until I put her back down.

I grope under my chair for her mesh bag of blocks, open the bag, and stack a few blocks into a short tower, grateful for the excuse to not look up at Dennis. "Help Mommy build a house."

She plops down on the damp porch, picks up a block in each hand, and claps them together.

Dennis squats beside her, and I instinctively straighten up in my chair. He stacks a few more blocks on top of mine. After a minute, Molly gets the hang of it, thudding her blocks on top. When it's several blocks high, she kicks gleefully and knocks it down. "Flat it," she says, delighted.

Dennis and I both laugh and for the briefest second, a smidge of the tension between us lifts.

"Flat it?" He asks without looking at me.

"I don't know where she got that—maybe from Uncle Nack."

The fog over the yard starts to evaporate as I sit here watching him play with Molly.

At lunchtime, he follows me into the kitchen. It's steamy in here with the aroma of fresh tomatoes and garlicky meat. Figures that as soon as Uncle Nack could get out of bed and stand up straight, the first thing he does is cook up a pot of his famous spaghetti gravy.

"Smells really good," Dennis says.

I strap Molly into her highchair.

Just then, Uncle Nack comes up from the cellar. "Well, look what the fog blew in." He deftly bolts the door and turns to clap Dennis on the shoulder. They shake hands. An odd look passes between them that gives me a little shiver, but then it's gone before I can figure out whatever it was.

"How's your back?"

"Gettin' there." Uncle Nack stirs the gravy and knocks his wooden spoon on the side of the pot before waving it at Dennis and me. "You two up for meatball sandwiches?"

I get dishes out of the cabinet to set the table. "I'll have mine on a plate."

"I'm in for the real deal," Dennis says, pulling up a kitchen chair.

Since we're having tomato gravy, instead of using one of Molly's baby bibs, I fasten an adult-size plastic Lobster House bib around her neck and tuck it in around her body.

Uncle Nack hands me a plate with two meatballs and mashes a meatball into Molly's Winnie the Pooh bowl. I blow on it for a few minutes, touching a piece to my lip to make sure it's not too hot for her.

"Beball, beball," she shrieks when I place the bowl on her tray and wrap her fingers around her spoon. Like always, she promptly flings the spoon onto the floor.

Dennis grasps his meatball sub with both hands and takes a huge bite, licking a drip of gravy off his bottom lip.

While we eat, I think I see *the look* pass between them again, but it's fleeting. Molly reaches her hand into her bowl, dumping teeny fistfuls of meat onto her tray and smearing it around. Eventually, she stops playing and starts eating right off of the tray.

"A finger painter, huh?" Dennis says between bites.

"Talented like her mother."

I have to say, I'm touched by the rare hint of pride in Uncle Nack's voice. I feel myself blush.

Dennis wipes his mouth with his napkin, peering in my direction but not quite into my eyes, more at my forehead, but it's as close as we've come to eye-contact since he got here. "How's all that going?"

"Good." I take a nervous sip of water. "I think."

"Get her to take you out to the shed to see the windows she's painting," Uncle Nack says with a little too much bluster in his voice.

I feel my cheeks go pink but before I can protest, Dennis pops his last nub of sandwich into his mouth and carries his plate to the sink. "I'm ready," he says, but something about the unease in his eyes tells me maybe, just like me, he's really not.

I get up slowly and wet a big wad of paper towel. "Just let me clean up Molly."

Uncle Nack swipes the towel from my hand. "You go. I'm good here," he says, taking one of Molly's hands in his and mopping it with the towel.

Outside, the sun is warmer than it was earlier and the fog is gone, but the awkwardness between Dennis and me is still heavy.

At the woodshed, I self-consciously hang back by the door. Dennis strides right over to my dog houses, stooping down to inspect every cranny and nuance. "You made these yourself?"

I nod.

"They're amazing."

"You think so?" I take a few steps closer—trying with all my might to see them through his eyes.

He strolls over to the corner of the workbench. "What's this?"

I follow his gaze to the wood-framed windows I've started to refinish. "The windows Uncle Nack mentioned. Poppi salvaged them from odd jobs over the years."

He picks up the porthole-shaped window and holds it up to the light. The sailboat floating on waves that I painted on the glass sparkles like a stained glass image. He whistles and his eyes meet mine—really looking right into me this time, reminding me of a look of Poppi's that I miss so much. The one that seemed to say *there is no one in the whole wide world that I am more proud of than you.*

I have to swallow to find my voice. "Do you think people will want to hang them like pictures—maybe on a wall that doesn't have a real window?" I pick up a larger, square window. I've already sanded and white-washed the distressed frame but haven't started to paint the glass. "I think I'll build a flowerbox on the front of this one—you know, like a planter, and then paint billowy white sheer curtains and a big sun on the pane."

"You *really* are talented." The heat in his eyes is achingly familiar. He tilts his head and his Adam's apple bobs, and instinctively my entire body knows that I didn't imagine that he was going to kiss me that night because every inch of me tingles with the same sensation now.

A blush washes over me. "Dennis?"

His expression is so intent, it almost makes me feel naked. I take a small step back, but manage to hold his gaze.

"Are we ever going to talk about it?" I murmur.

"It?" he asks uncertainly.

"I know I didn't imagine it. I know we almost kissed."

He shakes his head. "It shouldn't have happened."

"But it *almost* did."

He cracks his knuckles and nervously grinds his teeth.

"Is that why you didn't come home all those weeks?" I ask weakly.

"Yeah, but." He sighs and runs his fingers through his hair. "It's not just that." He studies his fingernails, his shoelaces, and some fascinating thing I cannot see on the floor. "I don't know how to talk to you about it."

My stomach clenches at the strain in his voice.

He leans heavily against a workhorse. "Your uncle told me . . ." he shuffles his feet and swallows before blurting, "I know about the drinking thing with the car."

"He's such a blabbermouth," I say so childishly that even to me, it sounds lame.

He waves his arm out over my dog houses, the crayon wall hangings in progress on the worktable, and my imagined flowerbox window. "Look at all this. You have *talent*."

Me? Talent?

He paces in a circle and pulls up short, shaking his head somberly at me. "And you're just throwing it all away."

I hug my arms around my middle. "Don't start."

Stepping over to the window, he unlatches and opens it a couple of inches, sucking in deeply. He turns and backs up against the sill. "You *have* to stop drinking."

"Do *not* go there." I spit out the words. Who the hell does he think he is? If he had bothered to ask instead of coming off like he knows it all, he'd know I'm more than halfway to my sixty days and have not had a drink. "What's it to you, anyway?"

"Molly was in the car with you."

It feels like a slap in the face.

"Every time you take a drink, you take a little piece of who you are away from her."

He sounds so ridiculously smug. If I wasn't so pissed, I'd laugh right in his face. "Don't preach at me." My tone is clipped.

He digs his hands so deep into his pockets, his shoulders hunch forward. "I can't do this anymore." His voice is strangled, like the words are choking him.

I clench my fists on my hips. "Who's asking you to? Go back to MarieEleana and live happily ever after." I stride angrily toward him, "And while you're at it . . ." I stop abruptly. His expression looks like he just got kneed in the balls.

He lets out a lungful of air. "We broke up."

"You *what?*" My body tenses in confusion. If I heard him right, what I should be feeling is overjoyed.

So why do I feel guilt?

I shag the rung of an old stool with my foot, drag it over, and slump down onto it. "Because of me?" I ask in a muffled voice.

He drops his head. I count my breaths going in and out, trying to control my racing heart.

"Because of *me*." He turns back to the window, blowing out a gust of air that puffs dust or bugs off the sill.

In the endless space of quiet, I watch his back until it starts to feel like time is standing still.

Finally, he turns around, catching my eye briefly before he looks away. "I've been going to Al-Anon," he says so quietly, I briefly think I must have heard him wrong.

"Al-Anon?" I blink, trying to comprehend.

"It's a group for."

"I *know* what it is," I snap, cutting him off.

His shoulders rise and then slump in some sort of apology. "I just wanted you to know." He slowly walks out of the shed, softly closing the door behind him, shutting out the daylight.

Because of me?

I know I should run after him and ask that question again. But sitting alone in the semi-darkness, the back of my neck prickles with fear, and I just don't have the guts.

Chapter 37

*O*n the long walk back to the house, my brain keeps arguing with itself—race into the house, away from those bottles—the other, obnoxiously loud side taunts me to screw the rest of the sixty days and beeline back to the shed.

Midway, I stop walking, cover my ears with my hands as if that will silence the nerve-wracking debate, and stare up at the smoky clouds blocking what little sun is left in this afternoon's sky. Sparse leaves are starting to bud on the zig-zagging tree branches overhead.

The pull of the umbrella bag is like a soul-sucking magnet.

It's an effort to push one foot robotically in front of the other until I reach the back kitchen door and fling myself inside.

Uncle Nack turns swiftly from the kitchen counter as I stalk into the kitchen. That fleeting secret that passed between Dennis and him blankets his eyes again, and I instantly know. *He knows.* The two of them are in cahoots, cooking up this scheme to ambush me.

I spin around. "It was Dennis who gave you those Al-Alon pamphlets, wasn't it?" I say accusingly.

He glances uneasily up at the ceiling as if maybe he'll find some defense written up there. "I'm the one who got them." He rubs his hands together in front as if they are really cold.

"You?" I slump against the doorjamb. "*You* go to those meetings?" I choke out the words, trying to swallow the panic rising in my throat.

He shakes his head. "I had to do *something.*"

Fury and shame collide in my head—how dare *these people*—him and Dennis, and I'm betting Ursula is in on this—go to these meetings and say God knows what about *Me.*

I feel like such a shit, it's impossible to make eye contact with him, and I can't think of anything to say. I guess he can't either, because for an awkwardly long minute, we gawk blindly over each other's heads.

Finally, he breaks the silence. "Do you want to talk about it?" His voice is low and gravelly.

Even if I could think of something to say, I'm too mortified and pissed right now to say it.

I shake my head, intent on leaving.

He takes a step in my direction, extending his hand toward a chair, inviting me to sit down. "We should talk." He sounds as worn down as me.

"I just want to lie down." Before he can say anything else, I head straight for the steps and wearily climb upstairs.

The angry tears start the second I lock my bedroom door. I tiptoe over and stand next to Molly's crib. Her chest rises and falls, rises and falls. Part of me wants to shake the crib rail until she wakes up and lets me hold her close. Instead, I place my hand over her heart and count her heartbeats with my fingertips. Tears leak off my chin and my breath makes little double-spaced hitches. I don't know how long I stand like that before I slink over to sit on the edge of the bed, wipe my face with a tissue, and rifle through my nightstand to pull out those brochures.

For the next hour, I sit rigidly, reading one after the other. When I get to the last one, I reshuffle so the AA ones—that I don't plan on reading again—are on the bottom of the pile and the Al-Anon ones are on top when I cram them all back into the drawer.

Later that night, when I finally fall asleep, Poppi comes to me in my dream, telling me it's time to shape up and get my act together. He calls me Scungilli and seems so real, I can almost smell his pipe smoke.

He stares right into my eyes. "You need to get your butt in gear, June."

"I'm not June, I'm Katie," my dream version of me reminds him.

His eyes fill up, and mine do, too. He slowly stands up to leave, but before he goes, he lifts my hand in both of his, smoothes his fingers over my open palm, and sings our goodnight song, "I love you truly."

I open my mouth to sing my part back to him, but no sound comes out.

I jolt awake. My cheeks are damp. The sun streams through the half-open blind slats so brightly this morning, no matter how tightly I close my eyes, I can't keep the light out. It's just as well. I don't want to fall back asleep and have that dream again.

Besides, Molly bounces in her crib, pointing at the crayon wall-hanging. "Geen, geen, geen."

"Green." I roll over, drying my cheeks on my pillowcase.

Molly shrieks, "Geen, geen," gripping the crib rail and shaking so hard, I'm afraid she might unhinge it and crash to the floor. I get up and lift her out, carrying her to the open window to pull up the blinds. She babbles and points to a ladybug crawling up the outside of the screen. I unhook the screen, reach around to catch it for her, and open her hand to lay it on her palm. My eyes sting with tears again, remembering how Poppi stroked my hand the same way in my dream.

The next week passes in a blur. Most nights, I dream of Poppi. Every morning, I reread the Al-Anon pamphlet with the list of questions that are supposed to help me decide if I've been affected by someone else's drinking and if Al-Anon is for me. By now it shouldn't surprise me that I get enough yes answers to totally ace the test.

Did Dennis and Uncle Nack ask themselves those same questions and get this many yeses about me?

On Friday afternoon, when I'm sure Uncle Nack will be outside for the next hour, I settle Molly into the playpen with her favorite toys. After putting a Big Bird tape into the VCR, I head upstairs, stretching the hall phone into my bedroom, and locking my bedroom door. While it rings on Dennis's end, I drum my fingers nervously on the receiver. By the time he answers, I am such a keyed-up human jumble, I don't even say hello.

"Will you take me to one of those meetings?" My heart races so wildly, it feels like an explosion in my chest.

On the other end of the line, Dennis noisily lets out a breath as if he's been holding it for too long. "There's a ten o'clock one at the hospital Sunday morning."

"Are you coming home this weekend?"

"I'll come home if you want to go." His voice is so protective, it gives me goose-bumps.

"I'll ask Uncle Nack to take Molly with him for breakfast at your mom's."

"I'll pick you up around nine-thirty," he says so decisively that fear and regret instantly start dogging me and I almost change my mind and tell him to forget it.

My hand shakes, and my stomach churns, and it takes all the willpower I've got not to back out. I say a hasty good-bye and hang up the phone.

On Sunday morning, by the time Dennis arrives, I have paced from one end of our driveway to the other about a zillion times.

I get into the Mustang at the curb. He must have just gotten his hair cut in the last day or two. It's crew-cut-short. And, yikes, what's with the reddish-blond fuzz on his lip?

"You're growing a mustache?"

"Yeah." He flicks his tongue over the corner of his lip. "What do you think?"

I wait a beat too long. "I like it."

He smirks to let me know he heard the fib in my tone. "No you don't."

I suck some air. "You caught me off-guard."

He scrunches his eyebrows, wagging his head. "Yeah, tell me about it."

I turn to him. The sun glares off the windshield into my eyes. I squint. "We're not talking about your mustache anymore, are we?"

He fidgets uneasily in his seat. "I'm really glad you're coming."

"Wish I could say the same." I cackle nervously because I can't think of anything else to do.

His eyes narrow sharply, but his smile is kind. He opens his mouth but before he says anything, I cut him off.

"Can we not talk about this now? I'm kind of a basket case."

He hesitates only a second before nodding and putting the car in gear.

The entire car ride, my stomach is one big knot, worrying the other people in the meeting already all hate me because of stuff that Dennis has said.

What if they ask me to talk? It scares me shitless it will all get more real if I have to admit anything out loud.

The visitor part of the hospital parking lot is nearly empty. I guess that's not unusual this early on a Sunday and at this time of year when there aren't many tourists getting stung by jellyfish or overdoing the sunburn.

I numbly follow Dennis into the hospital lobby, down the spic-and-span hall, and into the stairwell that goes to the basement. At the bottom of the stairs, we turn down another long hallway and pass a metal grate window rolled halfway up. After we turn another corner, you can hear water running, the clang of pots and dishes. Dennis points up the hall at a sign that says Café Conference Room. "We meet in there," he says.

A few steps from the meeting room, I stop abruptly, gripping the handle on the ladies room door. "I've got to make a pit stop."

Inside, I let the water run until it's cool, splash some on my face, wet a paper towel, and hold it to the back of my neck until my stomach settles down. I dry my hands on another towel, pant deeply, and walk out into the hall.

Dennis slouches against the wall with his hands in his pockets. "You okay?"

"I've been better."

I follow him into the room. A few old ladies give him a hug. He introduces me, saying it's my first time. They all say

"Welcome" with warm smiles. My reservations must show on my face because they take one look and thankfully, none of them try to hug me.

I look around to make sure there's no one I know. One whole side of the table is women. There's one dressed in a Hawaiian muumuu over a turtleneck and wearing huge hoop earrings, one with straw-like bleached blonde hair and a tulip tattoo above her wrist, and one wearing a long-sleeved orange tee shirt with a chartreuse scarf around her neck. At the far end, the old ladies just look like normal old ladies in cardigan sweaters and polyester pants. On the other side of the table, a girl around my age has on denim overalls and she's sitting next to a middle-aged guy with a ponytail and a diamond stud earring in one ear. There's only one other man, and the fluorescent ceiling light shines off his head. Dennis sits next to overalls-girl, and I sit edgily in the plastic folding chair next to his, trying to look like I fit in, in spite of not being entirely sure I really want to be here.

The meeting starts and they go around the room intro-ducing themselves with their first names, so I say my first name when they get to me. It's kind of weird how they all say welcome in unison, like they practiced it.

After the last person introduces themselves, one of the older women acts like she's in charge, reading a bunch of mumbo-jumbo, and then she asks who wants to share. I shrink into my folding chair, trying to be invisible.

The bald guy raises his hand. "You know, I've spent so much time feeling sorry for myself, cussing my alcoholic wife up one side and down the other for screwing up our kids that I missed the fact that my anger was hurting them, too. I know I owe them an amends."

Amends?

He adds that for now he makes amends by coming to meetings, but someday he hopes he has the courage to tell them he's sorry right to their face.

Oh.

When he's done, the tulip-tattoo blonde says her name is Kitty and that she's a double winner. She grins, showing a missing bottom front tooth.

I press my lips near Dennis's ear. "What's a double winner?"

"She's in Al-Anon *and* AA."

From where I'm sitting, I'd call that a double loser.

Kitty's voice is deep, kind of smoky. "Talk about owing an amends. Yesterday, instead of letting go and keeping my mouth shut, I tore into my teenage daughter about being too drunk to take care of her baby. She reminded me I'm not exactly mother of the year and brought up how scared she was the time when she was a year or two old and I left her sleeping in the back seat of the car all night. It was like a hundred degrees and I was so drunk from my brother's wedding, I just forgot she was there. She could have suffocated. Thank God the windows were open." Kitty shakes her head. "You'd think by now I could shut my trap and remember it's a disease."

I feel disoriented. All around the table, people nod. The guy with the ponytail says, "I hear you."

I must have heard her wrong when she said how old her daughter was when she forgot her in the car. There's no way a baby could remember if she was only one or two.

Back outside after the meeting, the wind is gustier than it was when we got here. It whips through the branches of the cherry blossoms at the edge of the parking lot. Petals flurry across the vacant parking spots, like the butterflies fluttering in my stomach. Dennis and I are quiet walking to the car.

He revs the engine a few times and turns sideways in the driver's seat. "What did you think of the meeting?" he asks anxiously.

I shrug, staring straight ahead, still mulling over what Kitty said. He seems to sense I'm not ready to talk yet and starts driving.

A few blocks later, we catch a red light and I drum up my nerve. "What's the first thing you remember?" I blurt out.

"From the meeting?"

"No. Like your first memory, from being a little kid?"

"I don't know."

The light changes. He shifts gears and the car grinds for a second. His eyebrows knit together. "Why?"

My lip trembles and just like that, I lose my courage. "Nothing. Never mind."

He shoots me a curious sideways glance for a second before returning his eyes to the road.

When we get back to the house, Uncle Nack's car is already in the driveway. Dennis drops me off without coming inside.

In the kitchen, Uncle Nack clears his throat and awkwardly asks me the same question about what I thought of the meeting. It makes me wonder if asking that question is part of the brainwashing they teach, just like how everyone says welcome in unison.

"It was okay." I look down at my hands, embarrassed. When I glance back at his face, there's such a sincere mixture of hope and worry and caring that something in me wants to reassure him. "I might go again," I say impulsively, surprising myself because it dawns on me, I might actually mean it.

He exhales noisily and looks a little relieved. "I go to the one at the library on Monday nights," he says self-consciously.

"Don't you play pinochle with Tony the Barber on Monday?" My voice drops off before the words are out of my mouth as it sinks in that's a white lie he's been telling me.

He shrugs apologetically and it hits me: he didn't tell me he goes on Monday as an invitation to go with him— more a heads-up so I know which meeting to avoid.

For the next couple of weeks, if Uncle Nack is around to babysit on Tuesday and Thursday nights, I walk to an Al-Anon meeting about a mile away on the other side of Cape May at the Lutheran church.

Tonight is my fourth meeting. Outside, the early May breeze is about seventy degrees, but in the church meeting room, something must have gone fluky with the air-conditioning and heat because it feels like ninety degrees in here. Around the table, people fan themselves with the leaflets. Tonight, Kitty wears a sleeveless shirt so, besides the tulip above her wrist, you can see the peace sign tattoo on her upper arm. She raises her hand to share, and like always, she starts by saying she's a double winner as if that makes her special. "My eighteen-year-old daughter just told me she's pregnant. *Again.*" She folds her arms on the table in front of her, elbows pointed out. "Says she doesn't know how it happened." Kitty leans so far forward, she's almost laying on the table. "Don't get me wrong, I love my kid, but you'd think after following in my footsteps and getting knocked up the first time at sixteen, she'd know that getting shit-faced drunk causes pregnancy."

Everyone but me laughs. For me, it hits too close to home. I never blame being drunk for getting pregnant. I always blame getting pregnant on Jake.

After the meeting, Kitty's words replay, replay, replay in my head. To give me more time to think, I take a detour down the Washington Street mall instead of walking home the more direct route.

It's one of those early May nights when the stores are having a sidewalk sale and lots of people stroll on the mall. It's early in the season for tourists, but a few young kids in flip-flops and souvenir hats sit on benches, slurping water ice while their parents shop nearby. Teens hang between the music store and the nut store, splitting pumpkins seeds with their front teeth, vying to see who can spit the shells the farthest.

My throat is dry from the stifling heat in the church, and I decide to get fresh-squeezed lemonade, waiting in a line so long, it snakes in front of the sidewalk bistro next door. The bistro's exhaust fan spews cooked-whiskey-smelling steam right into my face. I fill up my lungs, hungry to drink the smell in. Beside me, a couple at a small, round table orders two Manhattans, one straight up, one rocks. Needing a drink hits me out of nowhere, like a bug going splat on the windshield. I suck in more of the steam, wildly imagining that the waitress turns around and asks me if I'd like a Manhattan, too. Yes. Yes. Yes. In my mind's eye, I see myself stealing the couple's drinks when the waitress brings them, dashing away, ducking into an alcove to chug them. I can almost taste the burn going down.

I bolt from the line, darting blindly down the alley between the stores. My shins burn and I pant, but I don't stop running until I'm at home.

I mumble a hasty goodnight to Uncle Nack and climb right up to my room. It's not until I'm standing next to Molly's crib, watching her perfect lips pucker in her sleep that I finally calm down.

Molly clenches her favorite Chickie in her sweet grip. I bend into the crib to unravel her fingers and lift her. She whinnies and her eyes open briefly. I clutch her to my chest, wrap her tiny hand around a tuft of my hair, and settle into the rocking chair.

I don't care if she does wakes up. I'll hang on to her and rock her all night if that's what it takes to stay here where I belong and guard us both from the bottles in the shed.

Chapter 38

On Mother's Day, even though the group home where Mama lives gives me the heebie-jeebies, my conscience gets the best of me when Uncle Nack and Ursula urge me to visit her.

Mama sits on the sofa—the kind with nubs in the fabric that always makes you itch—in a cloud of her own cigarette smoke. Like every other time I've been here, her group home smells like dirty ashtrays, mothballs, and cooked cabbage. Mama's lips move endlessly, so I know she's counting.

"Happy Mother's Day," I say guardedly.

Her eyes never leave the ancient Shirley Temple movie on TV. Every few seconds, a black line runs across the TV screen. It would drive me nuts to watch the picture keep blipping like that, but she doesn't seem to notice.

"We brought Molly to visit." I keep my distance on the other side of the big tree stump they use as a coffee table, bouncing Molly on my hip to keep her still, but she just keeps squirming. In spite of myself, I yearn for Mama to just once open her arms eagerly to embrace Molly—and me.

Out of nowhere, Mama's housemate, Catherine, appears and turns off the television. She wears a plastic Lobster House bib, like the one I sometimes use with Molly, over a faded-mauve velour dress and ballet slippers. The way she snuck up behind us to turn the TV off makes me think what they say about her being here because she tried to burn down her house while her husband slept inside just might be true.

Mama flings her cigarette clear across the room at Catherine. "I'm watching that," she rants.

"Now, now, June." Uncle Nack picks up her cigarette and stubs it out in an ashtray.

"You have guests." Catherine's syrupy voice gives me goose-bumps, the way she sounds like one of the crazy old biddies in *Arsenic and Old Lace*. A few weeks ago, I watched that movie in the middle of the night when Molly had the croup. I walked her around the living room all night, afraid if I put her down, she might choke in her sleep.

Mama stands up and starts wringing her hands, circling the tree stump, muttering. Her voice has a thick, guttural sound, like she's gargling with words.

"TV's rude with company," Catherine scolds, making a tsking sound with her tongue.

"We don't mind," Uncle Nack says meekly, like maybe he believes the story about her husband, too, and doesn't want to piss her off.

Catherine's cheeks turn crimson. She chants, "It is rude, rude, rude," tucking her hands up under her bib and backing out of the room like a shifty nun.

Maybe this visit would be going smoother if Martha who runs the place was here, but she's visiting her family in Philadelphia. The fill-in houseparent, Tom, is nowhere in sight. You'd think someone responsible enough to be a houseparent for nutcases would stick around during visits.

Uncle Nack keeps readjusting the dials in back of the TV, but now there's so much snow on the screen, it's like watching a blizzard. He stops and says, "I'm going to the bathroom."

Molly thumps my chest with her balled-up fists to get me to put her down. To quiet her, I undo the buttons on the pink Easter coat Uncle Nack bought her and wave her terry cloth rabbit in her face. She reaches for it, but at the last second grabs my hair and pulls so hard, she bends me nearly in half.

"Ouch," I yelp.

Mama laughs a tittering little laugh. Do not ask me why Molly pulling my hair calms Mama, but she still giggles to herself as she settles back down on the couch. With no TV to watch, she peeps over at Molly and me. There are dark circles under her eyes. She has this new habit of sucking in her lips, so her chin sort of shrivels and gives the appearance that she has no teeth. Her hair is all gray at the temples. If you didn't know better, you'd never guess she isn't even forty.

"Pretty baby," she says in baby talk, stretching her arms to Molly as if she might want to hug her. The way she keeps her hands flat out in front reminds me of when I was four or five and Poppi taught me to float in the ocean. I felt so safe in the water, with my back and legs straddled across his solid hands. More than anything, I want Molly to feel protected like that in Mama's arms. I sit beside her on the couch and slide the ashtray to the other side of the tree stump to keep the smoke away from Molly.

Mama strokes Molly's hair, coiling one of Molly's curls around her finger. "My mother's hair was that color," she mutters distantly.

"Uncle Nack says that, too."

She looks Molly up and down, more curious than tender. "She doesn't look much like you."

"I think she looks like Poppi."

"God forbid." She scrunches up her face until there are deep creases in the corners of her eyes.

"What's wrong with being like Poppi?"

She puffs up her cheeks. Air hisses through her lips. "He was evil."

"Poppi?"

"Big fat liar." Thick spit dots the corners of her mouth. "He *stole* you from me."

A fiery flash of anger explodes in my head. "You *let* him."

Her face twists up and turns almost purple. "You better agree with me."

I jut out my chin. "I won't say anything bad about Poppi."

"You know what it's like to lose your baby girl?" She grips Molly by the shoulders and shakes her. "If I smash this baby's head against this tree trunk, you'll know."

I pry open her fingers and grab Molly so quickly, she howls. "What is wrong with you?" I scream.

And what is wrong with me?

It feels like we're in slow motion. Mama's eyes go blank. I back away from her, pressing Molly's body tightly to my chest, soothing her until her heartbeats feel like my own.

What was I thinking? There must be a piece missing in me somewhere, something really screwed up with my brain because after all I've seen, with all I know about her, I still absurdly pretend she can act like a rational mother.

Uncle Nack comes back from the bathroom, rubbernecking dumbly from me to Mama. "What happened?"

Mama's face is so vacant, like she's locked up somewhere inside her head and doesn't hear anything.

"What the hell is going on?"

"We're leaving," I shriek.

Uncle Nack throws up his hands. "We just got here."

I keep backing up closer to the door, buttoning Molly's coat. "I didn't want to come in the first place. I only came because you and Ursula guilted me into it."

"She's sick," he says not unkindly.

"She's sick all right." I yell over my shoulder, letting the door slam good and hard behind me.

At home, Uncle Nack tries to sweet-talk me to go to Ursula's with him to have a late Mother's Day lunch with her and Dennis like we planned.

"I've had enough of *your* version of Mother's Day, thank you," I snarl.

He winces like my jab hit the mark. He sucks in his cheek and chews for a few seconds. "You sure you're okay here alone."

"I'm not alone, I'm with Molly," I snipe.

"You know what I mean," he says, more kindly than I probably deserve.

I try to sound less snitty but without giving him the satisfaction of backing down or looking at him. "I have plenty to keep me busy in the shed."

When he finally leaves, I put Molly down for her nap and recheck the calendar where I write the days every day, even though I just wrote 53 on it this morning and know it can't have changed.

Half of my brain is so ready to march out to the shed, unzip the umbrella bag, and call it a draw—fifty-three days is close enough to sixty. The wimpier half of my brain pulls out the sheet of phone numbers they gave me at my meeting, sniveling that I should call someone in Al-Anon or maybe find a meeting to go to instead.

The push and pull rumbles in my head. I grip the phone list with both hands, staring down at Kitty "the double winner's" phone number for so long that the edges of the paper are creased and sweaty.

I reach for the phone. The tug-of-war in my head gets louder. My hand trembles.

Decision made, I crumble the phone list, fling it into the trash, and charge down the stairs.

Chapter 39

$\mathcal{I}$ walk briskly across the yard, trying in vain to out-pace the nagging thoughts willing me to turn back. In the woodshed, I shove aside some pickets, a few half-refinished windows, and the KATIE's KRAFT KORNER sign, yanking the umbrella bag out of its hiding place. Grasping the neck of the vodka bottle, I unscrew the top, turn around, and suddenly freeze.

A shiver runs up my body. It's like the Katie's Kraft Korner sign is Poppi incarnate watching me. Irrationally, I can't bring myself to drink from the bottle in front of it.

Without bothering to re-zip the bag, I recap the bottle and carry it outside. A chilly breeze stirs the trees. The swishing sound of branches brushing the roof shingles and a boisterous blue jay hopping along the rain gutter draw me to the carriage house.

The carriage house.

It's been years since I set foot inside. What better place to get blotto on Mother's Day than Mama's and my short-lived, hardly-home-sweet-home? It's so ironically perfect, I almost scoff out loud.

Step by step, as if I'm on auto-pilot, I tread across the back lawn, find the key under the weathered old mat, and jiggle it into the lock. The door sticks and I heave it with my shoulder. The odor of mildew is so pungent, for a minute, I can taste it.

Abandoned gardening tools and the old lawn ornaments Uncle Nack stopped displaying years ago haphazardly line the walls. In spite of the clutter, memories rear up everywhere. I halt mid-step and slump against the door.

I can almost hear Mama's Beatles music, see her foot jiggling under the table, and smell her overfull ashtrays. No matter how many times I close my eyes, I cannot erase the eleven-year-old at that fogged up window desperately watching Mama's shadow fleeing across the lawn.

I twist the cap off the bottle and hold it to my lips. "Happy Mother's Day, Mama," I quip irreverently.

The glass bottle clinks against my front teeth, but before I take the first sip, the wimpy side of my brain that is usually easily bullied into submission ramps up the volume. Suddenly, all I can hear is Kitty's story about what her daughter remembers from when she was one or two.

I lower the bottle to my side and vigorously shake my head, but I can't silence the nagging question stuck on replay. Will Molly stand in this doorway when she's my age, with the same messed-up memories as me?

But it's *my* mother's day too, and I want this drink— I earned it. Another irksome question buzzes my brain;

can I give Molly a different future by making a different choice?

I should have planned this better. I should have had a Plan B.

As my mind whirls, something unexplainable starts to happen. It feels like I'm watching a movie reel with another possible future unfolding scene by scene.

At first, what I'm thinking seems ludicrous. But what if it's not some harebrained, pie-in-the-sky fantasy?

What if?

I turn in a full circle and imagine customers browsing through the carriage house—the kitchen area full of hand-made wooden towel bars, mug trees, and carved napkin rings. Over there by the alcove hangs a gay assortment of birdfeeders in every shape and color, blue-bird and slanty-roofed birdhouses, picture frames on every tabletop, sturdy wooden mailbox copies of real Cape May Victorian houses, and every wall lined with multi-colored crayon hangings, refurbished windows, and flower boxes.

There's space in the bedroom for a half-dozen doghouses. I twirl in another circle and back out onto the porch. If I build an overhang, I can display more doghouses and maybe some customized address signs out here.

In my mind's eye, I see my own sign—Katie's Kraft Kottage.

Is what I'm thinking possible? Am I frigging out of my mind?

I gaze up at the fast-moving clouds in the sky, feeling so strongly that somehow, Poppi planted this seed in my head. And if I can pull it off, I know it will make him proud.

I'm still desperately craving a drink, but right this second, my stronger urge is to be with Molly. After one more hopeful glance around the carriage house, I recap the bottle for a second time, close the carriage house door, and head back into the house.

In her crib, Molly is asleep on her back, her lips slightly parted and her tongue peeking out. I tiptoe over and stare down at her.

Asleep like this, with her face so still, you can see her full bottom lip and the thinner top one. Mama said she doesn't look like me, but her lips are just like my lips. She has my ears, too, and even though her hair is auburn, it has my frizz at the ends.

Mama gave all of those things to me, and I passed them on to Molly.

I suddenly realize as I stare down at her that I'm humming Poppi's goodnight song. Barely whispering, I sing the words, "I love you truly, truly I do."

I can't imagine why I never sang Poppi's song to Molly before.

I gently touch her eyelids and trace my finger across her soft cheek. She scrunches her nose, sucking her lips into a tiny rosebud.

What if I'm wrong and everyone else is right and besides inheriting Mama's lips and frizz, I inherited her drinking gene, too?

And if I do have that gene, how do I keep from passing it to Molly?

I brush a wisp of hair away from her eyes. She is such a beautiful baby.

I may have Mama's lips and hair, but I have Poppi's hard-work hands. If I'm really lucky, just maybe I have *his* soul.

It's Poppi's soul and his heart I want to pass on to my Molly.

And I suddenly see clearly what I think somewhere inside, I've always known. For Molly to have the mother she deserves, I have to let Mama go.

I tiptoe away from Molly's crib and carry the vodka bottle back to the shed to riffle around in the umbrella bag for what's left of the airplane brandy bottles. I carry them all to the drain beside the back porch. Quickly, before I lose my nerve, I empty every one, rinsing the bottles out with the hose. I'm just tossing the empties into the recycle bin when Uncle Nack pulls into the driveway.

I walk over and wait for him to get out of the Caddy. "How was lunch?"

"Good." He starts to walk toward the house.

I pause a few seconds before catching up to walk beside him. "I'm sorry I was, you know, pissy with you earlier."

He stops and squints sideways at me, shadowing his eyes with his hand. "You had a rough morning."

I blink. "I guess."

He starts walking again, and I walk with him. "You might find some empty bottles in the recycle bucket, but I didn't drink them."

He stands still but doesn't say anything. His expression is unreadable.

"I poured them out."

He turns to face me and rests his hands reassuringly on my shoulders. His eyes are tearing up. My eyes feel watery, too. I have this sensation like I can finally breathe after holding my breath underwater for seconds too long. That relief you feel when you finally break the surface and come up gasping for air.

"Can you babysit tonight if I can find a meeting to go to?"

"Sure, Number Two." His voice catches. He squeezes my shoulder. "I'm really proud of you, kid."

I have to bite my lip not to cry.

Inside, I pick up the hall phone and dial Dennis's number, swallowing the lump rising in my throat each time their telephone rings. Finally, on the fifth ring, he answers.

"Do you have to go back to school tonight?"

"What do you need?"

"Can you take me to a meeting?"

"Hang on while I go to my bedroom for the schedule." There's a clunk when he puts the receiver down and in the background, he says, "Mom, will you hang up in here when I pick up in the bedroom?"

I stretch the phone cord to its limit, peeking through the dining room blinds. The sky looks bluer and the wind must have died down because the lilac branches with their heavy blooms hardly sway.

"Got it, Mom," Dennis yells. We both wait for the click.

"There's a seven o'clock meeting at the hospital."

"Do you mind taking me?" I'm itching to ask him if there's an AA meeting there tonight, too, but my throat closes before I muster the guts.

"I'll pick you up around five so we can catch up before."

Warm relief floods through me. "Thanks, Dennis," I say and gingerly hang up.

At a little after five, since we have almost two hours to kill and haven't had dinner, we stop at the custard stand on the promenade. I sit in the car while Dennis goes to the counter and orders us fries and milkshakes to go.

He drives along Beach Drive to the Cove, and we sit on a bench, munching our fries. The sky is cloudless and blue, but the sea breeze is downright cold and we both wear hoodies. I'd let my ears freeze off before actually putting the hood up, but I bunch it around my neck and tightly tie the string. I tug the sleeves down over my hand to pick up my shake. "Can I ask you something?" I ask nervously.

"Unum."

"Do you still miss MarieEleana?"

He inhales loudly and then is quiet for so long, I don't think he's going to answer me. He munches a fry and wipes his greasy fingers on his napkin. "Why?"

I hug my knees to my chest and wrap my arms around them, resting my chin on my knee. "I know I messed everything up, that it's my fault you broke up."

He takes one long deep swig of his milkshake and slowly turns to face me. "Is that what you think?" He rests his hand on my shoulder and inches his fingers into the gap between my hoodie and my hair at the base of my neck. He doesn't move his fingers or say anything else, lost in some secret thought.

His fingers are chilly from holding his milkshake, but they leave a warm imprint on my neck long after he moves his hand.

I spend the ride from the Cove to the hospital staring out the car window, wondering exactly what just happened, but too keyed up to ask him what his fingers on my neck meant.

The hospital parking lot is more crowded than when we come to morning meetings. Dennis parks all the way in the back near the border of evergreen trees. You can smell the pine when we get out, hear a songbird trilling overhead. Across the street, kids in zipped-up jackets run to an ice cream truck playing a jack-in-the-box tune. I trot ahead of Dennis, between rows of cars until we reach the wide path that leads to the front door.

Inside, we sign the book at the desk and head for the stairwell. About halfway down the first flight, the door at the top of the stairs opens and Kitty starts barreling down the steps, two at a time.

"Hey," I say hugging the wall to let her pass.

"Hey, yourself." She smiles and keeps going, calling over her shoulder. "Sorry, I'm late. I'm supposed to set up the chairs."

"We can help you," Dennis says.

She looks up from the landing. "I'm going to the AA meeting tonight." She shrugs. "Thanks anyway." She disappears through the door.

I am absolutely sure that Kitty showing up at this exact moment is some kind of cosmic sign.

On the fourth step from the bottom, what has been in the back of my head ever since I dumped every drop in those bottles down the drain hits me full force. On the landing, I turn around. Dennis is two steps up from the bottom.

"Do you mind if I go to the AA meeting tonight instead of Al-Anon?"

"Do I mind?" He steps onto the landing and caresses my cheeks in his hands. He can probably feel my heart thumping where his pinky rests on my neck. Everything stops while we stand here. His lips touch mine, just brush across them, mustache tickling, and then he tilts his head up and locks his eyes on mine. "You know I love you, right?"

My whole body quivers as if I just woke up from the longest sleep. I nod but don't say anything, not wanting to move my lips until they memorize everything about that fleeting first kiss.

Part of me wants to stay right here in this stairwell forever, kissing him back. "I don't want to be late," I murmur.

He lets go of my face and holds my arm to walk out into the hall, giving my elbow a little squeeze when I turn right in the direction of the AA meeting. Without turning around, I can feel his eyes on my back.

When I get to the room, they are already going around saying their names. Kitty waves me over to the empty seat next to her. My chair is under the window, and when I look up, a wren pecks at something on the windowsill. I swear he stares straight at me before soaring up into the sky.

After Kitty introduces herself, it's my turn. The enormity of what I'm about to do sticks in my throat. I make a teepee with my fingertips, press them to my lips, and swallow. Heat floods my face.

"Hi. My name is Katie. This is my first meeting." I close my eyes and concentrate on breathing. "And I'm an alcoholic."

"Welcome," they say in unison.

Kitty lays her hand on mine. I move my other hand and rest it on top to sandwich her hand. I feel all warm inside. For the first time in forever, it feels like I am home.

If you enjoyed *Cape Maybe*, please take a few minutes to rate it on Amazon and Goodreads.

Amazon: http://www.amazon.com/dp/0615741010

Goodreads: http://www.goodreads.com/author/show/6924892.Carol_Fragale_Brill

Acknowledgements

How lucky I was to have Vincent Fragale for my father. He died much too young, but my memories of his steadfast love influenced my development of Poppi. And to Clara Matteo Fragale, my mom, I attribute Katie's determined hope against troublesome odds for a better, happier tomorrow.

Thank you to my early readers—Jeanne Fragale Keller, Chris Jackman Brady, Janine Begasse, Donna Michael-Ziereis, Ron Rollet, Julie Russell, and especially Terese Svoboda for generous mentoring and editorial support. Special thanks for cover photos to Bella Cameron, Risa Kane, Malorie Massaro, and Matt Massaro.

And always I am grateful to Jim—for love, friendship, and encouragement beyond my wildest dreams.

Also by Carol Fragale Brill
The following is an excerpt from Carol Fragale Brill's novel, *PEACE BY PIECE*

Chapter 1

Ever since I can remember, I wanted to be near books. Losing Thomas changed just about everything else, but at least it did not change that. Growing up, when the library door closed behind me, I would stand in the vestibule to let the calm sink in, the air permeated by parched paper, old dust, and the Murphy's Oil Soap used to polish the high, wooden shelves. No one hollered or threw things or slapped their open palms on tables at the library. No one called you names or raised a voice louder than a hush.

I arrived early this morning to recheck everything for the vacation reading club. The head librarian, Mrs. Keller, says my idea for the children's club shows initiative and that one day I could be a good librarian if I change my mind about becoming a teacher—assuming that at 25, I finally have enough sense not to blow it again, and I can actually finish college this time.

Tunnels of sunlight stream through the tall windows. I catch my reflection in the glass. What possessed me to buy this cream-colored skirt? It makes my hips look huge.

The heavy wood door huffs open, framing Izzie lugging her Barbie lunch box. It probably holds her favorite fluffer-nutter sandwich and a thermos of apple juice. She comes right up to me and hugs me around the waist.

"You're here early today, Izzie Bee."

Isabella Gabriella Bannon is how she introduced herself the first time we met—a heavy, dark-complexioned kind of name for a little blonde-haired girl. The spunky, self-assured way she lifted her chin to tell me just who she was belied the hunger for acceptance in her gap-toothed smile. The attraction was instant, as was a kind of instinctive knowing that someone or something had broken her little girl heart.

Today, Izzie's ponytail is off-center, with fly-away strands at the sides. She must have done it herself. She smells like Juicy Fruit gum, an indulgence I suspect her father would not allow before lunch. I do not know him, but on the days he picked her up at the library after school last spring, he would pull up his shiny black Buick out front at the end of his work day and honk—two short beeps—the signal for Izzie to scurry and meet him outside.

"I wanted to be early for reading club. Rose dropped me off," Izzie says.

Rose is the widowed neighbor who sometimes watches Izzie. A few times last winter, she came by to take Izzie home. There was a grandmotherly softness in her Scottish accent and her big-bosomed body and in the way she gathered Izzie under her fleshy arm to nudge her to hush up and pack.

During the school year, on the days Rose was not home to take her in after school, Izzie came to the library to wait for her father. After the day she introduced herself, she started sitting near me to brag about winning her classroom spelling bee, her dancing solo at an annual recital, her father's important job and fancy new car, and about how no matter who else plays, she always wins at jacks. I looked forward to her visits, speeding through my work in the early afternoon to make time to sit and read with her or help with her homework if the circulation desk was slow. The days without her felt empty.

One day, I asked about her mother. In all her boasting, she had never mentioned her. Her round eyes widened. Usually, they are an unremarkable blue, but popped open like that, you could see flecks of silver-gray. She had lost another front tooth and her tongue poked through the space pensively before she blurted out, "My mother is a big, important star in California." She said it in her show-offy tone, but as soon as she blinked, her bravado evaporated. The frozen expression on her face told me she knew she had been quietly caught in a lie and that she was trying to figure out how much to say.

I slid my hand under her palm on the table and placed my other hand on top to wait, hoping she would decide I was someone she could trust. You could tell she had polished her own nails: the cuticles were smudged, the chipped polish streaked and lumpy in spots.

"Her band has its own bus. She misses me so much, but she's too far away." She pulled her hand away to dig into her binder. "See what she sent me for my birthday?" The card had a furry bear cub blowing out a bunch of candles on a cake. Not a card carefully chosen for your daughter's birthday, but the kind you get in a box at the drugstore—or in the mail from the missionaries asking for a donation.

"You didn't tell me it was your birthday."

"It was October, before you knew me." Izzie's fingers worried at the card's worn, curled-up edge. "She misses me all the time."

Eight months. Had she carried the card all that time?

"She wants to visit me when she can get off." She thrust out her chin. "Daddy says don't count on it, but she'll come, you'll see. Probably my next birthday, when I'm nine." She smoothed her hand over the card before placing it carefully into the pouch in her binder. Chewing on her lip, she beckoned me closer with her finger and looked directly into my eyes. "You think she'll come, don't you, Maggie?"

It was all I could do to hold her gaze. "Sure, Izzie Bee."

She let out her breath. "I bet she will for sure."

Here is what I do know for sure: If she were my little girl, nothing could keep me away.

Two hours later, I cannot stop grinning about the 11 children who joined reading club. The head librarian, Mrs. Keller, has already repeated three times she would have been overjoyed with six. Now, all but Izzie are gone. She sits alone at the small square table closest to the circulation desk, thumbing through *Little House on the Prairie*. At over 300 pages, it is advanced for her age, but she passed up a few shorter chapter books to not look babyish in front of the 9-and-10-year- olds in the club.

Mrs. Keller looks over her half glasses and pushes a stray strand of gray-streaked hair behind her ear. Almost every time she sees Mrs. Keller, Izzie cups her hands around her mouth to stifle a giggle and whisper that she looks like the Prince Valiant poster in the children's room. I purse my lips in disapproval, but with that squarish haircut, she reminds me of him, too. Mrs. Keller taps her watch face. "Why don't you take a longer lunch during this lull? You earned it," she says approvingly.

The brown bag I packed this morning holds a peach, a handful of cherries, some cut-up cheese, and seven whole wheat crackers—one serving, according to the box. It is a very colorful lunch for me, but not because I am back to fasting or refusing to eat anything white: white bread, white sugar, white rice, cottage cheese, plain yogurt, potatoes, and rolls—anything made with white flour. In fact, today, my cheese is white American, validation of how far I have come from what my best friend Lilly refers to as the white curse.

I grab my lunch from the drawer and jiggle the bag to get Izzie's attention. "Ready for lunch?"

She claps her hands to her face. "Please, please, can we eat outside on our bench?" The bench she refers to is in a tiny courtyard bordering the parking lot.

"A picnic it is," I say.

Most of the little courtyard is surrounded by trees and bushes, so passers-by do not see us sitting here. The air is humid for early June and heavy with the scent of lilacs. There is hardly a cloud in the bright, cornflower blue sky. Izzie takes a big bite of her sandwich. Marshmallow fluff sticks to her lips. I nibble a wedge of cheese. Izzie rips her crust, licks off the peanut butter, and tosses the crust to a pigeon at our feet.

"Do this," I say. I run my tongue over my top lip to show her where to lick off the fluff.

"She told me inside you hens were out here."

I squint up at Izzie's neighbor, Rose. Her floral cotton dress is a cross between a shirtwaist and a house dress. The way it is belted in the middle, you cannot tell where her waist actually starts, her bust is that billowy.

"We're having a picnic," Izzie says.

"Don't be talking with your mouth full." Rose pulls an ironed, white linen hankie with a border of embroidered daisies from her pocket. She hands it to Izzie to wipe her mouth. Izzie whips her tongue back and forth over her lips and hands back the hankie without using it. Rose flutters it at me. "Every time I see you, you remind me of somebody." She dabs the back of her neck with the hankie. "Her name is on the tip of my tongue. That pretty wisp of an actress who played Jackie Templeton on my soap."

I raise my shoulders, shaking my head to let her know I do not have a clue who she means.

"You never watched *General Hospital?*"

I shake my head again. In college, my roommate Lynn cut half her afternoon classes to watch it, but between work study and homework, I never got into soaps.

"You know the one." She fans the hankie in the air between us. "She was Michael Caine's daughter in that comedy last year, the one where he plays fast and loose with his best friend's daughter."

"*Blame It on Rio?*"

"That's it. With hair a bit darker, you'd be the spitting image of the skinny hen that plays his daughter."

"*Demi Moore?*" Rose must need her eyes checked. Has she seen my butt in this skirt?

"That's the one. You could be sisters." Rose points at Izzie. "You got two shakes of a lamb's tail to finish eating. My church ladies need help setting up for tomorrow's white elephant sale in the church basement."

"Can't I stay here?" Izzie whines.

"You've been in Maggie's hair enough for one day."

"I hate the church basement. It smells like wet socks." Rose snorts.

"I want to stay with Maggie and read my book."

Rose tilts her head at me, raising her eyebrows in a question. Izzie puts her hands together in prayer, batting her eyelashes. "Please, please, please?"

"If 5:30 isn't too late, I can walk Izzie home after work."

"You sure her Nibs won't be a bother?" I have noticed Rose calls Izzie *her Nibs* or *her majesty* when she is about to let her have her way.

"She'll be fine."

Rose cups Izzie's chin, lifting her face until their eyes meet. "You let Maggie work. She doesn't need to feel like a one-eyed mouse watching two mouse holes."

Izzie plants loud kisses on Rose's hand.

Rose writes her phone number and address on a crumpled, old K-Mart receipt and hands it to me. She throws Izzie a kiss, turning to go.

Izzie puckers her sticky lips and makes smacking-kissy sounds.

Rose shakes her head. "Isn't she one for the chuckle muscles?" You can hear her giggling softly as she walks away.

When I finish work, the sun is still bright yellow and just starting to move lower in the sky. On the walk to her house, Izzie and I play one of my secret childhood games, making up stories about the people we pass. The stout old lady with the babushka on her head and stockings rolled around her ankles is really a Russian princess, disguised so no one will try to steal the diamond tiara she carries in the worn canvas bag slung over her arm. The young woman leaving the Chinese laundry with shirts wrapped in brown paper and string is hugging a package of love letters from her boyfriend, a soldier off at war. The collie two young boys walk on a leash has magical powers. His name is Skooty and he is really not a dog at all, but a wizard with a crush on the boys' older sister, content to live in a dog house just to be near her everyday. In the midst of Izzie imagining how Skooty gets the girl, we turn onto her block, lined with sets of twin homes. One or two lawns look straggly, but most are well-kept, with plump green grass. The kind of thick-trunked old oak trees the city planted a half-century ago form a leafy arch at the curbs.

We are halfway down the block when the black Buick stops near an empty parking space a few houses up. It is a tight spot with a station wagon in front and a VW bug behind, but one three-point turn and Izzie's dad lines up the Buick perfectly parallel, just inches from the curb.

He gets out of the car clutching his briefcase. His suit jacket is draped over his arm. His keys dangle from the other hand. He pushes the door closed with his elbow. He is shorter than the impression he gives sitting behind the wheel. I would guess five ten. The squared off way he holds his shoulders makes you think he left the hanger in his shirt. His pants still hold their crease and his shoes have a mirror shine, as if he is the kind of man who reads his paper at lunch sitting on the shoeshine bench in his office building's lobby. Izzie walks up to him. The way he touches her shoulder is part enchantment and part fear she might break from his caress. He looks like a person who stays awake at night worrying, like me, about all the things that could go wrong.

He glances at me through his wire-rimmed glasses. There is no mistaking the resemblance in his gray-flecked blue eyes. "Rose called. You must be Maggie," he says.

"Yes. I've seen you picking up Izzie at the library." I catch myself twirling my hair around my finger and clasp my hands in front of me.

"I hope she wasn't too much trouble for you today."

Something about the dubious tone in his voice makes me defensive. "Not at all. I enjoy her company."

The look on his face suggests that when he has an entire day to spend with her, he does not have a clue what to do. Izzie holds up her book. "Maggie's helping me read *Little House on the Prairie*." She makes the tiniest move toward him. He pats her on the head.

I am not sure where to fix my eyes in the awkward silence between us. "Well, I should get home." I sound inane.

"Do you live around here?"

"Over in Hillcrest."

"Hillcrest?" Something flickers in his eyes but vanishes just as quickly. "That's the opposite direction from the library. I could have stopped there instead of you coming out of your way."

"Really, it was nothing." The truth is, I am not sure where to get the bus around here, but the evening is comfortably balmy. I can retrace my route back to the library and catch my regular bus from there.

"Bye, Izzie."

She grips my wrist in both hands. "We have to finish our wizard dog story," she pleads.

"We'll finish it next time."

She wraps both her arms around one of mine, rubbing her face against my elbow. "See you later, alligator," she says reluctantly.

"In a while, crocodile." I tickle her fingers to extract my arm. "Bye, Mr. Bannon."

"Donald."

"Um?"

"Call me Donald."

"Can I walk Maggie to the corner?"

He inventories the parked cars. "Didn't you drive?"

"We walked from the library."

"How are you getting home?"

"I'll take the bus."

"I can't let you do that." He walks to the porch steps. "I'll just put this stuff inside and drive you home."

"You don't have to."

He waves my words away. On the porch, he unlocks the front door and takes his jacket and briefcase inside. Walking back down the porch steps, he unbuttons the top button of his shirt and loosens his tie before opening both passenger doors. "Get in back, Izzie." You can tell he is comfortable giving orders.

I met my best friend, Lilly, when she was my high school English teacher, and have lived in the small apartment on the third floor of her house for almost four years. When we pull up out front, she is on the porch, watering her geraniums with the beat-up metal watering can she bought at a yard sale a few weeks ago. The houses on her block are attached row houses, but Lilly's is on the corner and the only one with a wraparound porch. Her floral peach silk kimono shimmers in the sunlight, darkening her complexion from its usual light mocha to the same deep brown as her eyes. For the second time in the last half hour, Donald's eyes narrow in something that might be disapproval. It is quick, and it is gone by the time he shifts sideways in his seat to say goodbye. His lips crease into what I suspect for him passes as a smile. Sitting this close, it is hard not to notice the deep forehead, the touches of gray in the light brown hair near the temple, and the V where the hairline is receding at the part. He is handsome in a prim sort of way.

Izzie reaches through our seats. I give her hand a squeeze and get out of the car. I know Lilly watches from the porch, wondering who these people are who have driven me home. The polite thing would be to introduce them, but what would I say? Here is the little girl I wish I could adopt? Instead, I close the door and stand on the pavement to wave at Izzie through the back window. The air is smoky sweet from the place around the corner on Germantown Avenue that barbeques ribs in a sawed-in-half trash can and sells them in the John's Bargain Store parking lot on Wednesday and Friday nights.

Coming home from work, there is no better perfume than that emanating from Lilly's freshly ground coffee. She buys the dark, roasted beans a few pounds at a time from a big barrel at the neighborhood co-op. On the porch, she hands me one of the extra-tall mugs painted with exotic birds her friend Mitch bought her the day they took his grandbaby to the zoo. Mitch is the art teacher at Holy Cross High School, but he did not teach there back when Lilly was my English teacher in my junior and senior years.

Back then, Lilly was Ms. Whitestone to me. She is the one who convinced me to apply to college in spite of my mother fretting that we could not afford it. Lilly helped me research scholarships and drove me 70 miles to the open house at Godfrey University at the South Jersey shore because back then, my mother did not drive and my father was not very dependable.

Mitch is more than just her friend, he is her boyfriend, but Lilly says that is a ridiculous term for people over 40. The first time I met Mitch, his commanding, James-Earl-Jones voice and football fullback stature intimidated me, but it is clear from the way he dotes on Lilly that his heart fills up every inch of his barrel-size chest.

Lilly sips from the mug with a widespread peacock tail. "I made pasta primavera. Have dinner with me out here." Although I am technically her tenant, she treats me more like a family member.

My finger traces over the flamingo on my mug. I would rather eat inside, but Lilly is a free spirit and likes to live out in the open. I could make up an excuse like the gnats are biting or my allergies are acting up, but Lilly always sees right through me. She will just tell me to tough it out.

Lilly twirls pasta on her fork. "I had the weirdest dream last night about Val being in a casket under the backboard on Holy Cross's basketball court."

The way she blurts it out, I almost drop my fork. Val was Lilly's fiancé. She was a senior in college when he died in Viet Nam. Even though he died over 20 years ago, I glance up to see if talking about him is upsetting her, but she just looks matter-of-fact. That is the thing about Lilly. She has this way of staring life square in the eye, even when she is being sentimental or looking back. Of all the things she has taught me over the years, life would sure be easier for me if she could teach me that neat little trick.

Lilly holds the pasta on her fork in midair, creasing her forehead as she remembers more about her dream. "Oh, get this— there was a DJ playing "Blue Velvet" of all things, as if I'd ever intentionally listen to Bobby Vinton."

"Where do you think the dream came from?"

She sops up the olive oil on her plate with a crusty end from a loaf of fresh Italian bread. "Girl, I don't have a clue."

"Do you want to look it up in my dream book?" I live by the dream book I keep in my bathroom. All you have to do is find a key word to learn what your dream means.

"I doubt we'll find middle-aged teenager sees casket on basketball court in the index."

She probably has a point.

I remember my dreams all the time, but Lilly hardly ever remembers hers. Last night, mine was about being in a train station with these three really narrow escalators and no signs to tell where each track went. I started down one of the escalators to ask someone at the bottom for directions, but halfway down I remembered my bag was up top under a bench. No matter how hard I tried, I could not push through the crowd to get back up there. Even before looking it up, I knew my dream book would say this dream is about feeling trapped.

"With all the dreaming you do, do you ever dream of Thomas?" she asks.

I am now acutely aware of the heat rising from this wrought iron chair. Somewhere nearby, a car motor grinds incessantly, and the pungent odor of exhaust hangs in the air. I shake my head no, opening my mouth to form the word, but nothing comes out.

From time to time, Lilly asks me about him: about why I never talk about him, about how she can count on one hand the times she has heard me speak his name in the last five years. Her question always seems to hit me out of nowhere, as if I ran smack into a sliding glass door, and I am numb and achy at the same time. Sometimes, it happens at night when the heat makes it hard to sleep and the two of us sit out here with the light off, slapping at mosquitoes in the dark and listening to the sounds of an urban nighttime:

sirens, souped-up mufflers, and squealing brakes. It could happen over coffee at the diner following a meeting, or walking to her car after a romantic movie, the kind that makes you laugh one minute and the next has you sobbing and stumbling up the aisle, hoping no one notices you are a complete human mess. Usually when she asks, I either change the subject or say there is nothing to talk about—which is about as far as you can get from reality. Knowing Lilly, she sees through my lame attempt to hide the truth. The thing is: What good does talking about him do?

What good will it do to tell her there are still days that a little thing like getting out of bed and dressed for work seems like the biggest chore? How would it help for her to know that so many thoughts of him rattle around my brain, it is as if there is a regret machine stuck on replay, replay, replay in my head?

"Earth to Maggie." Lilly waves her fork to get my attention. "It's hard to believe you *never* dream of him."

How will it help for her to know he inhabits my mind so often during the day, he ought to be paying me rent?

Lilly always says life has no room for what-ifs and coulda, woulda, shouldas. She preaches looking ahead instead. To remind me, she asked her boyfriend, Mitch, to calligraphy a quote from a fortune cookie onto an index card, and tacked it on my upstairs door. It says, "Comparison is the thief of joy."

In spite of everything Lilly says, my thoughts are plagued by what-ifs.

What if I had not quit school and blown my scholarship, or the biggest what-if of all—what if I could go back to that night and instead of obsessing about Thomas being 53 minutes late and hunting him down at the gym, I could wait sanely for him in my dorm room? If I had one more chance, I would stay put, or if I did go look for him, I swear I would get it right this time. I would trust him enough to stuff down the panic and swallow my doubt, stride across that parking lot to where he held Maria in the shadow cast by the building.

I would find the courage to look into his eyes and let him explain, instead of giving up and running away.

Made in the USA
Charleston, SC
14 October 2013